KT-153-380

"I was a soldier. Bound by oath to serve Rome."

"Then I do hope Rome kept you warm at nights. I hope Rome healed your hurts and loved you."

He kissed the fragrant shell of her ear. "By day I fought for Rome. By night I dreamed of you."

She crossed her arms and slanted her eyes to him. "How charming."

His jaw tightened. "Those dreams were the only thing that kept me sane. You will not make a mockery of them."

"Oh, I'm not, Donatus. I'm so pleased you had something beautiful with which to fill your time. Because I'm quite certain that I did not."

Author Note

Writers are sometimes asked where their ideas come from.

With me, it usually starts with researching the time period. Rarely does a character emerge quickly, and almost never does the story begin to tell itself. WARRIOR OR WIFE was that rare book that did, and Lelia was that character.

She came quickly, and in astonishing detail, while I was watching a documentary that told of a new and most unusual archaeological discovery in London. In 2000, a team of archaeologists unearthed a grave dating back to the late first century A.D., when London was a thriving commercial centre for the Roman province of Britannia. The grave was surprising because it was the resting place of a gladiator—an amazing find. Even more spectacular was that the remains discovered within it were those of a *woman*.

A gladiatrix.

And the big question burning me alive was: *Why?*

Why would a woman want to fight to the death in an arena?

Question by question, answer by answer, the story revealed itself to me, until the gladiatrix named Lelia stood, proud and noble, within my mind.

It had taken only a few minutes to find her, but her story would ultimately shake me to pieces.

I like to think of that unknown female warrior from Roman Britannia, and imagine that she might be pleased with this story she inspired. I hope you like it, too.

WARRIOR OR WIFE

Lyn Randal

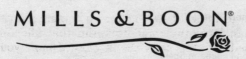

DID YOU PURCHASE THIS BOOK WITHOUT A COVER?

If you did, you should be aware it is **stolen property** as it was reported *unsold and destroyed* by a retailer. Neither the author nor the publisher has received any payment for this book.

All the characters in this book have no existence outside the imagination of the author, and have no relation whatsoever to anyone bearing the same name or names. They are not even distantly inspired by any individual known or unknown to the author, and all the incidents are pure invention.

All Rights Reserved including the right of reproduction in whole or in part in any form. This edition is published by arrangement with Harlequin Enterprises II BV/S.à.r.l. The text of this publication or any part thereof may not be reproduced or transmitted in any form or by any means, electronic or mechanical, including photocopying, recording, storage in an information retrieval system, or otherwise, without the written permission of the publisher.

This book is sold subject to the condition that it shall not, by way of trade or otherwise, be lent, resold, hired out or otherwise circulated without the prior consent of the publisher in any form of binding or cover other than that in which it is published and without a similar condition including this condition being imposed on the subsequent purchaser.

MILLS & BOON and MILLS & BOON with the Rose Device are registered trademarks of the publisher.

First published in Great Britain 2007
Harlequin Mills & Boon Limited,
Eton House, 18-24 Paradise Road, Richmond, Surrey TW9 1SR

© Leigh Randal 2007

ISBN: 978 0 263 85190 8

Set in Times Roman 10½ on 12 pt.
04-0807-83112

Printed and bound in Spain
by Litografia Rosés S.A., Barcelona

Lyn Randal grew up on a farm in rural Mississippi, where long, hot summers away from school and friends meant entertaining herself with books and her own imagination. Now, years later, she lives on a farm in rural Alabama, where long, hot summers mean entertaining herself with—you guessed it!— more books and an even bigger imagination. She considers herself rather fortunate that her husband, two children, two cats and one dog have all become quite accustomed to her strange writing habits, hardly noticing that she mutters odd lines of dialogue while doing household chores or disappears to take over the computer for hours on end, sometimes even managing to avoid huge mountains of laundry in the process.

Lyn especially enjoys the research that goes into writing historical novels, and she loves hearing from her readers. Contact her by visiting her website: www.lynrandal.com

WARRIOR OR WIFE is Lyn Randal's first novel for Mills & Boon® Historical Romance.

To Randy, the real-life inspiration for all my heroes. I truly could never have found success without you, nor would I have wanted to.

Prologue

Rome—July 10, 106 A.D.

For the first time in his life, Donatus was glad his father was dead. A dead man could not sob to see a son in this place, or the shame brought upon an honorable name.

Donatus was not supposed to be here. He was, after all, Marcus Flavius Donatus, owner of that patrician name as ancient as the bloody sand beneath his boots, that noble name carried by a father and grandfather as esteemed senators. He should have followed in their footsteps. He would have made a good senator. In his politics he was conservative. In his friendships he was cautious. He enjoyed good food and fine wine, but he never partook carelessly of either. He was fond of many women, but he had loved only one.

So Donatus could never have predicted this moment, not once in his thirty years. He was a cavalry officer, a veteran of the Dacian Wars. He was a decurion, a leader of men, decorated twice for bravery—once by Emperor Trajan himself. The Emperor had smiled at Donatus as he handed over the gold crown, the *corona aurea,* because he knew well the noble name the younger man carried.

The Emperor was not smiling now, though he sat with his entourage in the comfortable, shaded seating of the *pulvinar.* Donatus could even now remove the helmet that hid his identity. He could plead for leniency. It was his right as a Roman citizen. But then…there would be questions. Too many questions.

The irony was that the opponent now circling Donatus on the hot sand knew nothing of fine names, nor would he have cared. All he cared for was his glory as a gladiator, this *retiarius* who fought with net and trident. He was known to Donatus only as Hermes, a combat name. Donatus had watched him train—had watched them all—and knew Hermes was not the best among them, even though he'd killed twice already. Untrained criminals, men easily killed.

But Donatus had been to war. He knew how to kill, with right hand or left, with javelin or sword or bare hands. And he fully intended to kill Hermes.

He hefted the familiar weight of the sharp-bladed *gladius* as he circled, watching with wary eyes. Hermes threw the net.

Donatus crouched, making himself a smaller target, using his shield to deflect it. He was pleased that the gladiator's eyes had narrowed just before he'd attacked. A good warning, that.

Donatus moved in aggressively with his own weapon, his shield managing the trident's longer thrust. Hermes fell back beneath the power and speed of the assault, his brown eyes widening in surprise. The *retiarius's* concentration wavered for but a moment, but it was long enough. Donatus drew first blood, slashing across the right forearm. Donatus heard Hermes grunt as he stumbled backward, his arm dripping blood. The crowd roared with disapproval.

Hermes glanced uneasily toward the stands. Donatus knew then what the gladiator would do next. He was prepared when Hermes rushed at him with the trident. It was long and heavy and Donatus could not counter it with his *gladius*. Helpless behind his tall shield, he watched in frustration as Hermes maneuvered himself toward the net and scooped it up again, spreading it with practiced hands.

The eyes. Donatus watched the eyes. Circling, circling, watching those dark eyes. When they narrowed, he sprang sideways like an agile cat. The net flew past. Donatus bent and yanked at it, easily using it to pull Hermes toward him, since the arrogant *retiarius* had attached one end to his belt. Hermes struggled to free himself, fighting for balance. A dagger flashed and the net came loose, but not soon enough for Hermes to avoid the tight arc of the *gladius*.

Donatus thrust and feinted—fast strokes, powerful strokes. An opening came. He switched hands, surprising Hermes with a left-handed attack and a hard, numbing blow to his unprotected right shoulder. Hermes grunted and dropped the trident. He turned and ran, the only defense left to him.

Donatus moved toward his prey. At first he thought the roar of the crowd was meant for him, for the blood he was about to spill. The sound rolled across the crowd in an indistinct wave, a confusion turning into excitement, becoming distinct and sharper, becoming a name.

Her name, pulsing over and over. "Leda! Lee-dah! Lee-dah!"

Donatus did not turn to see, but he knew she had come. He felt her presence and it angered him.

And then she was beside him, her body taut with the crowd's energy. She was dressed in combat gear, her helmet beneath her arm. The *lanista* raced out behind her and held up his arms in the sign for the fighters to pause, angry confusion upon his face. Donatus looked past them both. Hermes stared at her, at him, at them.

"Why are you here?" Donatus gritted out, tasting his sweat.

"Take off your helmet, Donatus."

He glanced at her, and back to Hermes, who sidled toward the net. "Get out of here," he said, not gently. His fear for her, and the constricting hurt he felt each time he looked at her, made the words too harsh. "Let me fight. I will kill him."

Donatus pushed her aside and raised his sword. She stepped forward and put her hand over his on the hilt. Her voice was strong, urgent, pleading with him as if she cared. It pierced him that she seemed to care when they both knew she did not. "Trust me, Donatus," she said. "Take off your helmet."

Donatus shook his head and pointed the sword toward Hermes. The *retiarius* stopped, wary. The *lanista* moved forward.

Her eyes filled with tears. The tenor of her voice changed, grew tight. "Please, Donatus. Just for a moment. Only for a moment. Take off your helmet."

Donatus's jaw tensed. What game did she play now?

"The Emperor," she murmured as the *lanista* drew closer. "The Emperor must see your face. Trust me."

Donatus looked down at her, his breath hot and ragged within the confines of the metal visor. "Sweet mercy," he groaned softly. "If I die, then I die for you."

"There's no need to die, Donatus," she said. "Remove your helmet and face the Emperor."

He hesitated a moment, then lowered his shield and reached up with his left hand, unfastening the helmet's leather strap and drawing it off. He turned. His eyes found the

Emperor. Shock came into Trajan's face. Donatus wanted to speak, was opening his mouth to form the first word, when there came an explosion of blinding pain, of daylight splintering and bursting behind his eyelids. Then darkness came…

Chapter One

Four months earlier—Rome, March 19, 106 A.D.

Valerius Leptis had the oily smile of a jackal. He was just a little too smug, a little too cool, a little too calm as he considered Donatus from across the desk, fingers steepled together over his chest.

"My daughter…hmm," the jackal said with a slight narrowing of the eyes. "Interesting that you should come here now and ask about her. Want to know where she is, do you?"

Calm, calm, Donatus warned himself. *Don't rush into battle. Let the enemy come to you. Take your time. Consider your moves.*

"Where is she, Leptis?"

Leptis tilted his head and smiled. He avoided the direct question, pointing to Donatus's toga with a slight gesture. "I see by that crimson stripe that you've already taken your father's place in the Senate."

"Yes."

"He was a fine man, your father. Much esteemed. Sorely missed."

"Yes."

Silence filled the space for a long moment. Leptis eyed Donatus carefully. "So you're now the *pater familias* of your family? Doubtless you wish to marry and secure an heir?"

Donatus's jaw ratcheted with the tension between them. He did not answer.

"Doubtless you wish to find a wife of noble rank. How nice that you thought of Lelia. I was sure you'd forgotten all about her. Two years is a long time."

"Where is she, Leptis?"

Leptis's lips quirked a bit. Obviously he enjoyed the game of wits they played. "Ah, now…that *is* the question. I've heard you've been searching for her, Flavius Donatus. Heard you've been asking about her since almost the moment you returned to Rome. Couldn't find her, could you? And now you stand before me like the shameful coward you are."

"The past is just that. The *past.* Just tell me where she is, damn it. Let me offer her an honorable marriage."

Leptis raised one eyebrow. "How decent of you to make the offer now, two years after the fact."

"I could not offer for her then. My father had chosen a military career for me. I was pledged to serve Rome."

Leptis's eyes hardened. "You might have considered that a little sooner. Before you made a whore of her."

Donatus's hands clenched with the need to ram his fists into Leptis's thick jowls. "Lelia was never a whore," he said in a deceptively quiet voice. "Call her that ever again and I'll kill you."

Leptis snorted, rising from behind his desk. "Oh, this is a twist, it really is. Do you now feign love for her? Do you now demand respect for her?" His eyes raked Donatus with scorn. "A pity you are not like your father. A pity you're more like your mother, you worthless son of a—"

Leptis never saw the blow coming. He fell back down into his chair, stunned by the lightning strike. One hand jerked up to the cut that now marred his lip. He glared at Donatus over the blood he saw when he drew his hand away. His voice was quiet, but it quivered with rage. "Leave my home, you insolent dog. Leave my home and do not think to return here again."

Donatus stood over him now, anger searing his chest. "I'll find her, Leptis. With or without your help, I'll find her."

He turned and strode out of Leptis's presence, across the atrium with its colorful flowers and splashing fountain. The echo of his angry footsteps rang out and bounced among the marble columns.

As he neared the entrance to the street he heard his name called, hissed out in a bare whisper. He jerked his head around.

A young woman stood there, looking anxiously past Donatus toward the room he'd just vacated. She looked so much like Lelia that Donatus felt his chest lurch. Lelia's younger sister. She had to be.

She stepped out quickly from behind a column. "Go to the games today," she whispered. "You'll find there what you seek."

"How's that?" he asked.

She shook her head and glanced nervously toward Leptis's study. "Just go to the Amphitheater in time for the afternoon games. That's all I can say now. That's all I dare tell you."

Donatus started to ask her more, but she raised her hand to silence him, shook her head again, and left him as quickly as she'd come.

The streets were crowded now, mostly with clients on their way to seek the favor of their wealthy patrons. Donatus sighed and ran lean fingers through his hair. He should have stayed home himself, minding his own business, receiving his own clients.

He wondered at himself that he'd thought it necessary to endure such an encounter. He hadn't known Leptis had discovered his affair with Lelia. He'd hoped the older man would simply tell him where to find her and be pleased to entertain his suit. He'd obviously hoped for far too much.

The Fates had certainly tangled the threads of his life this time, he thought, and he'd helped them with the snarling. He'd done everything wrong two years ago, from the first moment he'd laid eyes on Lelia.

He should have gone to her father right then—should have invited him to dinner and plied him with gifts and fine wine. But to what end? The only honorable thing he could have offered would have been marriage, and he'd been a legionary, forbidden to marry while in the Emperor's service.

Honor had decreed that he turn his heart away. Lelia was not his to have. Yet Donatus couldn't do it. He was drawn to her, wanted her with a hopeless, helpless fascination.

He'd made his choice. He courted her secretly, knowing it was a serious breach of custom to do so without Leptis's permission. Such clandestine passion was dangerous, but he'd been lost to it from the moment he'd first seen her uncommon, statuesque beauty. He'd ceased caring for propriety the moment her violet eyes had met his. He'd risked all to stroke the silken fall of her ebony hair, to hold the delicious weight of her breasts in his palms, to have her long legs wrapped about his waist.

He should have been wiser. At twenty-eight he'd been a man full grown, old enough to have seen the trap.

In the end, he'd had to walk away. Lelia wanted to marry and he couldn't marry. She'd finally forced him to choose, not knowing what she asked, not understanding all he owed his father. For long weeks he struggled with the painful duality. He began to long for the respite of the Legion.

He was headed east with the Second Pannonian Cavalry and a strong detachment from the Seventh Legion by the time the numbness had worn off. By day his duties consumed him. By night he slept uneasily in his tent, the guilt devouring him.

He fought the Dacians like a madman; even his own men wondered at his sanity. It had won him glory, but it hadn't eased his pain.

He dreamed of her. He remembered her citrus taste, the silken texture of her skin, the husky-voiced laugh that made his nerves tingle.

He could not forget.

He'd been with Trajan's army deep in the Carpathian wilderness when news of his father's death had come. His commander had placed a kind hand on his shoulder and encouraged him to return home. "Decurions are expendable, my son," he'd said. "Senators are not. Go home, Donatus. Marry well and sire another generation of proud Romans. The wars are no longer yours to fight."

It had seemed strange to ride home without his iron helmet and cuirass of mail, with just a small escort and Lucan, the *vexillarius* who'd carried the standard for his troop of cavalry and who'd long been his most trusted friend.

It had seemed even stranger to assume his father's role, head of his own family, and to think of administering his father's estate, worth over ten million sesterces—the thought of it boggled the mind—and see to the welfare of hundreds of slaves and clients.

Most of all it had been strange to take his hereditary place in the Senate. *He,* Donatus, who'd sat a stinking horse in Trajan's Second Pannonian Cavalry just weeks before.

The one thing that hadn't seemed strange was his decision to find Lelia and make her his wife. It was time. He could offer marriage now, and he needed to make right the wrong he'd done her before. He needed an heir, and he could not imagine making a child with any but her.

Yet when he'd tried to find her he'd met a wall at every turn. Nobody knew where she was. None of their old friends had seen her, and they seemed oddly reluctant to speak of her. He'd gone to Leptis only as a last resort. Now his last resort had failed him.

Well, maybe there was one more thing he could do. He frowned as he pondered the whispered command of Lelia's sister. The gladiatorial games? An odd suggestion, that. He didn't remember that Lelia had often enjoyed them. But for now, that odd suggestion was all he had.

Donatus arrived at the Flavian Amphitheater early enough to watch two gladiatorial contests before his friend Lucan arrived. It had been a long time since he'd gone to the games. He'd enjoyed them in his youth but found them disquieting now. They reminded him too much of war, too much of blood spilt for vainglory.

He had some respect for the gladiators, for their strength and for their courage, but he had none at all for the crowds who appeased their bloodlust from the comfort of their seats, watching valiant men die beneath the hot Mediterranean sun before making their own way home to supper and a soft bed. He drew in a deep breath and rubbed the tension from the back of his neck. Maybe he'd changed, but war had a way of doing that to a man.

He realized just how much he'd changed when he ran into an old schoolmate, now a fellow senator, heading for the same row of seats.

Plinius Caecilius Falco was pleased to see Donatus. He'd shaken his hand eagerly and then took a seat beside him. He entertained both Lucan and Donatus with his ardent love of the gladiatorial contests, and with his knowledge of the competitors and the gossip that surrounded them. As a spectator, Falco was neither passive nor restrained. He roared, he jeered, he called out taunts to those combatants he disliked, and he cheered noisily for those he supported.

Donatus met Lucan's questioning glance once and shrugged. Perhaps if they'd not already seen so much death in the past two years they'd be much like Falco. As it was, Donatus could only feel a vague disquiet, wondering how any of this might bring him closer to finding Lelia.

He sat calmly, but his eyes darted frequently around the arena, especially toward the section where the women sat with their slaves. Would she be there? And if she did come, would he be able to find her in the crowd of faces?

As he scanned the section, row by row, trumpets blew to announce the next contest. Falco laughed and leaned forward, intently watching the two combatants as they entered the ring. Donatus glanced in the same direction.

Little wonder Falco's focus was so riveted. One of the fighters was a *woman*. Her opponent, a man, a hunchbacked dwarf. Both were armored, wearing the distinctly crested helmets and faceplates of Thracian fighters. They raised their swords. The roar of the crowd was deafening. Neither of the two previous contests had garnered such a reaction.

"The cheering—it's for her," Falco told them, gesturing toward the gladiatrix.

Lucan could scarcely conceal his surprise. His green eyes held distress. "A *woman?* The *ludi* train women to fight now?"

"Much has changed since you two left Rome. What

pleased the crowd two years ago is too tame today." Falco practically quivered with excitement. "But, ah, you'll soon grow to like it. To see a woman fight is damned arousing. Almost as good as bedding one." He laughed. "Almost."

Donatus found himself more in agreement with Lucan than with Falco. "And who is this woman that she would so defame her gender and decry the gentleness of her sex?"

Falco could scarcely pull his attention away from the ring. "She is called Leda. She began to fight nine months ago. So far she's fought five times."

"And killed?"

"Not a human. Not yet. Four beasts. Two lions, a bull and a tigress. Then she fought another woman, one who outweighed her by far. The Emperor himself watched that one, and was so impressed by Leda's valor that he called the result an even draw and rewarded both combatants with gold."

Falco returned his gaze to the ring, where the combatants now matched their skills with the ringing blows of serious swordplay. "She's skillful and has no lack of courage. And as you've seen, she is now the city's most popular gladiatrix. A fine-looking woman she is, too."

Donatus turned his own attention to the ring. He folded his arms and sat back, uneasy with the thought of watching a woman fight and perhaps die.

Yet as he watched, the soldier in him took over and he began to grudgingly admire her skill. She moved with an agility that was almost sensual, the lean muscles in her thighs wet with perspiration above the polished metal of her greaves. She was tireless, her sword flashing so rapidly that the dwarf was forced to maintain a constant defense.

As the fight wore on, Donatus found himself drawn in. The woman enthralled the crowd, weaving a spell of melancholy and passion over them, as if her soul cried out with the metallic wail of her sword. Twice the dwarf appeared on the verge of victory, using his superior strength against her. Twice Donatus held his breath, silently begging her to rise. When she somehow found the strength he breathed again, and heard the same sigh from the crowd all around him.

"She's good," Lucan said in a low voice beside him. "She's really good. But it makes me hurt to watch her. Why does she do this?"

Donatus nodded without answering. The same question plagued him, too.

How long the fight lasted, Donatus couldn't have begun to say. Time seemed suspended, held prisoner within a strange dimension of feeling. He couldn't look away. He felt each thrust as if against his own flesh. He tasted the rust, smelled the sweat, felt the blows numb his wrist. He lived each moment, and he understood the reason.

It was Leda, wooing the crowd with the force of her personality.

Something in her reached out to them, something they all recognized and felt in the deepest core of their being. She fought without caution, like a cornered tigress. Yet she seemed to await death, her movements somber and restrained.

Suddenly Donatus knew the reason she wielded the sword. She fought to live, and yet…she *wanted* to die.

Because he'd connected with her to a depth he couldn't understand, this knowledge grieved him. Without his completely realizing it, Donatus's hand tightened around the imaginary hilt of a sword, as if he could fight for her, as if his strength and will could somehow help her.

His attention never left her. He sat, still and tense, waiting for the end and fearing it. If she fell, he would know utter devastation, feeling he'd lost something irreplaceable, without even knowing what it was.

The contest wore on, interminable, frustrating, but that seemed to work in the woman's favor. She was not as strong as the little man, but her stamina was formidable.

In the end, this was not her day to die. The finish came with surprising suddenness. The dwarf, in his exhaustion, failed in his concentration and made one careless move. She took him down, holding her sword to his throat.

"Oh, mercy," Lucan groaned beside him. "Now she'll have to kill him."

Donatus watched. The decision went to the crowd, and today the spectators were in a generous mood. The dwarf had fought bravely. He'd given a good contest and they granted a reprieve, giving the sign for missus. The gladiatrix stood, sheathing her weapon. She helped her opponent to his feet, put a supporting arm around him and walked him off the field. The crowd cheered.

Donatus felt drained, as if returning to reality from a twisted dream. Strong emotions churned within him, but he couldn't label or explain any of them. He looked around. The entire arena was subdued. There was little noise, even less movement. The gladiatrix named Leda had cast an unusual spell.

The silence didn't last long. The crowd soon began a low, indistinct rumble. Falco picked it up, pumping his fist in the air in time to the growing crescendo. "Le-da! Le-da! Le-da!"

She entered the ring again, the bright yellow plume on her helmet bobbing with each step she took toward the center of the ring. Donatus leaned forward, spellbound by her presence despite his best intention to the contrary. She acknowledged the crowd's ardor with a deep bow.

The roar only increased. She returned to her full height and raised both fists high into the air in acknowledgement of their praise.

"Le-da! Le-da! Le-da!"

She bowed again, but the noise did not subside.

Donatus held his breath as the gladiatrix seemed to hesitate a moment. The crowd went wild when she stepped forward and reached up to the leather strap of her helmet with one delicate hand. They hooted and stamped and chanted as she unfastened the buckle and drew it slowly from her head, shaking her long braid free of the confining metal.

It took a moment for everything to register with Donatus—the long braid of glossy black hair, now dampened with sweat, the large eyes, the structure of her face. The woman before him was beautiful. She was the dream he'd dreamed for two long years, by night and by day, waking and sleeping. She was *Lelia*.

Donatus felt like he'd just taken a javelin through the gut.

Chapter Two

$\sim\!\!\curvearrowright\!\!\gg\!\!\ll\!\!\curvearrowleft\!\!\sim$

Donatus found Lucan in the popina, as they'd arranged. When Donatus approached the table, his friend smiled, stretching out long legs and sighing as he pushed away the remains of several dishes.

"I thought you'd never get back here," Lucan said. "And truly, had you lingered much longer, I'd have killed myself with this food. The *garum* here in the city is so good…and the wine!" He rolled his eyes in pleasure.

"You've been a soldier too long, my friend, eating a soldier's rations."

"Truly." Lucan leaned forward as Donatus gathered his toga into one hand and sat down. He lowered his voice. "But now what of you? Your grim expression tells me the news is not good."

Donatus shook his head. "No, it's not."

"You found out all you wished to know?"

"Mostly. Thanks be to the gods, Leptis has slaves who value gold above loyalty to their master. They were pleased to share what they could, although their knowledge is sketchy in places."

"Then you know how Lelia ended up in the gladiatorial ring? Did the slaves know that?"

"No, not for certain. But they were apt to conjecture." Donatus raised one eyebrow. "It seems I am to blame."

Lucan sat back abruptly. "You? But you were in Dacia!"

"And that's why." Donatus took a slow sip of wine, hoping to wash away the bitterness of the words he must speak. "I didn't know when I became involved with Lelia that her father had already promised her to another."

Lucan gave a low, drawn-out whistle.

"His name was Scipio Paullus. I know the man. He's a powerful, influential senator. It would have been a good match for Lelia's family." He met Lucan's gaze squarely. "It probably would not have been a good match for Lelia. Paullus is old and arrogant. He would have had to crush her to control her—and, believe me, he would not have hesitated to do so."

Donatus took another long draught of wine. "No matter now. It seems my relationship with Lelia ruined the match."

"How so? Leptis didn't know. She could have—"

"Paullus had stipulated that he receive a virginal bride."

Lucan met his gaze, then looked away. "Maybe it's not such a bad thing you ruined it, Donatus, if Paullus is as harsh a man as you say."

"You might think so. But in truth, it was a terrible thing. When I left, Lelia had to confess to her father that she couldn't wed Paullus, and why. Leptis was irate. She'd let herself be sullied. She'd disgraced the family."

Lucan made a soft sound of shared hurt.

"There was a terrible argument. Lelia's mother tried to placate Leptis, but his wrath would not be mollified. He ranted at Lelia, cursed at her. It must have been awful, because the slaves wouldn't even tell me all he said. Finally he disowned her before them all, and forcibly dragged her like refuse into the street. He told her that since she'd played the whore with me, perhaps she could earn her bread with what she'd learned."

Lucan's fist hit the table. "What father would do that to his child?"

Donatus didn't answer. There was no way he could cast blame. Not when he had his own share of the guilt.

For a long moment there was silence.

"You'll marry her, of course," Lucan said.

"Of course. I *will* make this right, Lucan. She'll be loath to trust me, and I'm prepared for that. But if I don't take her from the ring she'll be killed there. One fight, two…a dozen? I don't know when, only that eventually she'll die on that hot sand. And I couldn't live with myself if her life and her beauty were to be lost that way."

Lucan nodded and drew in a deep breath. "Then, my friend, you have work to do."

Donatus smiled for the first time. He'd already been thinking about that. Indeed he had.

Valeria Lelia turned down the narrow alley that led to her apartment. It was gloomy and smelled of urine, but at the moment she was too tired and too sore to care. The wound on her right thigh was deep; it would hurt to climb the stairs. The slave who'd stitched it together had told her she couldn't expect it to heal for at least three or four weeks. He'd also told Brocchus that she must not train or fight again until it did. She sighed, remembering the frown on the *lanista*'s face.

He must have been hoping to have her fight again soon, even though she'd already fought more often than was customary. Neither of them had anticipated her sudden popularity. It disturbed Lelia, but it pleased the *lanista* who employed her. *Owned* her, actually. His investment in her was paying off huge dividends—or it *had,* as long as she'd remained well enough to fight.

She hobbled up the stairs slowly, one at a time, balancing awkwardly and trying not to stretch the stitches too much. As she reached the top, a shadowy figure moved toward her. The sudden action startled her, and she jumped backwards reflexively. She teetered for one long, hideous moment on the edge of the step, then began to fall, her hands flailing outwards to grasp anything solid.

Her fingers caught in and clutched soft folds of fabric. The man who'd startled her now caught her, drawing her firmly against a broad expanse of solid chest. Lelia gasped, at once dismayed by her unusual clumsiness and thankful for his strong arms around her. He pulled her forward onto steadier footing and she glanced up, prepared to thank him for the help. Until she saw his face.

Her mouth went completely dry. "Donatus?" she finally managed to say. "It is you?"

"Yes, Lelia," he answered, his voice smoother and warmer than she'd remembered. Her heart clutched hard at the rich timbre of it.

Her back stiffened. Damn. It was Donatus, holding her against his body, making her breath come too rapidly, making her heart beat too quickly. She pushed herself from his hold and stepped away, smoothing her hands down her clothing so she wouldn't have to look at him.

He was handsome, so achingly handsome. The sight of him made her want to cry, and that angered her. She'd vowed to hate him. She *did* hate him. But the sight of him brought back those old feelings.

She forced her voice into submission. It came out just as

she'd hoped. Cool. Completely detached. Nothing like the heat that scorched her soul. "How did you find me?"

"One of the trainers at the *ludus* told me where you lived."

"Then you know." She looked away, surprised by the fire which suffused her face. She squared her shoulders. "I'm not ashamed of it. I am good at what I do."

"I know. I watched you today."

He said the words quietly, as if he were trying not to show emotion of any kind. She imagined she detected a hint of displeasure. It angered her that she cared what he thought.

She shrugged and hid her discomfort in impatience. "So you decided to come home. Back from your wars. What do you want with me?"

He studied her for a long moment. Lelia realized she held her breath only when he finally looked away. Those eyes of his, so green and fringed by such dark lashes, too beautiful to belong to a man. They'd always rendered her breathless, especially when he slept and those ebony lashes lay gentle as night against bronzed lean cheekbones. The memory of Donatus in warm, naked repose made her stomach churn with a sort of helpless anxiety, a flutter of hurt mixed with desire. And this, more than anything, angered her.

"We need to talk," he said. "Not here on the stairs. Is there a more private place?"

"Oh? Somewhere like my bedroom? Somewhere there's a soft mattress?"

His gaze swept up to meet hers. Surprisingly, it held a note of sadness. "We won't need a bed. Just a place that's quiet and free of interruption. Your apartment will be fine if it's nearby. You probably shouldn't walk down these stairs again with your wounded leg."

She frowned. So he'd noticed that, too. "Oh, well, come on, then. The sooner you say whatever you have to say, the sooner you'll leave and I can get back to the business of forgetting you." She led the way to her door, opened it, and gestured for him to walk inside. She noticed that he had to bend slightly to enter, his dark curls becoming even darker in the shadowed interior.

She left the door standing open, a not-too-subtle reminder that he'd be leaving shortly. Donatus took in the room quickly, surveying it, making the space his own with an air of quiet command.

There wasn't much for him to see. A pallet of straw covered by a blanket of wool. A cheap oil lamp etched with gladiators in combat—she'd bought that at the souvenir stalls. A low bench near a small hearth. A wooden box of food, and another with her folded clothes. The room was tidy, but then, keeping things in their proper places wasn't hard when there weren't many things.

As Donatus studied his surroundings, she studied him. He looked healthy, tanned and lean. He wore a senator's stripes. That must mean his father had died. That brought a pang of sadness. She'd liked Marcus Flavius Antonius. He'd been a good man, a kind man. His slaves loved him; his colleagues in the Senate esteemed him. Once upon a time she'd even imagined his son to be much like him. But that was before.

"It's nice, Lelia," Donatus said, gesturing around the small room.

She snorted. "Don't pretend to be impressed. I know it's only a dark, squalid room in a dark, squalid *insulae* in a dark, squalid part of town."

His eyes met hers. There was a flicker of pain, quickly veiled as he looked away and the dark lashes lowered. "You were not always so harsh," he said.

"I've learned to be."

He didn't answer. His lips tightened, the lines around them deepening. So that hurt him, did it? Well, she could tell him a few things about hurt.

"Why did you come?" she asked, crossing her arms.

"I came to apologize. I know it won't make everything right. I know it won't undo the wrong I did or the consequences that resulted, but—"

"You've talked to someone. What do you know?"

He frowned. "You've been disowned."

"And?"

"You've become a gladiatrix."

"And?" Lelia held her breath.

He shrugged. "That's all. Maybe you can tell me anything else I need to know."

"There *is* nothing else you need to know." Lelia didn't want him to say more. It had been easier to hate him when he'd been away, when she'd been able to pretend he was a man without conscience or honor. But he'd returned. He stood before her now, his scent filling the room. She could hardly bear to look at him, at his dark beauty.

He came closer. Lelia groaned inside and stepped backward. He noted her retreat and halted. He raised one hand. "I was wrong, Lelia. I knew… Believe me, I paid for what I did. Every day, every single day since I left you."

Lelia wanted to be moved by the pain in his voice. It seemed genuine, almost as genuine as the promises he'd once made. It helped to remember the day he'd left, how empty all those promises had seemed then. "You *paid,* Donatus? Oh, that's good. I'm glad you felt pain. I'm glad you have some small bit of conscience left. Maybe the next woman you desire won't have to suffer with lies quite as engaging as those I heard."

He closed his eyes. A long moment of quiet passed.

"Go away, Donatus. Just go away. I won't forgive you. I won't forget I lost everything because of you. I won't let you speak more lies and crawl into my bed and pretend the past never happened." She turned away, her legs quivering with agitation. "You're wasting your time. I never want to see you again."

He moved closer, so close she felt his heat all along her spine. "*Never,* Lelia? Never is such a long time."

"Never."

"It matters not." His body tensed, as if he battled within himself. "I'll give you back the things you've lost. I'll marry you."

Lelia twisted around. "I just told you I'd never forgive you, and you ask me to *marry* you?"

His smile was not what she'd expected. It was sad and tender. She didn't need that. Not when she was trying to hate him. She suddenly wanted to sink onto the straw mat and cry for that sweet, precious thing they'd lost. Instead, she stared up at him, unable to find the harsh words she needed. "Donatus, you lying dog. I don't *need* your pity. I don't want it. I'm surviving. Go whisper your lies to some other sweet young thing. I'm not so innocent anymore."

His expression hardened into hurt. "Then there is no love for me anymore?"

"None at all."

His eyes found hers. "I don't believe you."

She moved to the door, pushed it wider, and gestured an unspoken command that he leave. "Believe whatever you wish. Your belief changes my life not at all."

He raised one eyebrow. "Oh, but my sweet Lelia…*that's* where you're wrong." He stepped closer, took her chin in gentle fingertips, brushed his lips lightly across hers—and was gone before she could fully comprehend the words. Or ponder what he'd meant by them.

* * *

The night was cold in more ways than one. Lelia slept fitfully, her blanket twisted and not warm enough to provide protection after the small bank of coals in the hearth burnt out. She dreamed: the noise of the carts rumbling down the cobbled street outside became the clanking of the huge chain that raised the gates of the arena, and she rushed in to fight, fear pulsing through her veins.

Mercifully, she always awoke at the first slashing blow to her thigh and realized she fought nothing but her own fright and the pain of her stitches. Each time she pulled the blanket more securely around her body and tried to sleep again. At length she dozed, wandering darkly toward the maze of more dreams, more pain, more blood-churning racing of the heart.

The fourth time she awoke she finally gave up. She arose, put on her warmest tunic and *palla,* and opened the shuttered window to look out over the neighborhood in nightscape. The air was cool, but not frigid. Wrapped in the wool of her *palla,* she didn't shiver now. She breathed in deeply of the crisp air. It felt good, and cleared away the lingering melancholy of her dreams. Her restlessness was due to the pain of her wound. It had to be that.

She'd been injured before. The tigress she'd fought had ripped her back open with its claws. But Lelia didn't remember as much trouble sleeping then as now.

She sat down on the bench by the hearth with a sigh, and stirred up the beginnings of a small fire. The coals soon glowed with life and she turned away from the thickening smoke. She lit her small lantern and used its light to bathe and dress, coiling her hair into a simple but elegant braid.

Dawn would soon lighten the sky. On any normal day she'd be at the *ludus* soon after that, training with the *doctores* or battling other gladiators while the day was still cool. But now her injury prevented such activity. She was at odds with herself.

Perhaps that was why she dressed herself as a woman today, forsaking the plain and serviceable garments she usually wore in favor of the one expensive tunic she owned—the one she'd been wearing the day she'd been sent from her father's home.

That day seemed almost a lifetime ago. She slipped the tunic over her head, sighing at its softness, marveling at its rare color—purple, the color of a queen. Donatus had bought it for her, and a *palla* of embroidered gold to wear with it. But she'd left the *palla* behind, so hurried had been her flight.

She'd chosen the purple tunic that long-ago day because she'd badly needed to feel Donatus with her when she talked to her father. Even though Donatus had gone, she had still believed he'd return.

Lelia pushed aside the memories and moved toward the hearth, enjoying the feel of the garment as it slid sensuously against her skin. It made her feel feminine. It made her remember the way luxury felt. She closed her eyes and dreamed, swaying so that the fabric flowed over her body in a whisper. Absentmindedly she rubbed her hand down her hips, wincing at the scratching of her callused palms against such finely woven cloth.

In that moment she knew she was a mocker, a pretender, a low-bred purchased slave who wielded a sword to kill men and who had no right to clothe herself in a garment so delicate, or to pretend even for a minute that she was a queen. She sucked in her breath, caught by surprise at the pain.

She fought tears as she snatched the garment over her head, leaving it in a wadded heap upon the floor. Her breath was ragged as she dressed in her usual plain tunic of coarse cloth, cursing herself for the dreamer she was. Cursing Donatus, too, for making her want to dream.

* * *

Severina hadn't arrived yet. Lelia was relieved, knowing she had to catch her friend before Severina entered the *ludus*. Once she checked in with the trainers Severina's day would be a tight schedule of regulated activities. There'd be no time for talking.

Lelia knew this well. Normally she'd be following the same regimen of physical exercise, mental training, warm baths and hot food. It was a demanding regimen, and exhausting. But when she put aside all thoughts of the end to which it took her she found it enjoyable. She never felt more full of health than she did during her training. Only the fact that she was training to kill, or perhaps be killed, put a pall over the entire enterprise.

Most of the time she could put such morose thoughts aside. Severina had taught her to do that, had helped her enter a place within herself that was untouchable, that did not feel and did not fear. Severina had learned it herself years ago, as a slave to a cruel master, long before her time with the *lanistas* here. She'd taught herself to lie passively beneath the man while he rutted upon her, and to endure his beatings without so much as a whimper. She'd taught herself to *survive,* and now, in the oddest joining of two very different people in friendship, she'd taught Lelia the same.

Lelia awaited her now beneath an arched portico, pacing nervously until she spotted her friend. She called her over, rubbing the pain from her thigh while Severina made her way across the crowded street.

"Lelia?" Severina said when she joined her. "What are you doing here? You should be home, resting that leg."

"I have to talk, and it couldn't wait. I know you don't have long, that Brocchus won't be pleased if you're late."

Severina waved her hand in a gesture of dismissal. "He'll

get over it. Besides, I'm a little early today." She lifted one eyebrow. "Why are you so agitated? I've only seen you this nervous before a fight."

"He's here, Severina."

"Who?"

"Donatus."

Severina drew in a sharp breath. "How do you know?"

"He came to see me."

"So he knows?"

"Yes… No… I mean, I don't know. He's spoken with somebody, because he knew about the fighting and he knew about my being disowned. But he didn't seem to know about…everything else."

Severina gave her a sharp glance. "He doesn't know about his child."

"No."

Severina frowned at her.

Lelia frowned back. "Don't start with me, Severina," she cautioned. "I have good reasons for not telling him."

"I know, I know. I'll not berate you—though I think you're wrong. He could help you. With his family connections…his father, the rich senator. I've told you before, they can help you."

"His father's dead. Donatus has inherited it all. The family estate, the money, the seat in the Senate."

Severina gave a low whistle. "Then the gods are giving you good fortune. Just back him into a corner and make him pay."

"It's not like that. I… It's not like that."

"What is it, then? Don't tell me you still love him."

"Of course I don't. What kind of fool do you take me for?"

Severina looked unconvinced. "So what did he say? That he still loves you? That he misses you in his bed?"

"He came to apologize."

"Hoping you'd forgive him and let him take up where he left off. Hoping you'd spread your legs for him."

"Donatus asked me to marry him."

"He didn't!" Severina looked stunned. "I can't believe it. I didn't think him the sort."

"Neither did I."

Severina glanced at her quickly. "Will you marry him, Lelia?"

"No."

"You'd be a fool not to, no matter the past. You might hate him, but…for what he's offering you! Freedom, Lelia! Freedom from the *ludus,* from the *lanista,* from *death!*"

"I don't want his pity. I saw it in his eyes. He feels guilty."

"And he should." Severina snorted.

"I want no part of that. It wasn't his fault that I fell in love with him, that I lay with him and that we made a child together. That was my decision. He does not bear all the blame for that."

"But he bears the blame for leaving you."

"He didn't know."

"You should've told him. Maybe he would've stayed."

"And that's precisely why I did not tell him. Should I have been a chain around his neck? If he didn't wish to marry me, should I have captured him with a child, Severina? Oh, no. Resentment would have coiled like a serpent in his breast until he finally despised me for having so ensnared him."

"He loved you. You carried his child. He might have grown to love you more."

Lelia shrugged. "It wasn't a chance I was willing to take."

"And now?"

"Nothing's changed."

"Nothing except that he's returned and wants to marry you."

"Donatus hasn't truly considered the consequences. Not yet. He hasn't realized what marrying me would mean. He'd be the laughing stock of the Senate. He'd endure the derision of all the nobility."

"Maybe he'd consider you worth it."

"I doubt that. And, besides, the *lanista* would never allow it, even if I were willing. Which I am not."

"I'd get out of the *ludus* if I were you." There was silence as Severina looked away, lost in deep thought for long moments. "I'd get out of here. The *lanistas,* they've purchased elephants." Severina's gaze met her friend's. "Elephants, Lelia. A clerk told me last week. Four elephants, coming from Africa. We're to fight them when they arrive."

Severina's eyes filled with tears. "It's not that I'm *afraid* of elephants. It's that…I saw a gladiator kill an elephant once. I was only ten at the time, but I've never forgotten it. That elephant—you could read the emotion in her eyes. I'll never forget the way she looked at us all, with so much confusion, so much hurt, so much pain at the betrayal."

Severina shuddered. "I know killing is what we do. We train, we fight, we kill. We know when we enter the ring that that's what we're there for. So we just get down to business and do it. You learn to put it aside. But with an elephant I don't think I could. I'd see those eyes. I'd always see them, Lelia."

Severina swiped angrily at her eyes. "I don't want to kill an elephant, and I don't want you to have to, either."

The tears caught Lelia by surprise. Severina never showed such weakness. She'd killed six wild beasts already, and had never once shown fear. Lelia's heart tightened with concern.

"I want my freedom," Severina said hoarsely. "But if *I* can't get out, then at least I want *you* out."

The truth hit Lelia like the blow of a gladius. She understood in that moment that, no matter how well the *lanistas* taught them to set aside reality, there would remain, for each of them, a fundamental piece of humanity that could not be subdued or ignored. It would return. It would haunt them.

Worse, Severina's emotion reminded Lelia of her own worst fear—the fear which stalked her and sickened her each time she thought of it. Soon she would kill more than tigers. Soon she would kill more than elephants. If she stayed with Brocchus much longer, soon she would kill *men*.

Chapter Three

Brocchus the *lanista* pushed himself back from the books spread open upon his table and sighed with satisfaction. Things were going well, far better than he'd hoped. His wealth was increasing. Life was good. He scratched his head and arose, adjusting the patch he wore over one eye to hide the scar received from the curved sica of Astinax years before, when he'd been a young gladiator fighting in the arena at Capua. Normally he didn't think much about the scar or the patch, but lately he'd been amazed to discover a vanity within himself that cursed them both. And even more amazed to discover that that vanity had a woman as its cause.

Brocchus moved to the large window which looked out onto the training fields. He absentmindedly watched the men sweating in their exertions, hefting the wooden swords with which they battled, before he realized suddenly that his eyes were searching for *her*. He grunted at the sharp twist of his heart. *Leda.* The fiery young gladiatrix had ensnared him, and he didn't know what to do about it.

He was no fool. She could do better than he. He'd discovered enough about her to know she'd been reared a noblewoman. What strange fate had cast her penniless at his door, he did not know.

And any moment now she'd come here, to his personal apartment, where he could feast his eyes upon her, smell her soft scent, and imagine the feel of her body beneath his. She couldn't train but she would still work, and he'd pretended to need her help with the accounts.

Soon, very soon, he hoped to declare his feelings. Perhaps after she'd thought on the matter she'd see the wisdom of becoming the *lanista*'s woman rather than his warrior.

He was still lost in the reverie when he heard trumpets from the direction of the front gate. He sprang to his feet, slamming his account book shut. Trumpets usually meant good news for him—some wealthy, powerful person leading an entourage to the *ludus* to contract a private combat for the entertainment of friends. The price was negotiable, and almost always, because the gentleman was in front of his peers, he'd wish to appear generous.

Brocchus hurried out. Even he was awed by the splendor of the sight before him. Whoever this unexpected guest might be, he was obviously a man of wealth. Just one of the purple garments upon the slaves who bore his litter would have cost Brocchus a year's wages. He began to breathe harder, excitement churning.

A guard came forward, a handsome Roman at his side. The stranger's eyes were friendly and without guile. They contained merriment, as if he were inwardly laughing at some private joke. The stranger held out his hand. "I am Titus Livius Lucan, spokesman for Marcus Flavius Donatus whose entourage this is. Would you be the owner of this establishment, sir?"

"I am," Brocchus said, extending his own hand and smiling. "Welcome. What can I do for you today? Might you wish to arrange a combat of gladiators for your amusement?"

"No, our business is of more import than that. My friend wishes to purchase one of your gladiators."

Brocchus cleared his throat. "Well...you might see, sir, how I'm reluctant to discuss such an important matter out here, surrounded as we are by so many onlookers, and sweating in the sun. Would your friend care to leave his litter and enter the building?" At Lucan's nod, Brocchus turned to a nearby slave. "Refreshment for my guests. And be quick about it."

Donatus had never been so emotionally involved in any battle before. Not even in the wilds of Dacia, with warriors howling and dying all around him, not even when javelins had flown so close that his lips had felt the hissing wind of their passing.

This was a battle of a different sort, and in its way more fearsome. This was a battle of wits, of mental strategies, a battle that would ultimately be decided by how well he out-maneuvered the stranger before him. Donatus forced himself to breathe, to appear calm, to relax his stance and seem unaffected by the *lanista*'s frown.

"Leda's the best gladiatrix I own," the man said slowly. "I hadn't thought to sell her."

"I realize that," Donatus said. "I came prepared to be generous."

The *lanista*'s eyes narrowed. "Might I ask, sir, *why* you wish to purchase her?"

The barb was subtle, conveyed more in the tone than in the words, and it angered Donatus. He understood the question only too well, and supposed he should have been prepared for it. "My intentions are honorable," he said. "I wish to redeem her from this life of combat."

The *lanista* crossed his arms and studied him with his one good eye. "And why should her life of combat be of concern to you?"

"Because I knew her long before you did. She was never meant to be in the arena."

Donatus saw something flicker within the man's gaze, just a momentary flash of agreement before the harsh features become impassive again. He decided to pursue the advantage. "The gladiatrix you call Leda is of noble extraction."

"If so, how did she come to be in such penury that she'd sell her services to me?"

"She'd been cast from her home. Her father is a harsh man. He dealt harshly with her."

Donatus waited in the silence. The *lanista*'s face was granite, grim and unyielding.

Donatus looked around at their surroundings, realizing they were definitely in the *lanista*'s territory. Roman guards stood outside the door. Donatus could see several more through the window which faced the training field.

He studied the details in the room, noting the arms and equipment of the *lanista's* youth proudly displayed on the walls. There was a banner of silk, proclaiming the name of the familia of gladiators to which he'd belonged. And there, in the center, was the most cherished prize of all—the engraved wooden sword, the *rudis,* which signified the man's freedom.

"How much?" Donatus managed to say calmly. "How much did you pay for her? I'll give you that and more, enough to compensate for the loss of her skills in the arena."

"Leda is mine. I'll take care of her."

Something in his voice alerted Donatus. He glanced up in time to see the brief flash of emotion in the other man's face. In that moment Donatus understood.

"And what of Leda?" he questioned. "Does she return the love you feel?"

The *lanista*'s eyes narrowed. He crossed his arms. He did not respond.

"She is of the senatorial class. You…are not. What can you offer her?"

Again, there was no response.

Donatus drew in a long, exasperated breath. There was little choice left, even though what he was about to do might get him thrown out of the small apartment without ceremony. It was all he had left.

He named a price and heard the *lanista*'s sharp intake of breath. The amount was exorbitant, an unheard-of amount for any slave, especially for a woman. But Lelia was not just any slave, nor was she just any woman. She was *his* woman, even if she chose not to acknowledge that yet.

"You can't be serious," the *lanista* said, meeting his gaze as if reluctant to believe. "That's it, sir. You jest with me."

"I do not jest."

"Female slaves rarely cost more than two thousand sesterces. A good gladiator might go for five thousand. The very best might go ten thousand. And yet you offer me *fifty* thousand sesterces?"

"I do."

The *lanista* studied him closely. Too closely. "What is this woman to you, Senator?" he asked finally.

"The same as she is to you."

The *lanista* nodded. He drew in a long, deep, sighing breath. "Then she has ensnared the both of us, I see."

"More surely than a *retiarius* ensnares his opponent in his net."

"Of a truth," the *lanista* said, shaking his head in disbelief. "Poor mortal men that we are, surviving sword and javelin time and time again, only to be brought down by a woman's flashing eyes."

He held out a hand. Donatus took it, surprised by the sudden friendship being offered. He looked up into the other man's face.

"I'm a former slave," the *lanista* said gruffly. "I've made my wealth by the strength of my hands and through the blood of other men. I cannot offer her all that you can, and yet Leda must make the choice herself."

Donatus felt as if someone had kicked him in the gut. He heard the *lanista* call a slave, heard him give the order. Leda would be brought before them.

Suddenly Donatus understood that the battle he'd just fought had not been the end. Indeed, it was only the prelude to the one yet to come.

"No!"

Donatus felt the word rip into him. And if eyes could inflict wounds, then he was being pummeled to death by Lelia's long-lashed fury. Brocchus—for so Lelia had called the *lanista*—turned an almost pitying glance his way.

"No!" Lelia repeated, shaking her head. "You can't be serious!"

Brocchus moved to her and placed a gentle hand on her shoulder. "I know this is a surprise. Maybe you need a little time to consider."

Lelia whirled to face Donatus. "You! Of all the unmitigated nerve, to come here and try to *buy* me. Am I your slave, Donatus? Do you see the white chalk of a slave auction on my feet? Am I yours to possess?"

Donatus caught her wrist just before her palm made contact with his cheek. He wasn't as swift in blocking the kick of her booted toe to his shin, or the curse that was his immediate response to it, before he captured the other fist swinging toward his jaw.

"Stop it, Lelia!" he demanded, wrapping his arms around her tightly enough to hold her still. "Stop it! Listen to me."

She struggled against his hold, her breath hissing out

through her teeth. Even in his anger Donatus felt his body stir at the heaving of her breasts against his chest. He had to be a madman to want this woman so fiercely that even now he imagined her body against the wall—and himself kissing her into submission.

Oblivious to his thoughts, she continued to fight him, trying to twist within his arms, trying to free an elbow enough to crack his ribs with it. He let her struggle for a time, not giving her one bit of leverage or freedom, all the while making her more furious. He was only too aware of Brocchus's hulking presence, as he watched them with a mixture of concern and amusement from a few feet away.

"Oh, I hate you!" she said through clenched teeth.

"I know," Donatus answered. "But remember, my sweet, that love and hate are not too far apart."

"If you *think,* after all you've done to me, that I'll ever love you again, then you truly are a fool."

"It doesn't matter. But you should at least listen to me like a cultured lady, rather than behave like an uncivilized gladiatrix."

Her breath caught at the insult. "*An uncivilized gladiatrix! How dare you say such to me? You…stinking backside of an ill-begotten mule!*"

Donatus laughed. He couldn't hold it back, even knowing it would inflame her more. Her spirit hadn't diminished one iota. "I would let you go," he whispered near her ear. "Except that I'm enjoying the feel of your body so near to mine."

She gasped at the statement, then shoved her shoulder hard against his chest. "Brocchus!" she screeched. "Get this madman off me!"

Brocchus stepped forward, then hesitated at a warning frown from Donatus. "Perhaps if you promised not to slap him or kick him again, he'd release you himself," the *lanista* suggested with droll humor.

"Get off me, you ridiculous excuse for a warrior," Lelia said, twisting hard in Donatus's arms. "I'll listen to your stupid lies—just *let me go!*"

Donatus released her immediately and she retreated, rubbing her wrists as if he'd hurt her. He hadn't, but he saw Brocchus's eyes travel over her carefully, as if to make sure. When the *lanista* finally relaxed, studying them both with an odd expression, Donatus knew the big man had caught on to her fakery.

"Speak," she ordered, gesturing impatiently. "I said I'd listen."

"I offered Brocchus money for you," he said. "But not because I mean to enslave you."

She looked to Brocchus for confirmation. He nodded, raising one eyebrow slightly. The *lanista* cleared his throat and stepped forward. "Leda, I might be a fool for what I'm about to say, but you are my slave, are you not?"

Lelia's eyes grew wary. "You can't order me to marry him. I sold my services to you, Brocchus, but my heart is yet my own."

"True, but consider this. I may let fight whomever I choose, and I may let rest whomever I choose. If you do not fight, you'll be years earning enough to buy your freedom."

"Brocchus, no…don't say it. Don't listen to him. There's so much you don't know."

There was kindness in the *lanista*'s face as he took her hand and raised it to his lips. He kissed it softly, the gesture seeming strangely out of context, given his strength and gruffness and massive size. "I don't know all, that's true, but I see you together here and I know enough. Marry the Senator, Leda. Let him purchase your freedom, for I cannot put you into the arena again."

Her eyes squeezed shut. "No, oh, no."

She turned her back, hugging herself, her head bowed low. She walked to the window and stood there, watching the gladiators in combat. Donatus watched her, saw her eyes focus on one gladiatrix, a shapely woman with long chestnut hair in a heavy braid down her back. For long minutes Lelia watched, until the woman fell, overcome by the more powerful man she fought.

Abruptly Lelia turned, squaring her shoulders. Her eyes were hard when they met his. "You are a fool, Donatus, to want to marry me. You give no thought to the shame you'll bring upon your family honor to so link your name with mine. Yet, if you're willing to take the risk, then I'll marry you. But only if you agree to purchase Severina also. And for the same price you'll pay for me."

Donatus heard the *lanista*'s sharp intake of breath. The vixen played a game of wits, a game of will. She didn't know the price he'd offered, but she certainly knew it was no paltry sum.

"I am willing," he said. "But it will cost you."

"Cost me *what?*"

"You must marry me immediately. Right now. And you must agree that you will from henceforth act the part of the agreeable wife in public, whatever your private feelings."

Donatus could almost see her thoughts working furiously as she turned his suggestion around in her mind, viewing it from every possible angle.

"I'll agree to that," she finally answered. "But only if you release Severina from all servitude once I'm your wife. Give her freedom and enough money to begin a business of her own."

"Ah, but slaves are too dearly bought, my love. And especially this one, whose price will be equal to your own."

"You're not willing?" she asked, lifting her head, meeting his gaze with a triumphant expression. "Then I was right to suppose the price would be too precious for—"

"Oh, I didn't say I wasn't willing. I only said that such would be dearly bought. And you, my beloved wife, shall be the one to pay the price. One condition, and Severina will have her freedom and a new beginning."

Donatus moved to Lelia, so near he could smell her womanly fragrance. He leaned closer, his breath a mere whisper against her neck. "*An heir,* Lelia. You must give me one."

She closed her eyes, unable to speak for a moment.

Donatus lifted a finger to stroke the soft outline of her lips. "You must lie with me until you are with child. If you can't agree to this, then Severina will serve you as your slave. You may not release her."

"Donatus," she whispered. "Damn you for the bastard you are."

"I need an heir, Lelia. I owe that much to my father."

She lifted her head, meeting his gaze with angry eyes. "Then you'll have your heir. Go ahead. Call for the holy man. Do whatever you must do, and do it quickly."

Brocchus cleared his throat. "I think you'll not be sorry for this decision, Leda. The Senator can give you more than you could have gotten in the arena. And without the same risk."

She turned to him, her expression cold and unyielding. "Without risk? Then you understand nothing, Brocchus. I am more enslaved now than ever I was before. And, though I will be richer, I never shall have known greater poverty."

Brocchus frowned. "How can that be?"

"To you, I sold my service." She flung a haughty glance toward Donatus. "To him, I am selling my soul."

Chapter Four

"You look too beautiful for words," Severina said, stepping back to survey her handiwork. "I can hardly believe your good fortune—to have so captured the man's heart that he'd come for you with a grand procession and buy you from Brocchus like this!" She sighed dramatically. "And he's so handsome, with those dark curls and those long-lashed green eyes, with that cleft in his chin and those magnificent shoulders. You never told me he was so handsome."

"I don't want to talk about him," Lelia said, her voice flat. "I'll do what I must do. But to forgive him... That much goodness is not within me." She fingered the garment she wore, the *tunica recta* of a bride, secured at the waist with its girdle of wool, and over that, the traditional saffron-colored *palla*.

Severina came forward, holding the orange *flammeneum* of silk that would veil her hair. As her friend secured it over her braids, Lelia tasted the bitterness of defeat. Donatus had won.

She'd let him win.

He'd come for her, prepared even to the provision of these wedding garments, and she'd acquiesced as easily as ever any woman had given in to a man. That galled her. Though she'd felt compelled to do it, remembering Severina's tears.

There'd been no other way for Severina to be freed, and she owed her friend that much and more. Severina had saved her life in the dark days when she'd wanted to die, when her child was gone and she'd hated life—and hated herself, most of all—and had thought a sharp-bladed dagger held the peace she needed so badly. Severina had found her, staunched the bleeding, and brought a physician from the *ludus* to stitch her wound together again. Afterward, Severina had listened, understanding pain because she'd been through so much of it herself.

Lelia owed her more than she could ever repay.

For that reason she had succumbed to the terrible inevitability of marriage to Donatus. How she would perform all she'd promised, she did not know. For now, she couldn't even think of it. That one man could stir such a chaos of emotions within her—hatred as intense as anything she'd ever felt, sadness for all the losses she'd ever suffered, and…dare she admit it? Desire, too. She couldn't help but be stirred by this man's body, by the lithe grace with which he moved, by the memories they'd made together. Donatus had always known how to please her, how to touch her, how to ignite her soul, how to quench the fire.

She breathed in deeply, sensing the sharp edge of the precipice over which she was about to fall. Marriage to Donatus…and she'd promised him an heir. Whatever had she been thinking? Certainly she hadn't carefully considered what it would mean to make love with Donatus again.

Severina finished securing the veil over Lelia's hair. "It's time," she said. "They await us."

Lelia nodded, swallowing down the nausea that threatened. She thought of Severina, and of the moment when

Donatus would hand her friend the parchment that gave her freedom. Only by imagining the joy in Severina's gray eyes could she manage to put one foot in front of the other and move toward her destiny.

Six hours later, Lucan turned to Donatus with a frown. "You've got to stop her," he said, "before she plays the fool and drinks herself under this table."

"It's the wine." Brocchus shook his head. "She's not accustomed to it. I never let my gladiators drink anything but milk and water. I've always thought that fermented drink dulls the wits and slows the reflexes."

"You wouldn't know it to look at Lelia now," Lucan said. "No dull wit there. She's the life of this party. And I would guess she's forgotten that her *marriage* is the cause of the merriment, since she's surrounded by males so attentive you'd think she was the only woman in the city. And an available one, at that."

Donatus frowned. His friend's words had hit a nerve. He couldn't pretend that Lelia had any feeling for him. He knew that. Their marriage was little more than a business arrangement. In fact, he'd been surprised she'd agreed to his proposal at all. But he knew her well enough to know she'd not forgotten her anger, nor come close to forgiving him. She'd agreed for some other reason, some reason he had yet to fathom.

But curse it all, he wouldn't sit forgotten at this table while his wife giggled like a schoolgirl at the attentions of fully a dozen other men—all handsome, well-muscled gladiators. They plied her with compliments, they danced her around the room in their arms, they leaned much too near, whispering against her smooth alabaster skin. And they kept filling her glass with wine, so that now her cheeks were too flushed and her laughter too loud, and her glances in their direction were too damned flirtatious.

"I'll order my men to their quarters," Brocchus murmured. "Maybe then you can capture Leda's attention and begin the procession to your home. It's getting late, and you must be eager to fulfill your obligation to your bride."

Donatus nodded without enthusiasm. Brocchus looked momentarily worried. Perhaps the jealousy Donatus felt was somehow apparent in his eyes, because Brocchus leaned forward. "She's not usually like this," he said in a gruff whisper. "She's not had lovers. Not any that I know about." He turned away toward the group gathered around Lelia. Another couple of minutes and Brocchus had put an end to their frivolity.

"What are you thinking?" Lucan asked Donatus quietly, as he watched the crowd of gladiators, friends, clients and family begin slowly to disperse.

Donatus took a drink and shrugged. "Nothing of import."

Lucan snorted. "Oh, come now. Even a lack wit could see the strong emotion that darkens your eyes."

Donatus grunted and raked lean fingers through his hair. "You're right. I'm angry. She's making a fool of me, and doing it on purpose."

Lucan laughed softly. "Ah, but you love the challenge. I imagine you'll find *pleasurable* ways to bend her to your will. Especially tonight."

"My wife is drunk, Lucan. A wife who hates the sight of me. And what would the morrow bring if she awoke and discovered I'd used the situation to satisfy my own ends?"

"She promised you an heir, did she not?"

"She did. And I fully intend that Lelia will someday take my seed and bear my child. But I'm yet a young man, Lucan, and the need is not an uncontrollable one. I prefer to woo her gently, to let time and kind treatment heal the wounds I dealt her in the past."

Lucan nodded and reached up to squeeze his friend's shoulder. "Then I'll pray that the past can be forgotten quickly."

"Do that, and get your Christian brothers to pray for me, too. Maybe the god you serve will help me more than the Roman ones have."

Lucan smiled. "He can, you know. And without the obligatory sacrifices your Roman gods require."

"Maybe. Though if I understand your faith, your god does not demand a goat or heifer. He demands my heart."

"Only so he might heal it, my friend, only so he might heal it." Lucan stood to leave, glancing toward the other end of the room, where Lelia laughed with a Roman guard, both of them swaying a bit unsteadily on their feet. "From the looks of things, you're probably going to need it."

Donatus watched his friend go, gulped down the last of his wine, and stood. Lelia didn't see him approach until he was beside her. She started, and looked up at him fiercely when he placed his arm around her waist. Over Lelia's shoulder, he saw Severina's eyes widen before she turned away.

"Get your hands off me," Lelia said in a low growl.

"No, I will not. You've let every other man in this room touch you freely tonight. Will you now deny the same to your husband?"

"Being my husband does not mean you can maul me at will."

"Being your husband means I can touch you whenever and however I damn well please."

Her eyes flashed fire at that, and Donatus was glad. To taunt her this way helped assuage the hurt he felt.

"You may have the legal right to take my body, Donatus,

and I know only too well what I've promised you. But you're a downright fool if you think you'll ever make me like it."

The words cut him. His hand came up to her neck, his palm warm against her spine as he brought their faces close together. Lelia gasped at the sudden unexpected contact, her eyes fastening on his lips, her own parting slightly as if she anticipated a kiss. "Don't push me, Lelia," he said. "There is a limit to a man's patience." He let her go and retreated a step.

Her eyes narrowed. "And there is a limit to mine as well, Donatus. Be careful. I'm not the woman I was before you left me."

"No, you're not. Your eyes are cold when they look at me. And yet I do remember the warmth I once saw in them."

"Do not hope to see it again."

He reached a hand up to caress the smooth skin of her shoulder, giving a short, bitter laugh at the shudder that went through her. "And your body that was once soft is now muscular and sleek. Surprisingly, I like that. I find it provocative."

"Contain your wayward lusts and leave me alone."

Donatus laughed, a short sound strangely devoid of humor. "Have no fear, my love. I won't force my attentions on you. Not yet, anyway."

Triumph flashed in her eyes. It made him angry, to know Lelia manipulated him. He stepped forward and caught her arms so quickly that he startled a gasp from her. His lips descended and smothered the sound. She struggled for a moment; his arms tightened around her, pressing her body against his in a pleasure so excruciating it felt like pain.

It took a moment for him to realize that she'd stopped resisting, that her lips were now soft beneath his—not answering, but certainly yielding. His mouth grew more gentle, seducing her with a tenderness that made his chest ache. He heard her groan and caught the sound in his own throat. His tongue parted her hesitant lips and tasted the wine on her breath.

Then she was kissing him, too, her tongue stroking across his, all honey and liquid flame. His body leaped in response. Blood hammered in his veins. It no longer mattered that they were surrounded by guests.

It no longer mattered that he'd meant only to subdue her for a moment. His hold on her changed, drawing her closer to the need throbbing through him. He heard her whimper. The sound excited him.

He kissed her brow as he would a child, and left her, feeling her sway slightly as he withdrew his support.

Her eyes opened to reveal a confusion of unsated desire, fear and anger. "I hate you, Donatus," she whispered.

"I know," he said quietly. He turned and walked away, thinking that her body had belied everything her lips had said.

Her body had betrayed her. That was the only explanation. Her body had betrayed her, and the wine, and the relief she felt at no longer having to fight in the arena. It couldn't be that her feelings for Donatus had softened, even after the kindness he'd shown when, alone together at last, he'd given her the parchment that freed Severina.

She'd looked up at him in confusion.

"Take it," he'd said, closing her palm around it. "I want you to know the joy of that moment when Severina learns she is free."

She had looked down in near disbelief to the scroll of paper in her hand. "You should do it. Your money purchased her."

An ironic smile had lifted the corner of his lips. "But you, sweet Lelia, *you'll* be the one to pay."

And now she feared she was about to, for she rode with Donatus in the litter that carried them closer to his home, and to his bedroom, and to her fate. He'd promised not to force himself upon her, but that had been before she'd responded to his kiss, making herself more the fool for not having slapped him like the arrogant ass he was.

Her face flamed at the memory of how she'd let her tongue enter him, of how she'd groaned at the familiar hardness of his muscled thighs against hers. Of how she'd grown weak with desire for all those things Donatus could do to her. It shamed her, the way her body had not been controlled by her mind. Though she wanted to think it was only the wine that had dulled her ability to harness her emotions, no wine was as potent as the need she felt.

Donatus had once awakened her to passion. He'd taught her how exquisite a woman's response could be. And now, in his presence once again, that powerful memory had over-taken reason and reminded her of how good it had felt.

Except that everything had changed. In those days, she'd loved Donatus past all caring. She'd trusted him. He'd held her hand and whispered, "Fly with me," and she had soared. Fear hadn't existed then. Only Donatus and his taste on her tongue, his touch on her skin, and his magnificent fullness sheathed within her. She'd never once been afraid.

Tonight she was scared to death. Tonight she'd tasted Donatus and wanted more. His body had stiffened against hers, and she'd wanted more. She knew how he'd hurt her, how he'd used her and deserted her and left her in shame. She burned with hate for him—but she burned with need for him.

And soon, much too soon, they'd be alone and he'd know it.

Donatus was quiet during the ride home, and he was careful not to touch Lelia. He was quiet when she was welcomed into his home, watching her with wary eyes as Faustina and the boys showed her around and introduced her to the household slaves, at least those who'd stayed up so late. He was quiet, baffled by the fear he'd seen in her eyes.

He'd seen such fear before, on the faces of men who'd just taken a *pilum* through the chest—a disbelieving, startled fear followed by a resignation so grim that even now Donatus shuddered at it. And he'd seen that same play of emotions on Lelia's face when he'd released her from the kiss.

Damn it all, he hadn't even meant to kiss her. It wasn't part of the strategy he'd planned. He'd meant to show restraint, to win her with patience and care. Whatever had he been thinking, to be goaded into an action so hasty and so selfish? He knew instinctively that it had been too much, too soon.

Now he'd have to retreat and show more self-control than any mortal man possessed. He'd have to share a room with her and not touch her, share a bed with her and not give in to the desire which already wrenched his gut.

The worst part was knowing that she'd responded. Lelia had wanted him.

That thought made his breathing quicken. He hadn't forgotten, could never forget, the fierce passion they'd once shared. He'd had lovers before her, but none like her. And, because there'd been none like her, he'd had none since. His body felt the need for a woman, but he wanted no other. Only Lelia and the passion she could stir. Only her dark hair twining around him, only her silken flesh beneath his, only her breath sighing his name, telling him she loved him.

That was the reason he could not make love to her yet. Lelia hated him. He'd seen that in her eyes, too. He was a man with a man's needs, but he knew it was possible to win a battle and lose the war.

He might satisfy his lusts with Lelia this very night, but

when passion was spent she'd still look at him with loathing. That he could not bear, not when he wanted so much more.

Donatus made his way to his sleeping quarters. There was no help for it; he'd have to chain the hounds of his need and woo her gently. His jaw tightened as he imagined her body beside his in the bed, the soft fragrance of her as she rolled toward him in sleep.

A most fitting punishment for the way he'd left her before.

If he'd put her through two years of hell, it was nothing like the torment he was about to enter when he stepped over the threshold into his bedroom.

He entered quietly. Lelia was already in the bed, the bed-clothes concealing all but the soft outline of her form. He hoped she slept already, lulled into the arms of Morpheus by the wine she'd consumed. But when she turned to him, alerted by the soft fall of his footsteps, he knew the Fates had not deigned to be kind.

"I'm sorry. I hope I didn't wake you."

"You didn't," she said quietly. "I was awaiting you."

"You should try to sleep. We've had an exhausting day."

"I'm not tired."

"Well, I am." Donatus raked his fingers through his hair, half turning away from her intense gaze. "I hope you don't mind that we'll be sharing this room. We must keep up appearances. The slaves…"

"It's all right. I did promise we'd appear a happily married couple. I anticipated sharing the room with you, and all that might involve."

His breath stilled at the words, at the implication of them. "You take the bed," he said. "I'll make a pallet on the floor for myself."

"No. You'll share this bed with me."

His gaze flew to her face. Her expression was shadowed

and he couldn't read it. "I've been a soldier. I've camped in primitive conditions and I'm used to discomfort. A pallet will be no inconvenience for me."

"But it would be an inconvenience for me."

Again he searched her face, cursing the dimness of the fire in the hearth that would not let him discern her expression. "How would it inconvenience you?"

"I dislike cold stone on my naked backside."

Donatus felt his heart tighten. His body followed suit. He turned away before she could see the effect she had on him. "I said I'd not force you. I'll honor my word. You need not be concerned about your promise to provide me an heir. Not yet."

There was silence.

"Donatus," she said, so quietly that he strained to hear it. "Donatus, come to me."

He turned, but moved no closer. She sat up in bed, her eyes capturing his. Then slowly, deliberately, she lowered the sheets in a sensuous rustle of silk. Donatus realized then that she lay naked beneath the bedclothes. Her breasts gleamed with the soft, white luster of twin pearls in the dim light. His throat tightened. "What game do you play with me?" he asked.

"I promised you an heir. And, like you, I keep my word."

"No." He said nothing. If he said anything, the words might be transformed by her strange magic into that which he struggled to resist. Already the torment was a hideous thing. Already he could see himself across the room, his mouth upon the dark beauty of her nipples, his hands cradling the softness of her womanly flesh. And because he could see those things, and feel the emotions that went with them, he stood rooted in place.

"No?" she asked. "You would deny yourself pleasure, my husband?"

"Yes, Lelia. I deny myself pleasure. I promised you."

"You promised you'd not force me. This is not force, Donatus. I offer this freely."

He turned away, the sound that came from him something between a growl and a groan. "Have mercy, Lelia. I know not what game you play, but this…this is not the way it will be." He looked back at her, knowing the strain must show in his face. "Why are you offering yourself to me?"

She didn't answer.

He moved closer, trying to read her expression. "Answer me. Why do you torment me?"

"I mean to please you, Donatus. Not torment you."

He shook his head. "No. You hate me, Lelia. There's no warmth, no love remaining to wish me pleasure." Donatus folded his arms and studied her. He saw her eyes narrow. Anger flared within them.

"All right, damn you," she said. "The truth."

"That's better. Out with it."

"I want to get this over with. I know… Donatus, we've been lovers."

"And the important word is *lovers*."

"We cannot remain in this room together and not make love."

"And the important word is *love*."

"Shut up, Donatus, and listen to me." She clenched her hands into fists in her lap. "I don't love you and I never will. But you taught me…" She halted.

"I taught you what happens between two people who love," he said quietly.

"Yes."

"And that's exactly why I won't take you tonight, however much we may desire one another."

"What madness is this?" she whispered harshly. "What

game do you now play with me? I know you want me, Flavius Donatus."

He laughed, a bitter, self-mocking sound. "Yes, Flavia Lelia. I do want you. Even now my body throbs with the need you've aroused. Even now my heated blood cries foul and castigates me for the fool I am. I'll lie alone on cold stone tonight, and curse myself for turning away from you."

"Then do not turn from me. You know how inevitable it is, and that we will not rest, either of us, while this unspoken thing lies between us, a promise unfulfilled and awaiting its time."

"So that's how you see this thing? As an outstanding obligation you must yet fulfill?"

"Yes. I wish it done and finished."

"Hmm. A child who eats her sweetmeat too quickly. And would you then welcome the stomach ache which would follow?"

"What do you mean?"

"Are you so eager to carry my child?"

He saw her eyes widen in the dim light.

"You hate me. You admit it. And you don't want to bear my child." He knelt down beside her and took her hands into his larger ones, feeling their softness and the skin so cool against his. His chest constricted with sadness.

"I've never been one to consume a sweet too quickly," he said. "Even as a child I was careful to savor the things I treasured. And I do treasure you, Lelia, whatever else you might think."

He let go of her hands and stood abruptly, looking down at her, fighting the urge to stroke the beautiful curves of her breasts. "And, since every babe deserves the love of both his parents, I think it best that we wait until you *want* to give me a child."

"Then you'll wait until the sea turns to glass."

Donatus turned from her without comment. He gathered the feather mattress and extra blankets he'd ordered brought to his room and spread them before the hearth, settling himself into them without undressing, thinking that the cold stone beneath his back was nothing compared to his wife's cold stone heart.

What small sound awoke Donatus, he did not know. He lay in the dark, his breathing halted, wondering if his imaginings had been part of some nightmarish dream.

Then he heard it again—Lelia's whimper, a long, keening cry, followed by her thrashing in the bed. She lay quiet for but a moment, then cried out once more. "No! No! He can't be gone!" Her movements grew more agitated and she began to sob.

He went to her at once. His hands found her slender shoulders, forcing her into stillness even though she struggled against him. "Lelia!" he said gently. "Wake up. You're having a dream. A bad dream."

Immediately she ceased fighting.

"It was a dream, my love." Donatus knelt beside her, smoothing the fevered skin of her brow, wondering if he should give in to the urge to hold her. "You're awake now. It was just a dream."

She groaned and fell backward into the twisted bedclothes. "No, it isn't. I wish it were, but it isn't."

If anything, her waking words cut him more deeply than those sleeping words had, for their anguish was more piercing and sharp-edged. Donatus was overcome by the realization of something so wrong that the hair raised on the back of his neck.

"What is it? What?"

She did not answer.

"Who's gone? Was it…was the dream about me?"

He held his breath, afraid to hear the answer.

"Go back to sleep, Donatus. I'm sorry I disturbed you."

He leaned closer, until his lips brushed against her hair. "I must know. Did you dream I'd left you? Was the dream about me?"

Awkward silence followed, a silence that expanded and grew until he felt engulfed in the hot breath of waiting. "Yes, Donatus," she said at last. "It was about you."

Chapter Five

A knock on the door awakened Lelia the following morning. She shifted in bed, pulling the coverlet higher about her neck just as the door opened and a young girl of perhaps thirteen stuck her head through the crack.

"Are you awake?" the girl asked. "And more important, are you decently clothed? Mama says I'm to wait until you're decently clothed. She said… Oh, I suppose I shouldn't repeat what I heard her say to Livia. Not that I'm ignorant about men and women, but you'd think I was, the way Mama tries to hush up all talk of such things when I'm around."

Lelia raised one arm over her eyes. The girl must have taken that as a yes, for she slipped into the room and closed the door behind her.

"I'm sorry," Lelia said, lowering her arm again and trying not to grin at the girl's cheekiness, which somehow reminded her of herself at that age. "I don't think we've been introduced."

The girl smiled, and Lelia realized that she was really very attractive, with hair of warm chestnut, amber eyes, and flawless skin. "I'm Druscilla," she said pertly. "I'm the younger sister—the *only* sister—of Donatus. And I'm pleased that you're here, because until now we ladies have been seriously outnumbered. Your arrival should even things up a bit—especially if Donatus loves you as much as everyone says he does."

That got Lelia's attention. She raised an eyebrow. "Everyone is saying that?"

Druscilla grinned. "Oh, yes. Mama says no man goes to all the trouble Donatus has been through unless he's mad with love for a woman." She sighed. "Donatus spent lots of money buying pretty things for you."

Lelia struggled to sit up, still clutching the blanket over her naked breasts. She imagined how disheveled she must appear, and wondered if there were some discreet way she could get into her clothing. Then she remembered that she had no clothing except the wedding apparel she'd worn the night before.

"My goodness, but you're frowning," Druscilla said, studying Lelia's face far too intently. "Do you not like the idea of having your new husband buy things for you? I should think you'd like that. I'd *love* it if my husband were to do that for me—especially if he bought me the kind of things Donatus has bought for you."

"I'm sorry if I seem distracted, Druscilla, but the truth is, I need some privacy. You see, I'm *not* decently clothed."

Druscilla laughed abruptly, waving her hand in a graceful gesture of dismissal. "That's all right. I really didn't expect you would be."

"Druscilla," Lelia said, trying not to sound exasperated. "Would you please leave this room long enough for me to get some clothes on?"

"Certainly. But, you know, the thought occurred to me that you might want some of your pretty new clothes now. Donatus bought tunics and *pallas* and shoes—lovely things and all for you."

Lelia looked up, her hands clenching around the silk sheet she held. "He *what?*"

Druscilla giggled. "I told you Donatus is mad with love for you. He's had seamstresses working for the last three— no, maybe four days. And, oh, you should just *see* the finery he's bought! I shall pout for days that he hasn't bought anything nearly so elegant for me."

Druscilla turned and almost ran to the door, slipping out of it hastily. A moment or two later she entered again awkwardly, her arms laden with bundles wrapped in fabric, loosely tied.

She came forward and dropped them onto the floor beside the hearth. Lelia realized then that Donatus had gathered up all evidence of the pallet where he'd slept. She looked around the room and didn't see the mattress or blankets anywhere, nor any other sign of his presence. She wondered where he was.

"Thank you, Druscilla," she said. "You're being very thoughtful."

"Donatus said I must be especially helpful. He reminded us all, even the slaves, that you wouldn't know your way around at first, and that we must all help you fit in."

"How kind of him," Lelia said dryly.

"And he threatened to beat me if I talked too much or told you any family secrets you shouldn't know." Druscilla laughed. "He was teasing, of course. Donatus has never beaten anybody, least of all me. He adores me, you know."

"He does, does he?"

"Yes, he does. He says it's because I look so much like my mother—even though I don't act like her at all, more's the pity."

Lelia smiled at the girl's honesty. "Then Donatus must have a lot of admiration for your mother."

"Oh, he does. He says marrying Mama was the best thing Papa ever did. They married for love, you know, and Donatus says that even as a young man he could see the change Mama made in their world."

Lelia turned her head sharply. "Your mother is not also the mother of Donatus?"

"No, she isn't. Which makes us only half siblings, Donatus and me. Although I think I'm going to be tall like him." She straightened and posed, raising her head in an imperious manner. "What do you think? Will I be tall like Donatus?"

Lelia tilted her head, trying not to smile. "I think so. You are already taller than I was at your age."

"Are you quite tall, then?"

"Uhm…not quite as tall as Donatus, but close. Rather tall for a woman, anyway. I'd show you except I…I need my clothes on."

Druscilla laughed again, skipping to the door like a graceful deer. "Then certainly you must dress. But hurry, if you please. I want to measure my height against yours."

"Of course," Lelia said, laughing at the girl's demanding manner which, in spite of all, was really quite endearing. "Measure ourselves we shall—as soon as I find something to wear."

Druscilla opened the door and started out, but hesitated long enough to look back. "I'm glad you're here," she said. "And I'm glad you're tall. I can already envision all the proud children you and Donatus will make together."

Lelia nodded, not surprised that the thought should bring tears to her eyes.

She was clothed in a tunic of soft indigo linen by the time Druscilla returned. She'd hurried to dress, knowing the girl wouldn't be patient, and had chosen one of the first garments she'd come to. Now she sorted through the clothing more carefully, awed by the generosity of her new husband. He'd bought more tunics and *pallas* than she could wear in a month—all delicate, costly, and of a design to enhance her uniqueness. Many were embroidered or beaded, shimmering with light.

And there was more. One bundle contained delicate under-clothing and, though she wasn't one to be unduly embar-rassed, she did feel herself grow warm at the thought of Donatus in a shop, buying the *strophiums* that would bind her breasts. She pushed that bundle aside hurriedly.

Another bundle contained several pairs of shoes, most of them sandals of various colors and styles that, like the tunics, were of quality materials and elaborately decorated.

Her brow furrowed. Donatus had done all this himself? And in only four days? It was hard to imagine, and yet that was the impression she'd gotten from Druscilla. Something inside her did a strange somersault.

Tears came to her eyes, and she wiped them away with an angry hand. *"No, Donatus,"* she breathed. *"Don't love me."* The bitter taste of her own failures rose in her mouth. He couldn't love her. Not her. She'd only bring him shame. And disappointment, when he knew.

There was a knock at the door and Lelia hurried to compose herself. Druscilla entered, her mouth in motion, of course. But that made Lelia smile again.

"I see you've opened your gifts," Druscilla said. "Aren't they beautiful? And there are more in the atrium."

"More?" Lelia asked, her eyebrows winging up in disbe-lief.

"Yes. And the shopkeepers are still delivering."

"Merciful heavens. Wherever shall I put everything?"

Druscilla gave a short laugh. "We'll find a place. Or maybe

Donatus will build you a palace to hold it all. Mama says—
" The girl stopped, looking down at the sheets as she pushed
them aside to sit on the bed. "Oh, goodness, look at that. I
told Mama she shouldn't have used our best silk. But she told
me to hush, that only the finest would do for a bride's bed.
Now look at that. They've been stained. I knew they would
be. I should've told Donatus to lay you upon his cloak before
he…well, you know."

Lelia's eyes followed the girl's impatient gesture. There,
on the white silk, were flecks of blood. In a flash of intuition
she could see it—Donatus in the dark of predawn with a
dagger in hand, cutting his own flesh to give evidence of the
virginity she no longer possessed. Donatus spilling his blood
so she might hold her head high among the slaves and others
of his household. That he would care for her reputation and
shed his own blood to preserve it both awed and humbled her.

She drew in a steadying breath.

Last night. The wine. It had to be the lingering aftereffect
of so much wine that she felt like crying at every small thing
this morning.

Druscilla sighed, and turned her attention back to the
clothing. "This one," she said, pointing to a cream-colored
tunic. "I love this one—especially now that I've seen you."
She held it up.

It was of silk, a rustling fall of cloth that was not quite sheer,
yet not quite opaque. Lelia's eyes traveled down its length,
noting a wealth of embroidery—purple irises with leaves of
green—which adorned the hem. "It is beautiful," she murmured.

"The purple is almost the same as your eyes," Druscilla
said. "And look here. Did you note this?" She pointed to the
brooch that secured the shoulder of the garment.

Lelia drew in her breath, catching the glimmer of gold and
emerald and purple amethyst.

"The brooch goes with it," Druscilla said. "It has irises, too. And somewhere there are sandals to match, decorated with beadwork in the same colors." She sighed. "I think I'll have Donatus buy all my clothing from now on. He has such exquisite taste. Now, who would have expected that of him? You wouldn't think it of a soldier."

A knock on the door startled them both.

"Come in," they called in unison. Druscilla giggled, then sobered as her mother looked in.

"I hope I'm not disturbing anything," Faustina said to Lelia with quiet dignity. "I wondered if you might be hungry? I have brought food, if you wish to eat."

Lelia realized suddenly that she *was* hungry. Ravenous, in fact. She nodded, and Faustina pushed the door wider to admit two slaves, one laden with a tray of delicious-smelling food, another with a pitcher and glass.

Faustina hesitated a moment beside the bed, looking for the most convenient place to place the items. Lelia saw her eyes touch on the stained sheets momentarily before she gestured to Druscilla. "Up, daughter, and find a small table for our guest."

Lelia protested. "No, really. I don't wish to trouble you. I could take my meal in the triclinium, like everyone else."

Faustina smiled soothingly. "Except that everyone else has long finished, my dear. It is, in fact, well past the noon hour, and you have missed both breakfast and lunch. You must be half starved."

"My goodness!" Lelia exclaimed. "I had no idea! Please forgive me! I'm usually a very early riser. I can't imagine why I slept so long."

Faustina smiled. "It's really quite all right, but Donatus would never forgive me if I let you languish from hunger. You must renew your strength." The smile tugged at the corners of her lips. "He should be home in a short while."

Lelia ignored the implication. "I must have been sound asleep when he left. Where is he?"

"He's gone to the Senate. There's some rather important business being conducted today, I believe, and since he's been busy with other duties for several days now, he felt it important that he return to his work. He asked me to convey to you his most sincere apologies for leaving your side so soon."

Not that it mattered, Lelia thought. It wasn't as if there was any reason for him to stay in this bedroom with her.

Druscilla and the slaves had set up a small table and placed the food on it. Faustina gestured toward it now. "Come and eat, dear. Druscilla and I will return later to collect the dishes, and afterwards we'll get down to the business of deciding how you wish the household to be run."

"Me?" Lelia asked, eyebrows raised.

"Of course," Faustina said gently. "You're the mistress of this home now. As Donatus's wife you may make any changes you deem necessary."

Lelia shook her head. "Changes? No, no changes. I… Faustina, I really…" She held up a hand imploringly. "There's something you should know about my marriage to Donatus. I… We… I mean, we're not—"

A deep voice from the doorway interrupted. "I think my wife is trying to say that she'll need more time before she decides such matters, Faustina," Donatus answered smoothly.

Lelia's heart leaped at his sudden, unexpected presence. "Donatus. You've returned."

His eyes found hers, growing darker and warmer. "And just in time, I see, to share a meal with my beloved."

Faustina gestured, and the slaves and Druscilla hurried from the room. She followed, stopping at the door with a gentle half smile. "I'll see that your meal is not disturbed, Donatus," she said. "Eat well…and do enjoy yourselves."

She laughed softly as she pulled the door closed.

Donatus watched her leave, his expression stern and inscrutable. When the door was firmly shut, he turned to Lelia. "You would forget our agreement so quickly? You promised to maintain appearances, to be my proper wife." His lips tightened. "At least around others."

"I'm sorry. I was caught off guard."

"I see." He studied her carefully for some moments, his body straight, tall and tense. She looked away, anxious beneath his unwavering scrutiny.

He moved nearer, so close that Lelia was aware of the clean, masculine smell of him.

"Lelia," he whispered hoarsely. "Look at me."

She raised her eyes and lost her breath, drowning in the turbulent green sea of his gaze.

"You are my wife," he said. "And I am a senator of Rome. Out of respect for that office you will not shame yourself, or me. Or I swear by all that's holy—"

"Have mercy, Donatus," she said in exasperation. "It was an accident that I so nearly spoke the truth to Faustina. I know well what I promised you."

She turned away in a swift motion. She could barely keep the anger from her voice. "I understand the role of a senator, Flavius Donatus. I am the daughter of a senator, reared from birth to be wife to a senator. I know only too well how one so reared should conduct herself, and the brutal penalty if she should not."

He didn't answer.

She half turned, studying his passive features. "Tell me, Donatus. All these lovely clothes…are they part of the show? Part of my role as a noble senator's wife?"

A dark expression flitted across his face. "No," he said. "They were not meant for show. They were meant for you."

"Then *I* am meant for show." She waited, but he did not respond. She drew in a deep breath and turned away again, trying to lessen the impact of his nearness. "You've made a grave mistake, Donatus. The whole city knows what I am. The wanton child of a renowned senator. The rebellious daughter who slept in a soldier's arms and sullied herself for any other."

"They do not know. Faustina does not know. My friends do not know. You make too much of the past," Donatus said in a low voice. "There are one and a half *million* people in this city, Lelia. Even the senators are so numerous now they don't all know one another. Do you imagine they all remember your shame? Do you imagine they yet *care?* When far more salacious scandals are so plentiful and cheaply bought?"

He made a sound of disbelief. "Even a small storm can seem like a tempest to the lone sailor whose little ship is swamped. You are that lone sailor, Lelia, your life disrupted and put off course by the vagaries of the Fates. But the reality is that few know of your disgrace. Maybe friends of your father…maybe. *My* father didn't know, or he would have written to me, since I once introduced you to him as a special friend of mine. My family still doesn't know. But even if they did, would they care? I dare say they would not."

Lelia scowled at him. "Don't be so sure. If by chance they don't recall that, then they certainly know this—that I, Flavia Lelia, am also Leda the Gladiatrix, worthy of the gold and wreaths of victory, but never the respect of polite society."

"Lelia …"

"No, Donatus. Don't try to pretend these things don't exist. They are my reality. And now that you've wed me, they're yours as well."

"As long as you act the loving wife, none of those things matter to me."

She turned back to him. She raised her gaze, knowing it was full of challenge and self-mockery. "If those things don't matter, then they should...*Senator*."

Donatus didn't know when or how the change had been wrought in Lelia, only that he was disturbed by it. The Lelia he'd known before had been sometimes serious, but never morose. Pragmatic, but not cynical. And when she had smiled there'd been no self-deprecation in it, only a sincere enjoyment of life which *this* Lelia no longer seemed to know.

The most likely conclusion troubled him more than he cared to admit. It was his fault. Maybe if he'd married her... But, no, he refused to dwell on the past. There was no way he could go back and undo it, only move forward into a future that might yet be better—if he could somehow erase the lines of worry from her face and the shadow of pain from her eyes.

He watched her now as she sat across from him, devouring her food hungrily. And as always when he looked at her, his stomach tightened with the desire he felt. She had always been beautiful, but the physical changes of the last two years...they made him hurt with need. Her skin was not pale like that of other beauties. It glowed with health, with the golden warmth of the sun. Her body was leaner now, sleek and agile, though her curves had not lessened. If anything they were accented even more by the svelte gracefulness of her frame, by the definition of her muscle.

Donatus looked away, lifting a goblet to drink and ease a throat that had suddenly gone too dry.

He had eaten little, could hardly feel hunger. At least, not the usual kind. Neither had he slept, listening to her soft breathing across the room. Maybe that was why his mind seemed such a muddle and why he ached so much inside. It wasn't like him not to know the next action, to be unsure of how to move forward. But with Lelia… Well, nothing was the same anymore.

In the past she would have welcomed his most casual attempt to please her. Her eyes would have gleamed with joy over the clothes he'd purchased. But the only thing he'd seen in her eyes today had been a certain wariness, as if those beautiful garments came with obligation. That irked him, since he'd spent the better part of an entire day going from one shop to the next to find the wardrobe which would enhance her uniquely.

His goal had not been to put her on display, as she'd insinuated. He'd been even more selfish than that. He'd bought those beautiful garments for *himself,* every sheer, flowing, shimmering one of them, only because he wanted to look upon Lelia with pleasure. Not knowing when he'd be able to touch her, he considered it not such a far-fetched thing to do, to allow himself the fantasy of imagination, for now.

But looking on her with pleasure was like a sharp-bladed sword, cutting him both ways. She was his wife, but he could not lie with her. She was beautiful, but that beauty lay veiled in a sadness he couldn't heal. His insides were aflame, and he could do nothing to quench the burning.

"Where are you going?" she asked, when he stood so abruptly that he nearly overturned his wine.

"Back to the Curia Julia. The Senate will be back in session shortly. Today's business is of great import."

She looked at the dish of food he'd not touched. "You didn't eat."

"I didn't come to eat. I came to be with you."

"With me? But why?" She seemed startled. The frightened look had come back into her violet eyes.

He took her hand and raised it to his lips. "Because," he said, kissing it lightly, "you are mine."

She pulled her hand away. "I am not yours. Despite the words we spoke yesterday, I'm still owner of my heart. I'll give it to whomever I please."

"You will give it to me," he said. "For I'd have to slay any man who'd try to take you from me."

She didn't answer.

Donatus hesitated, wishing he could behave as any other husband, wishing he could stroke her arm with a lazy finger and smile, make some gentle comment about her beauty. But Lelia's eyes would narrow, and she'd spit some venomous reply in his direction.

He chose the middle ground. "I came home to be near you. Your presence much enthralls me." As expected, disbelief came into her eyes. "And also to tell you we've been invited to dinner tonight, at the home of Gaius Scribonius Firmus."

Her eyes widened. "No! Donatus, no. It's too soon. I'm not ready for that."

He'd expected this reaction, and had prepared for it. He crossed his arms over his chest and regarded her with a half-teasing, half-mocking expression. "What's this? Can it be that my fearless gladiatrix does indeed fear the pleasant company of my friend's household?"

He saw her swallow quickly. He saw, too, the fear and anger that fought for her face. "I fear nothing, Donatus. Least of all your arrogant friends."

"How do you know they're arrogant?"

"Because I know Scribonius Firmus. He's a friend of my father. Indeed, we entertained his family at our own home in the past. If they've invited us to dine, it's only for the purpose of gawking, to whisper on the morrow with their friends about the whore-turned-gladiatrix-turned-senator's-wife." Lelia's jaw clamped tight. "No, I'll not attend. Go alone, if you wish."

"You'll go with me," he said firmly. "Be dressed and ready when I return."

"I will not."

He stepped closer. "Lelia, you will."

Her eyes sparked at the low command. "Careful, Donatus. I'm not the same woman you left. You'll not find me so pliant beneath your hand."

He stood beside her at the table now, so near he could see the pulse leaping in her throat, could scent the soft, womanly smell of her skin. His hand moved of its own volition to the shadows of her neck, pushing aside the long silken curtain of her hair. His finger whispered along the sleek line of her jaw.

He felt her stiffen. She shifted slightly, her eyes darting in his direction.

"What are you doing, Donatus?" she asked, her tongue nervously flicking out to dampen the corner of her lips. He leaned down and touched his tongue to the same corner, hearing her sharp intake of breath.

"What are you doing?" she asked again, breathlessly.

"No, you're not the same woman I left," he said quietly. "But you are my wife, and you made a promise to me. And, Lelia, you've said you always keep your word."

Her eyes closed momentarily, and then opened again. He saw the truth settle in them. He saw honor claw for the throne and win it. And at its side, a fearsome companion. Frightened resignation.

Because Donatus was so near to her, because he felt pride swell at her courage, he loosed the hounds. He gave in to his heart's desire. He kissed her.

It was no simple kiss of gratitude for a decision well made. It was the kiss of a husband, a husband long without the succor of his woman's flesh. He drew her from her chair and into his arms, pressing her intimately against his body, making promises that caused the quicksilver of desire to flood their bodies. His heart was pounding when he finally released her. She was breathing hard, too, her face flushed, her hand pressed against her bosom as if to contain her rapidly beating heart.

"Be ready when I return," he said quietly. He turned and left, not giving her time to think of a reply.

Lelia spent the afternoon learning more of her new home. Druscilla had returned to accompany her, talking such a steady stream that Lelia had a hard time keeping up.

Nor was that the only difficulty. Donatus's home was so large she feared she'd be lost in it. There were corridors and more corridors, porticos and more porticos, and all of them columned in marble. They led to grand rooms, with floors of mosaic tile and walls decorated with murals, sumptuously furnished with couches cushioned in silk and tables carved with acanthus leaves or twining vines of grapes. Some were ornamented with gold.

"Across over there," Druscilla was saying, "is our largest banqueting hall. We've hardly used it, except when Papa hosted meals for the other senators and their families." She grinned mischievously. "That was usually when he was trying to influence a vote on some issue he thought important. But he loved the room, even overseeing its decoration himself. It's one of the most beautiful we have. He'd be so pleased it's being used now."

Druscilla lowered her voice. "Donatus's friend Lucan is using it. With Donatus's permission, of course."

Lelia's brow furrowed. *Lucan?* She didn't remember a friend named Lucan. "I must not know him."

"You don't?" Druscilla was incredulous.

"No, I don't suppose so. Describe him to me."

"Oh, you'd remember him if ever you'd seen him. He's younger than Donatus by about five years, and, oh, he's like

Adonis. He's so beautiful. His hair is the color of ripened wheat, lighter in places kissed by the sun. His eyes change, sometimes green and sometimes gold. His features are perfection, gorgeous lips smiling over perfectly white teeth. And his body…! It should be a crime for a man to be so beautiful." She rolled her eyes and faked an exaggerated swoon. "I'm thinking of becoming a Christian just so I can attend his meetings and look at him on a regular basis."

"A Christian?"

"Lucan is one of that strange group. That's why he's using the banquet hall. They hold meetings there, eating together in some sort of feasting ritual. They talk about and pray to their odd Jewish leader, who died and rose again. They speak much about blood and sins and, oh, I don't know what else. I've heard bits and pieces. It's quite curious."

Lelia tilted her head quizzically. "I've heard of Christians before. I've never met one. I know nothing of their beliefs."

"Donatus says Lucan's changed since he became one. He used to carouse and drink and spread his affections around among the ladies. If you know what I mean by that."

Lelia smiled. "I think I do."

"Donatus says he's changed. None of that. Not now. And in its place integrity and kindness, and a new self-control. All good things, impressive things. So Donatus allows the Christians to meet here—even though he says we must not, any of us, let that be known. It's illegal, you know."

"No, I didn't know."

"Donatus says that's because Emperors don't like mysterious groups and mysterious meetings. They fear dissenters."

"But Christians aren't dissenters, are they?"

"Not really. Not that I can see. Though they do refuse to worship the Emperor. Donatus told me it's because their god—and they have only one—forbids them to claim any other as their lord but he. And so they will not. Even though they could be killed for it."

Lelia nodded. "I've heard of that. My grandfather spoke once of Nero's torture of Christians after the great fire. He said the punishment was horrific and turned his stomach, even though he'd always thought their religion a ridiculous one."

"Just so. But that religion is Lucan's. And maybe I shall make it mine as well."

Lelia laughed softly. "One does not change religions simply to admire a man's pretty face."

Druscilla leaned forward, her face animated. "Oh, but it's not just his pretty face. You'll not believe what a manly form he has, not unless you see for yourself. I must introduce you to him."

Lelia laughed again. "Yes, you must. Only please do remember that I'm a matron now, and must be quite circumspect in my admiration of the manly beauty of any other but my husband."

Druscilla grinned, her amber eyes twinkling with mischief. "Donatus wouldn't have to know. I won't tell him if you don't. Just remember to keep your mouth closed. And don't gawk."

"I won't," Lelia promised with a smile. "I'll be most cautious."

They laughed together, and Druscilla took her hand, guiding her down yet another colonnaded portico.

"Come, look at this," the girl said a few moments later, sweeping open a door of screened lattice. "This is my favorite place in the whole world. I make my *paedagogus* give me lessons here, under the trees. If I have to be bored with study, at least I'd like to be bored in a place of beauty."

She pulled Lelia through the door and onto a stone-paved courtyard, surrounded by a garden just turning the green-gold of early spring.

"Oh, my goodness," Lelia breathed, surveying the panorama which surrounded them, just now realizing that the house was well-situated on the crown of one of Rome's seven hills, and that it overlooked the city on one side and the waters of the Tiber on the other. "Oh, Druscilla, this is beautiful! No wonder you love this place. And this home... Why, it's like the Emperor's palace!"

Druscilla seemed pleased. "Hardly that. But certainly more than adequate. My father had a great interest in architecture and engineering. He was forever designing and adding some new something. Thankfully, he'd completed most of his projects before he died, so at least Mama doesn't have to try to direct the workmen." She sighed. "Sometimes I miss him so much. He was a wonderful, gifted man. I'm sorry you never knew him."

"Oh, but I did. I met him once when—" Lelia halted in mid-sentence, remembering suddenly that she must have care in the things she said.

Druscilla was looking at her, waiting for her to finish. Lelia cleared her throat. "I met your father two years ago, at a banquet. And, yes, I liked him very much."

"Papa was handsome. Did you not think so?"

Lelia bit her lip, wishing she could deny the memory. But she *had* thought Marcus Flavius Antonius strikingly attractive. With his dark hair, graying slightly at the temples, with his high cheekbones and long-lashed green eyes, the father had been a slightly older version of Donatus, the son she had so desperately loved. "Yes," she said quietly. "Your father was handsome."

"And Donatus looks just like him—more than any of us," Druscilla said, regarding her intently. "So you must think Donatus handsome."

Lelia's throat closed up and she coughed, trying to clear

it. "Well…ah…a wife ought to think her husband attractive, I suppose." She coughed again. "Excuse me, Druscilla, but I really should go inside now. Sometimes the buds and flowers of spring make my head and throat ache."

Druscilla nodded. "That's all right. Perhaps you might come back later. This place is absolutely stunning in the summer, with leaves on all the trees and flowers in bloom. But come along. There's more for you to see. You won't believe all the improvements Papa made. Even indoor latrines, several of them, with water flowing underneath the seats to carry away the waste. Very few other houses have that, even those of the wealthiest families. And our kitchen has running water. Come, let me show you."

Lelia was happy to see anything—even the latrines of smooth marble, accented with gold clear down to the golden handles on the sponge sticks that cleansed dirty backsides. Anything, everything, just as long as she didn't have to talk about Donatus anymore.

It was in the kitchen, however, that she found Severina. Her friend was dressed in a plain tunic, dirty now from her day's labor as a scullery maid. She stood over a table with a weary expression, peeling the skins of small fruits.

"Severina?" Lelia said, rushing forward to capture the hand that wielded the knife. "What are you *doing?* You shouldn't be in here, and certainly not doing—" she shook the hand she held in agitation "—this!"

Severina's gray eyes held sudden confusion. "What else should I be doing? I was given this task by Livia."

"And who is Livia that she should order you about?"

Druscilla answered. "Livia runs the household. She directs all the slaves and freedmen who serve here."

Lelia turned sharply. "Severina's *not* a servant. Who told you she was?"

Druscilla looked startled. "Why, I don't know. I guess we just assumed it. She came with you, and we thought…"

"Severina's my friend. She's my *guest*. I'll not allow her to be put to menial work in my kitchen. I owe this woman my very life!"

A voice intruded, harsh with age and authority. "What is the problem, my lady? Do the kitchen slaves not perform their tasks to your satisfaction?"

Lelia turned. "There's been a grave mistake. This woman directed to work here is *not* a slave, mine or any other. She'll not work as long as she resides in this household, not even so much as to lift her finger unless she so chooses. She'll sleep on silk and dine on meals that others prepare for her."

The older woman frowned. "I don't understand."

"Severina is my friend. The dearest one I have. I'd have her be a guest in my home, not a servant under your hand."

"But she said—"

"I don't care what she said. I'll not have it." Lelia turned to Severina. "Put down that knife this instant and come with me."

The older woman raised a hand as if to stop her. "My lady, I wonder if the master would agree with your decision."

Lelia narrowed her eyes. "Of course he will." She looked the older woman over carefully. "Maybe it's you who doesn't agree. Who are you, that you should question my wishes?"

"I am Livia," the woman said, straightening her spine. "I direct the affairs of this household and have done so for nearly forty years."

"And do you wish to continue in that capacity?"

"I do indeed."

"Then understand this. Severina is a guest in my home and will be treated as such. Prepare the best room you have. And I do mean the best. Attend to it."

The old woman's jaw tightened, but she nodded curtly. "As you wish."

When the elderly servant had departed, Druscilla gave a low, drawn-out whistle. "You certainly told her."

Lelia shook her head, trying to quiet the blood still roaring through her ears. "A slave should never question the command of her mistress."

"Livia's not exactly a slave. At least not anymore. She may have been, years and years ago. But she was freed long before any of us can remember, and now she runs this household with an iron rod. Even Donatus is afraid of her."

That thought almost made Lelia smile. Almost. "Is he really?"

"Well, I don't know that he's *afraid* of her, but he is most careful not to anger her. I don't think he's yet forgotten the spankings she gave him as a boy. He'll be pleased you put her in her place. The old witch is much too full of herself and her own authority anyway. When I tell him—!"

"No, Druscilla. Not a word."

Druscilla looked unhappy. Lelia touched her hand lightly.

"Promise me. Not a word."

"If I must."

"You must. And now, if you don't mind, I need to prepare myself for a dinner party tonight."

"Of course. Do you need a slave to help you dress? Maybe to arrange your hair?"

"No, Severina can help me—if she doesn't mind."

"Of course I don't mind," Severina answered.

Lelia smiled. She turned to Druscilla. "Will you let me know when your brother arrives? And remember you're not to say a word."

Druscilla nodded. She watched Lelia link arms with Severina and lead her toward the suite of rooms Donatus had always claimed as his own. Watching them go, Druscilla smiled slyly, thinking that even if she couldn't tell Donatus what had happened in so many words…well, he could always *guess*.

Chapter Six

Lelia sat with her friend on the bed and squeezed gently, her arm around the other woman's thin shoulders. "Stop crying, Severina, or you'll smear the ink on the parchment."

"I know, I know." Her friend sniffed, wiping at her nose with the back of her hand. "I just can't help it. *Freedom.* He's given me freedom."

Lelia frowned, wishing she could tell Severina the truth—that it was *she* who would be purchasing it, and at a price very dear. But she couldn't. Severina would never allow her to do it, not if she knew. Her friend would sell her own self back into servitude before she expected Lelia to lie with Donatus and conceive his child…again. Better to let Severina think heroic things of Donatus, whether he deserved the praise or not.

"And that's not all," Lelia said quietly. "Donatus has promised to give you money, enough to start a business of your own. All you need to do now is decide what you wish to do. You'll have it, whatever you wish."

Severina shook her head. "No, no. Truly, he's done enough. I can't ask for more."

"Oh, hush. Donatus has been blessed with wealth beyond belief, and I can promise you he'll not miss it."

"Not miss it? How can he not miss this much money?"

The question caught Lelia by surprise. She arched her eyebrows.

Severina held up the parchment. "This money—so much money! Fifty *thousand* sesterces. My stars, but that's a fortune!"

Lelia leaned forward, trying to read the parchment. "Fifty thousand? He *didn't*."

"He did. It's there on the page, written plain as day. '*One gladiatorial slave, Cassia Severina, purchased this day from Publius Larcius Brocchus of the Ludus Magnus of Rome, for the price of fifty thousand sesterces...*'" Severina looked up. "There it is. I didn't read it wrong."

Lelia snatched at the paper. Severina let her have it, a puzzled frown upon her face. "You don't suppose it's a mistake, do you, Lelia? Fifty thousand sesterces for a slave? No, that can't be correct. No slave ever sells for that much."

Lelia looked away, tears pricking her eyelids. "It's not a mistake. That's the price Donatus paid for you."

And me, she wanted to add. Fifty thousand sesterces for each of them. Donatus had to be a certified madman.

Or else he did truly love her.

She handed the parchment back to Severina and moved to the window, hugging herself as she looked out at the lengthening shadows of late afternoon.

"Is something wrong?" Severina asked behind her. "Lelia? Are you all right?"

No, she was not all right. But the ache in her chest had nothing to do with Severina, with the parchment in her hand. It had everything to do with Donatus.

"I'm just tired and out of sorts," she said, half turning toward her friend.

"You probably got little sleep last night. Did you...? Did he...?"

Lelia shook her head. "You'd not believe it if I told you."

"I bet I can guess. Donatus made love to you and you *liked* it."

"Severina! Of course not!"

"Of course not *what?* He didn't love you, or you didn't like it?"

"He didn't love me."

"A pity, then."

"A pity? I thought you were on my side."

"I am, Lelia. Of course I am. But any fool can see the man loves you. Why else would he have sought you out? Bought you? Married you?" Severina shrugged. "The wonder is that he's chosen to deny himself what is his by right. He might have quickly done the deed. Perhaps he should have."

Lelia nodded. "I know. It yet lies between us, an obligation I am loath to fulfill."

Severina looked at her intently. "I wonder..."

"What's that supposed to mean?"

"I know you too well, Lelia. You're a woman fierce in your loves and loyalties. You made love with Donatus, carried his child. Can you truly say no feeling remains?"

Lelia looked down, wanting to deny the words. "I can't forgive him, Severina. He hurt me. Don't ask me to forgive him. Don't ask me to love him."

"I'm not asking it," Severina said softly. "I don't have to."

Lelia looked up sharply.

Severina sighed. "Love's not something one simply chooses to do. It's just there, like the wind. You can no more control it than you could an errant breeze."

Lelia drew in a long, wavering sigh. Severina was right. She hated to admit it, despised knowing it, but Severina was right.

* * *

Lelia sucked in her breath as she lowered her wound down into the warm water of the bath.

"Does it hurt much?" Severina asked, easing through the water to sit on the concrete ledge beside Lelia.

"Mostly at night. I should've been more wary of the little man. He had a powerful arm."

Severina nodded, looking pensive. "Odd to think those days are behind us now."

Lelia rubbed the ache out of her neck, then lifted warm water so that it cascaded over one shoulder. "It is odd, isn't it? Yesterday we were at the *ludus,* tasting the salt of our own sweat, gripping the handle of a sword."

"Last night I dreamed of it. I was in the arena." Severina shuddered. "Back there again."

"Don't think of it. That life is past. The Fates have conspired a different destiny." Lelia sighed. "And yet, for all that, I'll miss the physical exertion. I rather liked the activity."

"I did, too. And there was the added satisfaction of knowing that should any man accost me in the streets I could flip him over my back and grind my boot into his throat before he breathed again."

Lelia smiled, circling her left hand around her right upper arm. "I know. I like the feel of my own strength. I like the feel of this muscle. And Donatus..." She halted.

Severina's gaze met hers. She grinned. "Donatus likes it, does he?"

Lelia shrugged. "How would I know? He hasn't touched me."

"But he will. You know he will."

Lelia ground her teeth. She closed her eyes and leaned her head back against the wall.

"Maybe you should just give up the fight. Let the man love

you, be a good husband to you. Tell Donatus about his son. Let him help you."

Lelia's eyes flew open. "I don't need his help."

"I say you do. What have you accomplished on your own? You've poured every bit of your earnings, all the gold you've won, into the task, and yet no results have come of it. If Donatus is as rich as you say…"

"No."

"And why not? Only for the sake of your pride? What does that mean, Lelia? What does that mean? When every day that passes your son is still without his mother."

Lelia growled impatiently. "I know that. You think I don't know that? It's one of the reasons I gave in to Donatus's marriage proposal. Leaving the *ludus* means more freedom to seek out my son. But to tell Donatus…!"

"Would it be so awful to let him know? My stars, Lelia. The man has a *son*. An heir." Severina paused, a worried expression marring the beauty of her gray eyes. "I'm no expert on the ways of nobility, but it seems a safe bet to say that the child would mean much to Donatus. To his entire family."

Lelia looked away.

"I don't suppose you've given thought to how he'll feel when he discovers it?"

"He'll not discover it."

"Oh, come now. It will be found out. You can't keep the secret forever. Someday Donatus will chance upon it. Have you not thought about that moment? He's a man, Lelia, and a proud one. Honor matters to him, and truth, and justice. Would you risk losing his love because of your pride?"

"What do you know of it? You weren't there when I stood before my father, confessing that I carried Donatus's child. You weren't there to hear the things said, to see me dragged into the alley and tossed like trash into the street.

You weren't there when I begged to eat, enduring the offers of men for my body, knowing that if it weren't for the child within me I might have lowered myself to that to survive. Have mercy, Severina!"

Severina's eyes filled with tears. "I know. I'm sorry."

"And when the baby came, there was no husband to hold my hand, to brush back my hair and whisper encouragements. Donatus was not there to smile with pride at the son he had made so well."

"I know. I'm sorry."

"Don't talk of this to me again. I will not tell Donatus. He didn't offer me his help before. He'll have no part in helping me now."

"But he didn't know."

"And he'll not know. Not now. Not ever."

Severina frowned. "Well, if he does find out, remember I warned you."

Lelia scowled at her. "I'll remember."

Donatus was weary. The long, restless night and the long, interminable day had sapped his strength. Or perhaps it was the dread of this evening.

He'd tried all day to force Lelia from his mind. He'd tried to forget the haunted look in her face when he'd told her about their dinner invitation. But it had to be done. Challenges needed to be faced and conquered, and the sooner the better.

It would be the first step toward rebuilding her life. He wanted badly to give her that. It wasn't much. Not when he wanted to give her so much more. But a man had to start somewhere. If all he could do was hold her hand under the table while she faced the lions of public opinion, well…it was a start.

He entered their bedroom quietly. She was seated at a table, facing away from him. Severina was arranging her hair. Neither of them heard him, and he took a moment before he let his presence be known.

Lelia's tunic and *palla* were lying across the bed. She'd chosen well. The tunic with the hem of embroidered irises made him think of her eyes. He'd paid dearly for it, but the cost was fractional beside the pleasure he'd receive from looking at her in it. Even the thought made his heart skip.

He moved forward. Both women started, hearing his footfalls. "I'm sorry," he said quietly. "I didn't mean to startle you."

Severina had almost dropped the mirror. She put it down quickly and turned to face him. "I was just leaving."

"You were not!" protested Lelia.

Donatus smiled at Severina, his eyebrow quirking upward mischievously. "Of course you were."

"No!" Lelia said, pushing her chair back, struggling to rise. "My hair's not done."

"It is," Donatus said, not taking his eyes from Severina. She nodded, moving toward the door.

"Donatus, no!" Lelia wailed. "My hair's not done!"

Donatus looked at her. His breath caught in his throat, stuck there. Lelia was barely clothed. The garment she wore was of thin white cotton, and there was nothing beneath it. Nothing. Except her flesh, her warm and muscular flesh, looking womanly and attractive beneath its veil.

Severina left the room. For one moment he considered stepping to the door and calling her back. But what would he say? *Come back in here so I won't be tempted to make love to my own wife?*

He stood one brief moment in indecision, then turned to Lelia. She watched him warily, not seeming to understand the effect she was having on him.

"Sit down," he said. His voice sounded odd. Strangled, and much too harsh. "Sit down. I'll finish your hair."

She frowned. "And what do you know of hair?" But she dutifully sat, her back to him.

He moved to her, hesitating for one moment while he wondered at what he'd said and why he'd said it. He knew nothing of a lady's hairstyles. He only knew what he liked— her hair, long and silken, a curtain around him when he loved her. His hand hovered in the air, wanting to touch it and fearing to.

She half turned, suspicion in her face. "Do you know what you're doing?"

"Yes." He moved to stand exactly behind her. She relaxed a bit, as if she believed him.

He took up the brush and ran a test stroke down through her hair. The long ebony strands fell shimmering, catching the light of the coals in the hearth. He lifted the brush, pulling it free of the strands. A scent wafted up with it, the delicate scent of citrus and woman. He inhaled. He'd forgotten so much, but now the scent brought it back. He remembered lying with her beneath a grove of trees, her scent wrapping itself all around him, her hair smooth beneath his fingertips…

"Donatus?" she said, breaking into his reverie. Donatus realized he'd stopped brushing.

"I'm sorry," he said, resuming the motion of the bristles in her hair. "I was thinking."

"About what?"

"About you. About me. About the past."

She said nothing. The only sound was the brush as it glided through her hair.

"Do you ever remember, Lelia?"

"No."

"Nothing?"

"It ended."

He touched her hair, his left hand sliding down the silken cascade in the brush's wake, tracing the outline of the curl at the bottom. "It didn't end for me."

"Donatus, don't."

"Are you afraid to hear me, Lelia? Afraid of what you might remember? Afraid of what you might feel?"

He felt her tense. "There's no sense in reliving the past once it's gone," she said.

"I treasure the memories."

"Then do it silently. I don't want to hear them."

He wrapped the curl around his finger, tugging at it gently as he lowered his lips. She jumped like a nervous kitten when his tongue touched the shadowed place behind her ear. She tried to twist around, but was held captive by the fetter of her hair.

"Stop this, Donatus."

"I missed you, Lelia. My decision to leave you pierced two hearts."

"Of course it did. That's why you hurried back to me."

"I was a soldier. Bound by oath to serve Rome."

"Then I do hope Rome kept you warm at night. I hope Rome healed your hurts and loved you."

He kissed the fragrant shell of her ear. "By day I fought for Rome. By night I dreamed of you."

She crossed her arms and slanted her eyes to him. "How charming."

His jaw tightened. He straightened and loosed the curl. "Those dreams were the only thing that kept me sane. You will not make a mockery of them."

"Oh, I'm not, Donatus. I'm so pleased you had something beautiful with which to fill your time. Because I'm quite certain that I did not."

Donatus lowered the hairbrush. "I'm sorry, Lelia," he said. "I lied."

She snorted. "I should've known. There were no memories. There were no dreams."

"I lied about knowing how to dress your hair." He placed the hairbrush beside her on the table. Their eyes caught and held. "I didn't lie about the memories. Or the dreams."

Lelia was still staring after him when he opened the door and turned back to her. "I'll send Severina to finish your hair."

Donatus fought the urge to pull back the curtain of the litter and look out. He wanted to see his host's home as they neared it, as if that would somehow help prepare him for what they faced.

He hated feeling this way. Give him a sword, a javelin, a good horse, and he could wage war almost single-handedly. He could usually handle himself well socially, too. But he was no longer a bachelor with only himself to consider. He'd married a woman, a lovely creature, all mystery and shadow. He'd married Lelia, his forbidden love, and Leda the Gladiatrix, knowing full well how high the tide of censure would sweep.

Well, let it come. He'd anchor Lelia. He'd command the situation as he'd commanded his ala, using swiftness and skill to outmaneuver the enemy, daring the world to give her anything but acceptance. And if it were true that the friends of Lelia's father were the ones most likely to hold her disgrace against them both, then he'd chosen well for this first foray into enemy territory. Tonight he and Lelia would face the very senators most likely to remember, and most likely to care.

Lelia hardly looked concerned at the moment, her head held high, impervious as a queen. But he knew better. He'd felt her hand tremble as he'd handed her into the litter. He'd seen her lips tighten when he'd given her a smile of reassurance and told her that her beauty would outshine any other. She was frightened. Either that, or she detested his compliments. Or perhaps both.

Donatus's long hours in the Senate made their arrival at the home of Scribonius Firmus rather late—so late that darkness had already come. Torchbearers led the way through the dark streets, bearing weapons in case robbers thought Donatus's well-appointed litter easy prey.

Only Donatus knew that he'd *planned* to be so late. And as they entered the wealthy and powerful Senator's home, Donatus almost smiled. The banquet in progress had already become noisy. That was a good sign, just the sign he'd hoped for. Maybe Bacchus would be kind where the Fates hadn't been. Maybe ample wine and good food had taken the malicious bite from the assembled company. Perhaps they'd be disposed to gentleness.

"Come, my love," he said, placing his hand solicitously on her waist. He leaned near. "And remember, you promised."

She looked up at him, one eyebrow lifting slightly. In an endearing, wifely gesture, she reached up and straightened his tunic, appearing to be the loving partner that they both knew she was not. "Don't be an ass, Donatus," she said sweetly. "You don't have to keep reminding me that I'm a senator's wife. I can play the damn part." She patted the garment into place and smiled. It was all Donatus could do not to laugh aloud, crush her to his chest and kiss her.

A slave took them to the banquet hall. Firmus met them at the door, red-faced with the effects of wine, and smiling broadly.

"Donatus," he roared, too loudly. "I'm so pleased you've arrived. I feared you'd been *detained,* but I see your lovely wife hasn't kept you in chains for her pleasure." He guffawed loudly at his own joke before raising Lelia's hand to his lips. "Flavia Lelia. You're far more lovely than I remember."

Something in his eyes made Donatus wary, and when Lelia gasped and jerked her hand away from the man's lips, he knew how hot his anger could burn.

"I'll attribute your momentary lack of good sense to the wine which graces your table, Firmus," he said coldly. "Otherwise I'd remind you to be more of a gentleman in the presence of a lady."

Firmus laughed, his eyes raking over Lelia in a way that suggested he thought her anything but a lady. "Let it be the wine, then," Firmus said. "And let me guide you to your place so that you may have some, too."

He led them to a wide, comfortable couch, facing the table and covered in a square of orange linen tasseled with blue silk. Firmus motioned for Donatus to recline. "Enjoy yourselves. I think you'll agree that my slaves have outdone themselves with the food."

Donatus settled onto the couch and pulled Lelia down with him, his arm going about her naturally. He felt her stiffen and smiled into her face. "We're being watched," he said, nodding almost imperceptibly toward the other guests. "They surely think you're the most stunning woman they've seen."

She met his gaze. "Hardly that. They probably wonder what wickedness I'll do in their midst tonight."

His eyes captured hers. "Let them think what they will. We know the truth."

Inexplicably, her eyes filled with tears. Donatus didn't know what he'd said to cause that, but he knew what would happen if the others saw it. There'd be a feeding frenzy, as lions circling a weak gazelle for the kill.

He did what he had to do. He kissed her, pulling her hard into his arms as an impassioned lover would do in the privacy of their bed. He heard the guests gasp, heard the buzz of conversation cease completely.

Lelia went momentarily still against him, then began to struggle for release. He did not let her go, but slanted his kiss against her lips, demanding entrance. She resisted only a moment, then let him enter.

He wanted to moan at the taste of her, knowing he could not, knowing their audience would enjoy such fodder for their gossip on the morrow. But he drank deeply of her wine, loved her with his tongue, slid into her in a breathless foreplay of all he wanted to give her. She trembled against him, and Donatus realized that he no longer acted for the crowd. His manhood had grown heavy and full against her leg.

His tongue began to stroke her in a familiar rhythm, mating his breath with hers. She answered it, her tongue against his, pulsing with hungry reply. His hand rose to the back of her neck, lacing his fingers into her hair to pull her deeper into his mouth. She came forward into it eagerly.

"Newlyweds," he heard Firmus say loudly, gaining a titter from the crowd. But only a titter, for most were too busy gawking.

Time to retreat, as badly as Donatus hated to—especially when Lelia was responding to him so beautifully. He hadn't anticipated that, but then, there were always such surprises in battlefield maneuvers.

He pulled away, his eyes searching hers, finding them heavy with desire. "Trust me," he said softly.

He turned to the crowd, looking around as if surprised by the sudden attention. "Please…please forgive me," he said, raking his hair with lean fingers. "I fear my great love for my wife has made me forget myself." He heard the crowd murmur, but the sound was a pleasing one. There was soft laughter, mostly feminine. It bolstered his confidence that victory was imminent. If all of the world loved a lover, then they would soon love him, for he'd play the most besotted lover the world had ever known. Or maybe he wasn't playing.

Firmus grinned at him from his place near the head of the table. "I say, Donatus. You'll not strain my supply of wine tonight. You have a potion far more intoxicating."

Donatus glanced at his wife. "I do, Firmus. But is my lady wife not worthy of such adoration?" He surveyed the smiling faces of the women. "Two years ago I should have made her my bride, but the wars of Rome called me into duty before I could accomplish the deed. For two years I lay in a hard cot in a Roman army camp and dreamed of her. For two years the wind sighed her name to me, and every flower of spring reminded me of her beauty. I fought the Dacians like a man possessed. I won honors. The *corona aurea* was placed upon my brow by none other than Emperor Trajan himself. But, ah, I confess to you now that I fought our enemies with selfish intent, vanquishing them only that I might more quickly return to my beloved's side." He bowed his head in a humble gesture. "And now my duty to Rome is accomplished, and I've returned to her. I do beg your forgiveness for my forward behavior. I offer the only excuse I can—that I have been too long without the one whose love makes my heart beat."

There was a moment of stunned silence, followed by hearty applause. "Hear! Hear!" someone said loudly. Others seconded.

Donatus turned to Lelia, smiling at her. He took her hand, lacing their fingertips together before he raised it to his lips for a tender kiss. The roar of the crowd increased.

Someone pushed food before them, and silver goblets were filled with wine. Donatus laughed, and kissed Lelia's hand again. The noise of the banquet resumed, surrounding them, buoying them on a wave of goodwill.

It worked, he thought with elation as they tasted the food. He'd not been sure it would. It could have so easily gone the other way, and they'd have been outcasts for years to come. He'd considered that possibility with care, measuring the risk, finally deciding that one must engage the enemy to overcome them.

And it had worked. Tomorrow the talk all over Rome would be that of the hero returned from the Dacian Wars and of the love he'd left behind at such great personal sacrifice. And Lelia, as befitted the newest heroine of Rome's poetic soul, would be his beloved, his beauteous and most worthy wife.

He could hardly keep from grinning. Damn, it had worked.

"Donatus," Lelia whispered. "I should crucify you for that."

"It worked," he said, looking down at her.

"And what if it hadn't?"

"It did."

"You're impossible."

Donatus noted that her lips were threatening to turn up at the corners. And that reminded him of the kiss they'd just shared and her response to it. He leaned closer. "Impossible to ignore? Or impossible to resist?"

"Don't flatter yourself," she whispered, her eyes growing wider at the certain hunger in his. "But I confess your skill with rhetoric surprises me."

He smiled at the change of topic, recognizing it for the evasion it was. "It surprises me, too. Perhaps love makes poets of common men. Cavalry soldiers among them."

"Love?" she scoffed. "Hardly that."

He was silent.

She glanced up, drawing in her breath at his expression. "Donatus?"

He leaned into her and saw her eyelids lower as his tongue

touched the corner of her lips. "I said *love,* Lelia. I'll not recant the word."

She shuddered. "Have mercy, Donatus."

His lips moved softly against hers. "I shall, my sweet. I shall."

Chapter Seven

Lelia felt herself slipping into the spell, mesmerized by those green eyes. She told herself it was just gratitude she felt, because he'd so magnificently won some measure of respect for her from a public that only yesterday had spurned her. She owed him a kiss, surely. She wouldn't want him to think she didn't appreciate what he'd done.

Their lips met, passion tearing through the fabric of their souls in a surge instantaneous and blazing. "Donatus!" she gasped, drawing away from him.

His large hand captured her, twining through her hair, pulling her back. "No," he commanded. "Don't fight me."

His mouth was urgent, heat upon heat. His tongue, serious and demanding, urged her submission, stimulating her with a provocative thrusting rhythm that awakened memories, and needs.

She responded to him, pulling him deeper into her mouth, pulling his hardened body nearer to hers. Desire flooded her, until she wanted to arch herself against his swollen manhood. Her breasts tingled. She had to fight to breathe, to think, to remember that they were at a banquet, among a crowd. And that she couldn't do this. Not yet. It was too early. There might be a child. The thought sobered her enough to push at Donatus's chest.

He wouldn't let her retreat. "Come with me," he breathed heavily against her ear. "They'll understand. Come with me."

"Let me go, Donatus."

"Do you really want me to?"

She looked at him, aching at the sight of the taut skin stretched over the high cheekbones, the lashes lowered so seductively over those green eyes. Her whole body was burning. His too. She knew it. She could feel him, thick and hard against the soft folds of her tunic.

"Donatus, we can't."

"We can. Start anew with me, Lelia. Tonight."

She drew a long, quavering breath.

He looked down, his eyes tracing the curves of her breasts. Beneath that unwavering regard her insides tightened. Her nipples ached for his touch. He raised his eyes again to hers, and she saw the knowledge there. He knew.

"Do you want me?"

She licked at lips gone dry. "Yes, Donatus. I want you."

"Then let's forget all else. Who knows but that the Fates have decreed our destiny this way? Perhaps the joining of our bodies will unite our souls, and all we need consider now is our mutual pleasure."

He laughed shortly, running his brown fingers through his dark hair. "Last night I told you I'd wait for you, but now…"

Lelia was silent, her body tense with need. "Two years has been a long time, Donatus. For both of us." She bit her lip uncertainly. "Maybe it is time. Maybe we'll both feel better when this promise is fulfilled. One time, Donatus. One time. This can't be the start of anything. It's just our bodies, nothing more. You must understand that."

He was silent. She saw the battle within him. His fingertip traced her lips. She met it with her tongue. He sucked in his breath. "Are you sure?" he asked quietly. "It's not the way I wanted it to be, Lelia. I wanted…"

"I know, Donatus. But you can only take that which I willingly give."

He looked down, his lashes lying long and dark against his tanned cheekbones. "I'm sorry I couldn't wait until you loved me. But I'm a man, and I need you, Lelia."

He loosened his grip and slid away from her, rising, pulling her up beside him. "Wait for me near the door. I'll make our excuses to the host."

She nodded, feeling as guilty as on the first time they'd slipped away to be alone together. She watched him make his way around the table, then eased into the atrium on the other side of the portal.

Looking down at the tile floor, her thoughts so distracted by Donatus and by that which they'd just agreed to do, she didn't see the other guests coming in until she stumbled into one. He reached out a hand to steady her, grasping her elbow firmly in a grip of iron.

"Oh!" she gasped. "I'm sorry. Please forgive—!" She stopped in mid-sentence, her heart pounding. Her gaze had lifted to see the face she most dreaded in all the world.

Her father.

His gaze swept over her quickly, his expression hard. "Lelia. What are you doing here? Plying the trade you learned with your secret lover?" He gave her a small shove to set her away from him.

"Leptis." A familiar voice from behind him made Lelia turn in that direction.

"Mother?" she asked.

"I'm here." Her mother stepped out from behind her

father's tall, broad-shouldered form. She held out her arms. Lelia rushed into them.

"No!" Leptis said firmly. "Don't encourage her, Prisca."

His wife ignored him. She hugged Lelia tightly and then drew back, studying her face. "Are you well?" she asked.

Lelia nodded, not trusting herself to speak for the lump in her throat.

Leptis grasped her arm and pulled her out of her mother's grasp roughly. "I said *no!*" he growled. "And I do mean it. Even if I have to see it done with my own hands. As your father, I'm responsible for—"

A cold, mocking challenge interrupted his statement. "You're no longer responsible for her, Leptis."

Leptis turned. Over his shoulder, Lelia saw Donatus, standing erect in the doorway, arms crossed, face grim. "I should've known," Leptis acknowledged bitterly. "That's why she's here, acting for all the world as if she belongs among polite society."

"She does. She's the wife of a senator now."

Lelia heard her mother gasp, and turned to her. Some strong emotion crossed her mother's face as the older woman closed her eyes, her hand pressed to her breast.

Leptis frowned. "So you've married her, have you? Well, isn't that nice and decent of you, to make an honest woman of her now, two years after the fact? You'll be such a cozy little family now, you and Lelia and—"

"Father!" Lelia said, in a voice loud enough to cover his next words. "Please! For the sake of Firmus don't make a scene here among his guests. They're just within the banquet room there. They surely can hear your words."

Leptis's eyes narrowed. "You'd censure me, girl? I don't think so." He stepped forward menacingly.

Donatus stepped forward at the same time. "No, Leptis. It

is I who doesn't think so. Lelia's my wife now, and I'll not abide her mistreatment." He put his hand on Lelia's arm, drawing her closer to his side. "Come, my love. It's time we were leaving."

They were barely inside the litter before Lelia gave way to tears. Donatus seemed to be expecting them. He enfolded her in his arms. "Shh, my sweet," he consoled her gently, stroking her hair with his large hand. "It's over. He's not going to hurt you. Not ever again."

She didn't reply, couldn't explain that words could pierce more deeply than anything physical.

Donatus was surprised at the fierce protectiveness he felt, holding Lelia in his arms. He was surprised, too, that he'd maintained such calm when he'd wanted nothing more than to thrash her father. Indeed, he was familiar with the prelude to battle— the quick rush of energy, the roar in his head, the feel of his muscles bunched and ready and singing with anticipation.

But he hadn't touched the man. In some deep part of himself he realized now that what he wanted for Lelia had kept him from it. He wanted for Lelia—impossible though it seemed now—a full reinstatement to her position in society, and to her place within her family. He had taken it away from her. And he, Flavius Donatus, must somehow help her get it back.

Her sobs quieted, her body now resting softly against his. "I'm sorry," he said. "I didn't know your parents had been invited."

She shifted slightly, raising her face. "I don't blame you. I can't run from them forever. It was bound to happen sooner or later. It will probably happen again."

He drew her close again, soothing her with a touch. "You were brave, my sweet. You faced your fears tonight. You triumphed over them."

Warrior or Wife

She breathed deeply. "Oh, Donatus…"

He could hardly believe that she came to him then, her lips finding his in the darkness. He knew she sought comfort, and he did not withhold it. He kissed her until her world steadied. Then he kissed her until it tilted madly again, until her breathing quickened and she remembered what it was they had promised one another.

"I want you," she whispered.

"Soon, my love. We're nearly home."

When she would have returned to this passion, he laughed softly. "Patience, love. The slaves wouldn't understand if you left this litter only half clothed. Or maybe they would."

The words had the desired effect. She groaned softly, but seemed content to let him hold her close, his hand stroking down her hair and the sensuous curve of her back.

Slaves met them at their arrival. "My wife hasn't eaten," he said. "Bring food to our chamber. And wine—the best we have."

He lifted Lelia down from the litter, purposely letting her body impact hard against his, sliding down his length to the ground. He heard her sharp intake of breath and knew she'd felt his excitement.

"Come, my love. We have much beauty to rediscover."

She took his hand.

They'd barely entered their bedroom when she fell into his arms. Her kiss, her warmth against him brought a surge of desire to his loins. "Ah, Lelia," he groaned. "You press me mightily, when I would take my time in loving you."

"I don't want to wait," she answered, her voice low and husky. "I need you now."

There was a knock at the door. Lelia turned to it in disbelief.

"Our meal, my lady. You scarcely touched the food at the banquet. I thought you might be hungry."

"I'm not. At least, not for that."

He smiled. "Then you haven't considered what a sensuous thing a meal can be when shared between lovers."

He ignored her exasperation and opened the door.

The slaves entered with several dishes, and in just a short time had arranged them all upon a small table, complete with comfortable silk cushions on the chairs. Donatus closed the door behind them and returned to pour wine. He brought a silver goblet to Lelia.

"Drink. It will calm you."

"I don't need calming, Donatus. I need *you.*"

He smiled. "Then perhaps *I'll* drink it. I need calming very much. Your nearness devastates me." He raised the goblet and drank.

Lelia glanced down his length and then back up again. "I could grow to dislike that senatorial toga," she said with a sigh. "A wife cannot gauge the level of her husband's desire beneath its voluminous folds."

Their eyes met and locked. Donatus felt his breath still. "You'd like to see me, Lelia?"

"Yes," she said, her gaze never wavering.

Donatus swallowed hard and raised the goblet again to his lips, drinking the wine down quickly. He turned away, walking back to the table to pour more before he lost all control. "I promise you, my love, you shall have all you desire. But for now, humor me. Let us take our time and savor this experience."

He glanced up in time to see the exasperation cross her face.

"What game do you play with me, Donatus? Can it be that you expect more of our joining than the appeasement of our desire?"

He lowered the jug of wine and lifted the goblet, his eyes

watching her over the rim as he sipped. "I play no game. I simply seek to share my heart with you."

She snorted. "Keep your heart, Donatus. I want only your body."

Donatus ignored the stab. He moved to her, taking her hand and leading her to the table. "Ah, but it's not possible to separate the two," he said as he seated her.

She looked up at him. "Of course it is. How quickly you've forgotten. You pledged your heart before, then left with it again. Little connection then between your body and your heart."

"It surely seemed so." He took his time in filling a plate before handing it to her. "And yet, how deceived were we both. I thought I could put you behind me. You were convinced I had." He filled his own plate and picked up a spoon. "We were both wrong."

Donatus saw the words pierce her, but she chose to ignore them, concentrating instead on her plate. He did likewise, though it was hard to desire food when what he most wanted was to brush his hands across the soft curve of her shoulders and nibble the delicately scented place behind her ear, the place that had always made her grow limp with desire.

He drank more wine. "I did not forget you. I could not forget you. I held onto those memories like a drowning man holds onto a lifeline. I relived my moments with you again and again, each night for two lonely years."

"Donatus, don't do this."

"My favorite… It was when I took you to my father's river barge. Do you remember that, Lelia?"

He saw her eyelids lower, veiling her thoughts. She was instantly still.

Donatus took the pale hand that rested quietly upon the table. "Lelia," he whispered. "Do you remember that night?

The way the moonlight bathed our bodies in silver? The way the river rocked us as we slept?"

Lelia did remember. And now she fought against rising panic. Of all the memories they'd made together, that was the one she'd never been able to set aside completely. She had relived it even in her dreams.

It hadn't been the first time they'd made love. But it had been, of all their joinings, the most perfect union of their two souls.

Her parents had gone to visit friends at Ostia. For one night and one day she and Donatus had realized a dream, sharing something precious, something so exquisite that even now she hardly dared think of it, almost afraid that, like delicate rainbow-colored glass, it might shatter into worthless shards to make her weep.

She closed her eyes. "The past is gone. Let us not speak of it."

He pulled her hand to his lips. She felt their warmth against her fingers, lingering long.

"I want you to remember," he whispered against her skin. "Tell me you remember."

She could not answer. His low voice had brought it all back. She saw again the smooth sheets upon which they lay, the white curtains all around them, lustrous and shimmering with moonlight, billowing with every gentle breeze. She remembered Donatus's hands upon her, his groans, the emotion in his eyes as they loved, the answering tears in hers. She remembered the warmth in her heart as she'd drifted off to sleep at last, content to be in his arms. And the next morning, their bodies glowing golden in the dawn, naked and beautiful and alive with more than desire.

She sensed the expectant waiting in Donatus's touch, and

knew that he wanted to hear her say the words. And for once, she could not bear to hurt him.

"I remember," she heard herself whisper. "I never forgot that night, Donatus. I always thought it was then that we made—" She stopped abruptly.

Donatus raised an eyebrow. "We made…?"

Lelia picked up her goblet with a shaking hand and drank deeply, steadying herself. She forced herself to meet his gaze as she lowered it. "We made the most perfect love that night. Sadly, it did not survive."

"That's where you're wrong."

He stood and pulled her up into his arms. Lelia instinctively shivered as his hardness made firm contact with her softness, as his lips lowered to within an inch of hers. "It *did* survive, Lelia," Donatus whispered.

His breath was warm across her face, smelling of wine and desire. "It did *not* die. And tonight I will fulfill all the promises I made to you then."

She hardly had time to ponder the strange twist of her heart before his lips descended in a kiss both forceful and gentle. Everything seemed to culminate in that moment, and she felt herself wanting to respond, wishing it could be true.

Donatus groaned when her lips parted. Her body tightened with that remembered sound. His tongue invaded her mouth and she welcomed him, tasting him again. "Oh, Donatus," she breathed at last.

He pulled back and looked at her, his breathing ragged, his eyes wide and dark, as green as the depths of an ancient forest. He raised a finger to her lips, tracing their outline. "I know you don't love me, Lelia. But make me one promise. For this night, agree to set aside the hate. For this one night, trust me."

His gaze searched hers and she looked up, surprised to see

the intensity there. His voice was hoarse with emotion. "Promise me."

She nodded, looking down. For once she felt ashamed of herself, that she couldn't promise him more. Not her heart, not her love. Just her body, and that was all.

He lifted her up in one agile movement, taking her with him to the bed. His lips found hers again as he stretched himself over her, his weight supported on his elbows, but with his hips lying heavy and full against hers. She groaned at the feel of his body, at the burden that felt so primitive and so right.

Her hands found his shoulders, his chest. She tore at his toga and loosened it, needing to feel his skin.

"Have mercy," he breathed in her ear. "Don't rush this, Lelia. Let me savor you."

She almost groaned her frustration aloud, then drew in her breath sharply as his hand captured her breast through the gown she wore. His lips trailed hot fire down her neck, across her collarbone, but it was his fingertips upon her nipple that made her ache between her legs.

"I need you, Donatus," she urged. "Don't make me wait."

He laughed softly. "Ah, you remember it now. It was always like this between us, this white heat that fused us."

His weight eased. She opened her eyes as he stood. He drew off his clothing, one article at a time, until he stood naked before her. Her breath halted. She was lost, mesmerized by the male beauty she'd never completely forgotten.

Her eyes traveled him slowly, each hard, defined muscle and the glorious arousal of his erection, so large and so thrusting. Her throat tightened, remembering pleasure.

She jumped like a startled doe when his hand touched her shoulder, his fingers working against the delicate clasp of the jeweled brooch. He frowned. "They don't make these cursed things easy, do they?"

She laughed nervously. "I don't suppose they imagined the haste with which a woman might wish to disrobe."

The brooch gave way suddenly. Donatus made a short sound of triumph and tossed it without ceremony onto a bedside table. Then his hands were upon her, sliding her garment down, torching her skin, making her writhe with breathless agony. His weight came back, resting against her, half upon her, delicious with sensation. His lips were hot. His hands, too, hot and smooth as they stroked her skin, her hair, her breasts. She gasped when his mouth found her nipple, his hands cupping her while his tongue evoked all kinds of maddening sensations. She became molten liquid, searing volcanic lava poured upon sleek sheets, a heated river of desire against the even sleeker male blade.

"My love," Donatus whispered into her ear. His hand found her, her feminine flesh swollen and needy. She jerked at the profound ache that engulfed her.

"Take me, Donatus," she urged, opening her eyes to look into his, startled by the beautiful sadness she found there.

"Not yet. There's more for you, Lelia, my precious, my wife. I have so much to give you."

She groaned, grinding her teeth together, her head lolling back against the pillows, barely noticing that he shifted and lowered himself until his mouth touched her most sensitive place. She gasped and rose up, her fingers spearing into his dark curls and clenching. "By the gods, Donatus!" she gasped. "What are you doing?"

He didn't answer, only began to kiss her softly, lovingly, spreading her apart with his fingers, tasting every inch of her. The sensation was a new one, and like nothing she'd ever experienced. It made her delirious.

She heard her voice from afar, wondering at her strange mewling cries. Everything within her coiled around the blooming sensation that Donatus's tongue evoked. Need wound itself tighter and tighter, until she thought she would surely plummet over the edge of sanity.

She spiraled to a high place, each sensation keen as a needle and distant as thunder. She panted now, and cried. Her legs quivered and tightened, crushing Donatus's crisp curls against her soft thighs. She became sensation, gossamer-light and ephemeral, floating above reality. She was hot sun and cold ice, tidal wave and gentle sea, panting with need, dying in the pleasure of it.

She neared the sun, squeezing her eyes shut as her breath halted and the first shiver of feeling hovered on the edge of the precipice. At just that moment Donatus shifted again, covering her with himself, his full weight bearing her down onto the bed. She screamed as he plunged his heat into her.

Her nails bit into his shoulders as she lost control, crying out in an agony of pleasure as he held her, stroking her hair during the cataclysm of her climax. It came, wave upon wave, reverberating through her core, riding her along on a ferocious rising crest until it broke with terrible glory onto the rocky shore.

She returned to reality slowly, becoming aware of Donatus's weight upon her, of his fullness within her, of his gaze studying her.

She opened her eyes, almost losing her breath at the tenderness in his face. He brushed an errant curl from her face. "You're so beautiful," he whispered.

"Donatus, I…" She hesitated, not knowing what to say. The experience they had just shared had been wonderful beyond belief, and for the first time since he'd left she felt relaxed and at peace. But physical release was not love, and she couldn't feign that which she did not feel.

"Shh…" he said, placing a finger across her lips. "You don't have to say anything. There is time yet. Plenty of time yet."

She nodded and lay back into the pillows, content that Donatus somehow understood. His hips began to move in a long, sleek, unhurried rhythm. She concentrated on that rhythm, on the beauty of it, on the perfection. She opened her eyes and watched tension etch itself across his features. She stroked his chest, glorying in the restrained strength of his body.

But soon those small pleasures were drowned in the building of new desire. It rose within her again, the tide of passion. Only this time Donatus was with her in it, feeling his own need, straining with her toward that high place.

They were nearing it when someone pounded at the door, startling Lelia into a gasp and Donatus into a curse.

"Donatus! Donatus! Open the door!" a male voice called from the corridor, the sound nearly overtaken by pounding so insistent that the door rattled on its hinges. "Answer the door, Donatus!" their visitor roared.

Donatus let loose a string of curses as he withdrew from her and flung himself to his feet. He didn't bother to dress, but strode naked to the door and yanked it open, a fierce scowl upon his features. "Lucan, you'd better have one damned good reason for—!"

He stopped in mid-sentence, taking in the scene which met him.

Behind him, Lelia struggled to rise, startled by the speed with which Donatus had left her, still aching with needs he'd aroused but not yet appeased. She sat up just as he reached the portal, frantically trying to draw a sheet over her nakedness as Lucan's form appeared in the doorway. She felt rather than saw the stranger's quick perusal.

"What happened here?" Donatus asked, his voice suddenly subdued.

"It's the food," Lucan said, his eyes sweeping over the room. "Have you eaten the food? Has your lady?"

"We had something. But—"

"The figs? Did you eat them?"

Donatus looked around, seeming stunned. "No."

Lucan glanced down at Donatus's nakedness and gestured. "Get some clothes on, then, and quickly. I'll take care of the poor lad, keeping everything quiet for the present. I'll return shortly. Don't eat anything. Neither you nor your wife."

Donatus nodded and closed the door. His face was stern as he turned to face Lelia.

"What is it, Donatus? What's happened?"

He came to her, raising her face with gentle fingers. "A death, I'm afraid. One of the slave boys."

Lelia drew in a sharp breath. "Where? How?"

Donatus wasn't quick to answer. He had turned from her and begun to dress.

"Donatus?" she asked, feeling a nervous panic begin.

Donatus handed her the gown he had so hastily stripped from her earlier. "Here," he said. "Dress yourself, and quickly. I fear this will be a long night for us. There will be much to do now."

"Donatus, tell me what's happened."

He drew her into his arms, his expression filled with pain. "Someone has attempted murder within our house tonight."

"The slave boy was *murdered?*"

"Yes, but he was not the murderer's intended victim. That, I'm afraid, was an unfortunate accident."

Lelia drew in a sharp breath. She was putting it all together— what he said now with what Lucan had said earlier. "Then…?"

Donatus's answer was short, and not as reassuring as he'd probably hoped it would be. "Don't lose yourself to fear. All will be discovered. I swear it."

"It was *us,* wasn't it? We were the intended victims."

Donatus leaned forward and kissed her softly on the lips.

"Don't be afraid, love. We'll get to the truth of it." He turned quickly, but Lelia had seen the brief flare of anxiety in his eyes. He knew something more—something he wasn't telling her. The shudder she felt at that knowledge went all the way down to her soul.

Chapter Eight

Lucan returned with Faustina, and now stood looking at the bowls of food on the small marble-topped table. He glanced up at Donatus, his face serious.

"It has to be the figs," Lucan said quietly. "Troilus had two of them still clutched in his hand. The poor pilfering lad thought no more than to have himself a little snack."

Donatus nodded grimly. "Lelia and I tasted some of everything else. But if it were the figs…"

Faustina met his gaze. "Then *you* were not the one the murderer wanted."

"No."

Lelia looked from one to the other in confusion. "Why not? What have the figs to do with that?"

Faustina rubbed the tension from the back of her neck, speaking slowly. "Donatus can't eat fresh figs. From the time he was a small child they've always made him ill."

"My throat swells and the inside of my mouth itches," Donatus explained. "If I were to eat enough of them, my throat would close up and I'd likely die. Everyone in this household knows that. Certainly everyone among the kitchen staff."

"Are there any new slaves?" Lucan asked. "Someone who might not have known that?"

Faustina shook her head. "No, we've not purchased slaves in several years. In fact, Antonius had been systematically reducing their numbers for some time before he died."

Donatus shrugged. "Even if there were new slaves, that wouldn't account for the poison. Someone had to have deliberately put it there."

The others nodded. Lucan spoke. "It does seem likely, then, that whoever did that was trying to kill Lelia and not you, Donatus."

Donatus drew in a deep breath. "Let's go with that assumption, then, and reason this out." He turned toward Lelia. "Have you any idea who'd want to kill you, my love?"

Lelia felt heat climb her neck. "I can't imagine anyone would. My father's the only person angry with me."

Donatus sent her a look so stern that it reminded her the others knew nothing of her situation. "W-well…" she stammered. "If he wanted to murder me, I suppose he'd have done so two years ago, when…" She trailed off, not sure how to proceed.

"And there's no one else?" Lucan prodded. "No females so jealous of your handsome new spouse that they'd like to dispatch you posthaste?"

Lelia looked up in surprise. She hadn't even considered that there might be rivals for Donatus's love. Could there be? She glanced at Donatus to find him giving Lucan a fierce scowl.

"No, there are no jealous females," Donatus growled. He turned again to Lelia. "Lucan knows that well, if anyone does."

Lucan shrugged. "I'm just trying to consider all the possibilities. I didn't *think* there'd been others, but—"

"You didn't *think* at all," Donatus replied.

Lucan looked chagrined. "No, I didn't. I truly didn't. Your pardon, my lady, for my implying that Donatus might have been anything less than faithful to you. Please forgive me."

Lelia smiled at him graciously. "That's all right. This situation has rattled us all. And truly I do agree that all possibilities should be examined."

The look he gave her was relieved and full of gratitude, and for the first time Lelia was struck by the man's beauty. Lucan's appearance was unusual because it was so fair. His hair was of the lightest gold, casually tousled and thick with curls. His eyes were curiously shaped to a most unusual slant, darkly fringed and, as Druscilla had told her earlier, of a most enchanting shade of green-gold. His cheekbones were high, his chin firm and clefted. A golden tan accented teeth that were straight and very white. His lips were full and sensual. *A man of gold.* No wonder Druscilla was enamored with him.

There was something intriguing about Lucan. A kindness and a vulnerability that a woman could almost sense, mixed with a latent but breathtaking sensuality. She could imagine that many ladies sighed with real grief when this man turned from the pleasures of his sinful flesh.

He took her hand and held it for a long moment, studying her almost as intently as she studied him. Then, as if waking from a dream, they both became aware of Donatus's frowning attention. Lucan let go of her hand and withdrew, looking apologetic, almost guilty.

Faustina seemed not to notice the odd exchange. "I'll find out who prepared the food," she said. "Also the names of every person who was in the kitchen, and all those who carried the dishes here. They'll be questioned immediately." She turned to Donatus. "Do you wish to be present for that?"

He shook his head. "No. You and Lucan can handle it. My first priority is Lelia's safety, and since I have to believe that someone in this household has tried to murder her…" He raked his fingers through his hair, then looked from Faustina to Lucan and back again. "I'm taking her to the river tonight."

Faustina looked relieved. "A good decision. At least you'll be safe, and can sleep securely."

"We'll leave tomorrow for Hercuaneum." Donatus glanced toward Lelia. "I have a villa there, though I haven't visited it since my return home. We should be safe there."

He turned to Lucan. "I entrust you, my friend, with the task of finding the serpent who nests within my own home. Find this person and discover the motive for so foul a deed, and I shall reward you handsomely."

Lucan bowed his head. "Your safety is my only reward, Flavius Donatus."

Donatus acknowledged his reply with a softening of his features. "I'd prefer that no one but us four know where we've gone, but unfortunately that cannot be easily accomplished. We'll need some trustworthy men to form an escort. Choose them carefully. And no more than, say, six or eight. Provide them with horses and the necessities of travel. And weapons, as they must protect us from robbers on the road."

He turned to Faustina. "In the morning, send the *raeda* with four good horses. Have Severina pack up Lelia's things, and mine. And her own things, too. She'll come with us."

Donatus smiled at Lelia's surprised, thankful expression. "I didn't think you would trust anyone else. And I suppose I'll feel better, too, knowing that any murderer will face not just one, but two, well-trained gladiatrices."

Donatus moved across the room, opening the lid of a cedar chest in the corner. He returned with a bag, placing it into Lucan's hand. Lelia heard the clink of coins as Lucan's fingers closed around it. "Find the mother of the murdered slave boy and give this to her. Small recompense it shall be, I know. See to it that the boy has a decent burial, and that the authorities are duly notified of what's occurred here tonight."

Lucan nodded.

"I'll also need you to handle a few other matters for me. Instructions for the steward here, sending my proxy vote to another senator." Donatus sighed. "I'll need a short while to write them out before I leave."

"Then we'll go now, and return in a while. Faustina can gather food for you to take, and I…" Lucan's expression twisted in dismay. "I have a corpse that needs attention." He and Donatus clasped hands in a firm gesture of affection. "Bolt the door securely when we leave," Lucan said quietly. "A grizzled old warrior like you scarcely needs to be concerned, but your lady—"

Donatus's features relaxed for the first time since the whole unnerving situation had been discovered. He smiled, even if it did have an element of grim humor. "My lady? She fights better than I do, Lucan. Don't forget she's been trained at the *Ludus Magnus* of Rome. In fact, were the situation not so dire, I'd applaud her murderer for being sensible and using poison, rather than attempting to murder her with a blade."

Lucan nodded and headed for the door. Faustina followed. "Just the same, bolt the door. I'll rap four times when I return."

Donatus watched them leave and, as instructed, bolted the door. He didn't seem to notice Lelia, nor did he speak as he busied himself with parchment and ink at a small writing table nearby.

Now that the tension had dissipated somewhat, Lelia felt weary to her bones. The stitches in her thigh had begun to ache, too. She sat down on the bed and rubbed the wound, pondering her situation.

Who would try to murder her? She had no enemies that she knew—no reason that someone would want to get rid of her. Unless it had something to do with her marriage to Donatus... She sighed. That was the worrisome thing. Donatus was a wealthy man. She knew nothing of his household, of the personalities within it. If someone wanted to get rid of her before she could give Donatus his heir, she had no way of knowing who it might be. Donatus hadn't thought of any of these things yet. Nor had Lucan. The turbulence of the evening, the late hour and the emotional upheaval, all made simple logic a hard-won commodity. But soon enough they'd both have to consider that the enemy came from within their own ranks, and that she was being sought out only because she stood in the way of a murderer and his inheritance.

For now, they needed to sleep. Donatus had said they'd go to a place of safety at the river. The river barge, perhaps? Her heart clutched at the thought. Not that. Not there. Not tonight. It would bring back too many memories, beautiful and painful. And a time long gone, when love was not lost.

Oh, mercy. She couldn't think of it. Not right now. Instead, she jumped up and began to busy herself with gathering the things they'd need for an overnight stay. Her clothing hadn't yet been put away, so she was able to quickly find a fresh change of clothes for herself. But for Donatus, that was another matter altogether.

She looked across toward where he sat, bent over his parchments, furiously scratching words onto a scroll. His features were etched against the lamp's soft light, and without being able to control herself, Lelia drew in her breath at the handsome image he presented. A man, not of gold like Lucan, but of muscle and bone and the fires of Vulcan. A man dark like earth, dark as a cave, dark with mystery and depth. Her heart did a strange somersault. What was this, this *something*

she felt? This aching homesickness, full of nostalgic sweet-
ness and wretched bitterness in one draught?

Her hand came to her chest in an involuntary gesture, as
if she could push the hurt from her breast—and the fear, too.
For in that moment she knew with the most hideous terror that
something powerful had awakened within her this night.
Something like *love.*

In an effort to flee that thought, she turned away from
Donatus and went to rummage through the chests from which
he'd earlier withdrawn his clothing. She felt uncomfortable,
touching the soft layers of his neatly folded garments, moving
aside his *gladius* and other accoutrements of war. It seemed
such an intimate thing, to go through his possessions this way.
But just as she was about to close the lid, and wait for Donatus
to choose his own things, the glimmer of the gold band on
her hand winked in the reflected light of Donatus's lamp. She
stared at it. *His wife.* She was his wife.

The knowledge hit her forcefully for the first time. Tears
filled her eyes—though she didn't know, couldn't explain,
what those tears meant. Only that with them had returned that
sweet sadness. She drew in a steadying breath and returned
to her task.

Donatus was tidy, if nothing else. His chests were orga-
nized with the efficiency of a soldier, and it didn't take Lelia
long to find the things he'd require. She was about to close
the chest in which she'd found his shaving implements when
something unusual, tucked into a corner, caught her eye—a
small portrait, framed in ebony wood and garnished with
jewels.

She picked it up carefully, scarcely daring to breathe. It
was a likeness of a woman. A young woman, and beautiful.
The portrait was so skillfully painted that she almost seemed
living, as if in another moment her smile would deepen into

laughter. Her hair was dark and sleek, her lips red and pretty, her cheeks flushed with good health. But it was her eyes that conveyed the most of her personality. They were of uncertain color, dark and intense. Something about her seemed familiar.

Jealousy bit into Lelia's heart. Who was she, this woman whose portrait was obviously cherished, framed with rubies to match her lips, and pearls to match her skin, and—?

"What are you doing?" Donatus's voice was resonant and warm from across the room. Lelia jumped, and dropped the picture into the chest. It clattered against the other items as it landed.

"I...I was gathering some things for you. I hope you don't mind."

Donatus chuckled. "No, love. A wife would do such things."

Lelia reddened and closed the lid of the chest. She gathered up his clothing and carried them across to the bed.

"My *wife*." Donatus looked at her, his expression full of tenderness. "I'm pleased to say those words."

Lelia looked away. "You should have done better for yourself than me, Senator. Scarcely twelve hours wed and already you've fended off the lions of public opinion and drawn out a murderer. I'll surely bring you to grief."

She looked back in time to see his brows draw together in a frown. He appeared thoughtful, but thankfully he did not respond. Instead he rose, rolling the scrolls and securing them with a wax seal.

Lelia busied herself, bundling their clothing into a clean linen towel. Out of habit, she drew up the crumpled sheets and straightened them over the feather mattress of the bed, trying to ignore the feelings that flooded her at the memory of Donatus's body over hers, arrogant with manly desire.

She must be exhausted, she thought, for tears had filled her eyes again. She couldn't understand it, this sudden urge to cry at every small, insignificant thing.

Except that being married to Donatus and making love with him were far from small and insignificant things. In fact, they touched her to her very core. And that *did* make her want to cry.

It was risky, this going through the dark streets alone. Donatus's nerves were on edge already, and now every small noise, every darting of a rat through an alley, made him start and his hand move toward the hilt of his sword.

Ordinarily he'd not travel through the city at night—not unless the need were very great, and then only with many torches and armed men. But he'd had to weigh his options differently in this case. The danger of the streets seemed minuscule compared to the danger that lurked beneath his own roof.

And so it was that he and Lelia moved out quietly, two dark-cloaked figures slipping like wraiths through the black streets. Thankfully, the river was not far.

Lelia stayed close. Sometimes the tall *insula* blocked the moonlight, and he sensed her rather than saw her. He couldn't hear her footsteps. She didn't speak. She'd been strangely withdrawn all evening—or at least since Lucan had interrupted their lovemaking with his grim news.

Her reticence disturbed him. Though it was too late and he was too weary to delve into her reasons, he hoped there were no regrets for that which had occurred between them.

It had been too early for such intimacy. He was almost certain of it. There was no trust in her heart. But he was a man, not a god. To be offered that which he'd dreamed of nightly for two lonely years... Donatus shook his head in the darkness, thankful Lelia couldn't see the thoughts that ravaged him now.

He forced the fear down; he had no time for it. Nor would he waste precious time thinking of it. The past had been a mistake, and he would always regret the foolish choice he'd made. But at least he'd learned from it.

He was a different man now, changed forever by the sharp cut of the chisel. He couldn't yet call pain a welcome companion, but he'd grown wise enough not to begrudge its presence.

Had Lelia realized that? No, he knew she hadn't. Her imagination might give him all sorts of selfish motives for the lovemaking of this night. That knowledge was bitter. He'd meant to move so carefully, to give her time to discover that he wasn't the same man who'd left her. He wanted trust to develop, even if love did not.

He halted at the top of a hill, realizing the moonlight had brightened around them. They'd passed through the most crowded of the streets; the wharves were below. He chanced a glance at the woman beside him, breathing heavily from the rapidity of their progress.

"There it is," he said quietly. "The large one on the far right."

She strained for a glimpse. "That's not your father's barge," she whispered. "The one we shared was not so grand."

"No, it's not. When I returned home, I discovered that my father had sold the one we remember so fondly. That distressed me. I'd dreamed of it for two years. So I bought another, as similar to the old one as possible, though larger, slightly more ornate."

He brought up a hand to caress her cheek. "It was to have been a wedding gift for you. I regret these circumstances have spoiled the surprise."

Lelia's gasp pleased him.

Her eyes were wide, glistening with reflected starlight,

when she turned her pale face to him. "For me? But I've done nothing to merit so fine a gift."

He drew her closer. "You have," he said quietly. "You once gave me a gift, too. Something inestimably precious."

She looked up in confusion, panic flaring in her eyes.

"Your virginity," he said. "And your love. Even if you've forgotten them both, I never have."

She closed her eyes, her lashes making spiked shadows over her cheekbones. The moonlight gave her skin the luster of porcelain. Donatus wondered what emotion she veiled.

"Come," he said, pulling her down the hill. "The sooner we're aboard, the sooner we sleep."

The groan she gave made him smile. She must be as tired as he. That was good—very good. Maybe they'd be able to sleep like babies. They needed to forget for a while that they were adults, male and female, with all the appropriate parts and the natural desire to use them.

Lelia lay against crisp sheets, shivering. The night air upon the river was cool, even though it had the smell of spring. She wished Donatus would come and warm her with his body, but she understood why he hadn't yet. He'd hired experienced boatmen, four of them, to take the barge out into deeper water. Safer, he'd said. Once they'd found a suitable place, an anchor would be dropped and he'd come to her.

Lelia was tired. Her thoughts had grown confused. Worry plagued her.

Four days ago she'd lain in bed thinking of the combat scheduled for the following day. She'd been unable to sleep for the thought that perhaps it would be her last night on earth.

Now she lay in bed thinking the same thing. She'd thought herself saved from death, but the Fates had conspired a new punishment, snarling the cords of her life.

And what of Donatus? How did he fit into it?

She rolled onto her side and watched the billowing curtains as they caught the night breezes. White, like the ones she remembered, but even more lovely. These were beaded with silver. They caught moonbeams and shimmered with subtle, reflected light.

Lelia sighed and replayed the entire day, going quickly through the parts she'd spent without Donatus because they frightened her now. Even as she'd smiled at new faces, trying to remember the myriad of names, someone in the house had watched her. Even as she'd toured her new surroundings, laughing at Druscilla's pert remarks, someone had wanted her dead.

She moved ahead to more pleasant memories. Donatus had bought her gowns, lovely gowns. More beautiful gowns than she could wear in a month's time, and with all the accessories to match. Why?

He'd told her he loved her, not just once but several times. Did he? The thought was almost absurd. Perhaps he felt guilty. A guilty man might buy gowns and jewels, but... *barges?*

Lelia let her thoughts drift. The night air was cool, the sheets soft. Her eyelids grew heavy and lowered. Oh, Donatus. Donatus...

Who are you?

And then as if answering the call of her heart, the bed dipped beneath his weight and he was there. His heat came alongside hers. His arms came around her, a cradle of muscle and bone. Enveloped in his scent, in his warmth, she felt the barge gently rocking, rocking, and let herself be lulled to sleep.

Something woke her, deep into the night, either her own crying or Donatus's hands as they shook her gently.

"Shh," he was saying. "Lelia, don't cry. Sweet mercy, it rives my soul to hear you cry." He drew her closer. "I'm here," he whispered. "You were dreaming again. Tossing and crying out."

"I'm sorry," she murmured sleepily.

There was a long moment of silence before his weight shifted on the bed and his body came against hers, warmth against the chill. Without realizing what she did, her entire body stiffened. He must have felt it, for he halted. His voice gently filled the darkness.

"Relax, love. I mean only to comfort you."

She drew in a deep breath, forcing herself to breathe. Willing her taut muscles to ease.

"That's better," he said. One large hand came up and began to stroke her hair, the touch rhythmic and calming, with just the right amount of firm, massaging pressure.

Lelia relaxed completely, surprised by her own willingness to do so. Her eyes closed again, her mind slowed. She felt herself slipping backward into the gray. Slipping away until she was only passingly aware of his warm, masculine scent and the strength of his fingers as they moved, kneading the fear from her neck and shoulders and arms.

As if from a far distance, she heard him. "I would never have left you if I'd known."

Something worrisome niggled at the blurred edges of her consciousness. If he had known…? The words bothered her somehow, and she began the arduous climb back to lucidity, trying to rouse herself from the sleep which pulled at her with many-armed tentacles.

She must have stirred, for Donatus soothed her and pushed her back against the softness of the sheets. "Rest," he whispered. "No more bad dreams. Rest, Lelia."

She was tired, so tired. Too tired to think now of what he'd said... What was it again? Too tired to think of what he'd meant. Too tired to do anything but breathe Donatus's clean smell and rest against the heated wall of his chest. Too tired to do anything except sleep.

Lelia awoke the next morning to the sound of male laughter and the smell of roasted meat. She lifted her eyelids, found them heavy, and lowered them again. A sigh, a leisurely stretch, and she tried again, shielding her face from the slanting rays of a morning sun that suffused the curtains all around her with coral and gold.

Donatus had gone. Surprisingly, that saddened her, though she didn't understand why it should. She certainly didn't want more of the disturbing intimacies of the previous evening. She could hardly believe she'd allowed herself to be held and kissed and almost, *almost* let herself be used once more for his pleasures. She frowned, thinking of that. Whatever had possessed her?

Had she forgotten what it had been like, that day two years ago when she'd discovered he'd gone? Had she forgotten how desperate she'd felt, and how alone?

She must have, to let herself be seduced again. Heat rose in her face. She'd acquiesced far too easily. A wanton, wanton woman would not have been led to his bed any more quickly than she.

True, she'd felt a woman's need for his touch. She'd once known the most exquisite of flights within his arms, and now was tortured with want of it. But to forget all he'd done...

Lelia groaned in dismay and rose stiffly from the bed. At least nearly being murdered had given her a second chance to show some good sense. She could only imagine if there'd been no intervention. She'd have awoken this morning filled with fear that she might be with child. Even though she'd promised it, and even though she knew the moment would come…Lelia shuddered. She wanted the obligation met, but feared it just the same. She dreaded the moment when she knew another child rested within her womb. She dreaded that moment so much.

The aching that settled in her chest now made her want to sob, to curl into a tight little ball and cry until there were no more tears.

Instead, she swallowed hard and raised her chin. She was stronger than this; she wouldn't yield to the stealthy attack of hurt. It came, as it always did, whenever she thought of her son. She drew in her breath, almost feeling his soft baby curves against her, and the answering prickle of her breasts that ached to nurse him. She closed her eyes against the memory, against the wandering blue-green of his eyes, the gentle clutch of his fingers. She closed her eyes and waited for the ache to pass.

"Lelia?" Donatus's voice startled her, made her turn.

He entered, pushing aside the curtain wall. Lelia averted her eyes, afraid for him to see the tears, precariously balanced. He moved to her, his tread silent. Too late. He knew. He must know.

Donatus touched her, drew her cool hands into his warm ones, chafed them lightly against his calloused palms. The touch made her shiver. "What's wrong?" he asked.

"Nothing. It's nothing." She pulled her hands away and turned, angry with herself. Angry with him.

He studied her. She didn't look his way, but she could feel his eyes upon her. "Last night," he said. His voice was rough-edged, sharp as splinters, the words forced out. "I'm sorry about last night. It wasn't right. I knew it wasn't right. But by the gods, Lelia, I couldn't turn away. I wanted you. I've wanted you for two years, burying the need, burning with it. And there you were, all warm and sweet and eager."

Lelia didn't answer. She couldn't. The raw ache grew within her chest until there was nothing but heat and hurt, miserable companions to his.

Donatus's eyes didn't leave her. Long moments of quiet slipped away, whispering around them, between them. The curtains sighed with it, billowing sunlit gold and beaded silver in the rhythm of their breathing.

"I'm sorry," Donatus said again, the two words conveying a world of infinite sorrow.

"I'm sorry, too," she whispered. "Sorry that we can't go back. That it will never be like it was."

He looked at her, his eyes piercing and beautiful. He was mystery and contradiction, shrouded in light and exhaling darkness, a fallen spirit sculpted in bronze. He did not answer her.

"I thought I could do it, Donatus. I thought so. But I can't."

Dark lashes lowered, a fringed veil over green fire. The muscle in his jaw worked with powerful emotion.

"I promised to give you an heir, but I'm sorry. I just can't."

Again, the silence. Lelia waited within it, her heart pounding, willing him to understand and knowing well that he could not.

"What are you afraid of? You're my wife now, Lelia. I will not leave you again. I will cherish any child we make together." The veil of his lashes rose. His gaze met hers, solemn, demanding truth.

Lelia looked away. How could she answer? She didn't know herself anymore, couldn't understand why she hated Donatus and yet suffered at the hurt in his eyes.

He stood, waiting. The ache filled her, throbbed to the same rhythm as her heartbeat. He waited; she couldn't answer the question.

Donatus melted into a blur, huge and indistinct through her

tears. He made a low sound of protest, pulling her into his embrace as if he could staunch the flow with his fierce affection. "Lelia." He breathed her name, the sound resonating with all his need, his pain.

He held her and let her cry. Lelia buried her face into his hard shoulder and sobbed for the past, for dreams lost, for wounds never healed, for memories never forgotten. If only she hadn't loved him. If only he hadn't gone. If only...

At length her mourning quieted into sweet peace. Donatus held her in arms that were comforting and protective. He rocked her gently, one hand cascading down the dark fall of her hair in a soothing rhythm. Lelia let him hold her, reluctant to disturb the intimacy of this moment. They rested like lovers spent after passion. They rested, survivors tossed ashore by the fury of a storm. They rested, warm skin against warm skin, tasting the salt and texture of shared tears.

Donatus raised her chin until their gazes met. Lelia shuddered at the hideous longing within his eyes. "I can't help the past, or undo what I've done, but I swear I never meant to hurt you." He looked away, the muscles in his cheek tightening. "I'm not the same man I was when I left. I won't hold you to your promise."

Lelia could hardly comprehend the words. His gaze met hers. "You don't have to give me an heir. You don't have to sleep with me, make love with me, bear my seed, not now or ever. I can't hurt you again. No promise is worth your pain."

Lelia stepped backwards, stunned. "Donatus? I don't understand."

Donatus's expression softened. "I ask only one thing of you."

Lelia frowned, suddenly wary.

"Don't play games with me," he said quietly. "Understand that I have my limits. I also grieve for the things we lost."

Lelia's throat tightened.

"Don't ask me not to care for you. Don't ask me not to want you. But know that I'll never force myself upon you. You can trust me." He held out his hand. "Here, let us be at peace."

She took his hand and he pulled her to him, leaning forward to place a kiss upon her forehead. That action was so small, so insignificant, without guile. But as he pulled away Lelia shuddered at the fierce determination in his expression, and she understood in a sudden flash of insight.

He'd lowered the bridge—called retreat. He'd purposely lost the battle—because Donatus, the wily strategist, had decided to win the war.

Chapter Nine

The raeda was large, roomy and comfortable. It was also slow, or it seemed so to Donatus. He was used to traveling on horseback, fast and light, without the encumbrance of females and all their attendant accoutrements. He watched in amazement as Lucan loaded five wooden boxes into the wagon.

"I told Faustina to pack light," Donatus growled.

"She did. But she also said it would be important for Lelia to have the things she needed to maintain her appearance properly, now that she's a senator's wife."

Donatus frowned. "We'll be in the country. I doubt whether the slaves who work the fields will have much care for Lelia's high position. Or mine either, for that matter."

Lucan shrugged, grinning at his friend a little crookedly. "You're not a rough soldier anymore, my friend. You're a married man now. You'll have to get used to this domestic life, carting and hauling your woman and her things. And it'll only get worse when all those babies start coming."

Donatus felt the heat burn his neck at that. It had reminded him only too well of what he'd done. He could hardly believe his own weakness. He'd let Lelia's tears manipulate him into giving up the one thing he owed his father. Whatever had he been thinking? Now there would be no heir.

That knowledge hurt. It made him angry, too—angry with himself. Maybe he'd been a soldier too long; maybe all those years apart from family life had left him unprepared for love. He'd certainly botched every single thing in his relationship with Lelia. Every single thing from start to finish. And now this.

He'd married a woman who despised him, who so dreaded a physical union with him that she cried at the very thought of it. Worse, she'd sworn she'd never care for him, and he had no right to expect she'd change her mind. But at least he'd had the expectation of a child. He wanted one so much.

That loss hurt brutally.

His obligation to his father, to his ancestors, was only part of the reason. More important than anything was that Donatus hoped to replicate the loving relationship he'd had with his own father.

He'd been only seven years old when his mother had gone. Too young to understand the reasons, but old enough to cry alone in the shadows when they'd argued in their room. He hadn't understood the words. *Lovers…shame…adultery.*

He'd only understood that she'd left them both, and that his father's face had been etched with the same hollow loss that his childish heart had felt. He'd understood betrayal.

But his father hadn't let grief destroy their lives. He'd been wise and used the pain well. It became the glue that held them together, father and son against the cruel world. Life went on—not the same as before, but at least serene, more predictable without the woman's tantrums and vagaries to mar the soft passage of time.

Donatus hadn't missed his mother for long. Her affection

had been capricious at best, and sometimes he'd suffered because he'd been his father's child. He looked like his sire, with the same dark curls and green eyes. He possessed his father's inquisitive mind and boundless energy. He was the heir, so longed-for and so cherished.

But the more his father loved him, the more his mother turned away. Donatus hadn't understood. There was some flaw within himself, there must be.

It had taken him years to understand that she'd only used him as a weapon. Wounding Donatus had been the most certain way to wound his father.

When he thought of her now, all he felt was a dull pain. Anger had eventually been replaced by sadness. Donatus still remembered her—odd snatches of childhood memories, disjointed pieces of his past. He remembered her, but he couldn't say he loved her. She'd left him when he needed her, and he had no desire to reopen that old wound.

But his father deserved every bit of the *pietus* of his son, all his reverence and all his honor. Antonius had given all of himself to Donatus the child, even the part of his heart that could have gone to another woman. He'd not remarried until Donatus was a man full-grown. From his father, Donatus had learned of honor and justice and truth and faith. From his father, he'd learned to be a man.

Now it hurt Donatus that he'd given away the one thing he owed such a man. His father would have wanted Donatus to sire a child. He would have been pleased with a baby's bright smile. But Donatus had given in to a woman's fickle tears. And now there'd be no heir.

Donatus chanced a glance in Lelia's direction. She sat erect and composed beside Severina, her hair glistening blue-black in the strong midday sun. They'd been quiet most of the morning, talking seldom and only in low, hushed voices.

Donatus wondered what Lelia thought, what she felt, if she were pleased with herself to have gained all she wanted without giving up anything of value.

The voice of conscience intruded, warning him not to be angry. He had, after all, himself forged this distorted relationship in the fires of betrayal. If Lelia distrusted him, he'd taught it to her. If she dreaded making love with him, he'd caused her to fear it.

He'd hoped she wouldn't regret the love they'd almost made. He'd hoped she'd accept their new relationship and let it grow without ripping it up by the roots. But when he saw her tears, he knew he'd hoped for too damned much.

The journey ahead now seemed, strangely, a rather appropriate metaphor for his future married life. Long, dull, fraught with danger…and to a destination that would probably be a disappointment.

"It's not right," Severina said as she and Lelia carried their small bundles of clothing up the narrow stairway. "You should share a room with your husband, not with me."

Lelia made a wry face. "You know this marriage is anything but the usual."

Severina glanced at her and almost missed the step. "I also know you promised to keep up appearances. What will people say about the Senator's wife who refuses to share his room?"

"Since when have you cared about appearances?"

"It's not myself I'm thinking of. It's you. We're only a scant day's journey from Rome. All kinds of important people stop at this inn; it's the best one. Word might get around that you and he are not truly wed."

Lelia shook her head, breathing heavily from her rapid climb up the stairs. She looked down the narrow corridor and found it empty. "Donatus himself suggested this arrangement."

Severina joined Lelia on the landing, also breathing hard.

"He did? Now, that…" she looked accusingly at Lelia "…I can hardly believe. What warm-blooded man newly married to a beautiful woman like you wouldn't take every opportunity to enjoy his conjugal pleasures? You'll have to come up with a better excuse. That one's a little far-fetched."

Lelia made a short sound of mock irritation. "It's the truth, whether you believe me or not." She headed down the corridor until she stood outside the door to their rented chambers.

Severina soon caught up with her, fishing a key from a fold in her tunic. She handed it to Lelia, and in just a moment the heavy wooden door swung open with a groan.

The room within was spotlessly clean, and Lelia breathed a sigh of relief. Severina had been right. This was the best inn within twenty miles, but an inn was still an inn. At least now she could be content that the linens were not infested with lice and goodness-only-knew what else.

"So why in the world did Donatus want you to sleep with *me?*" Severina asked as she tossed her bundle of clothing onto the mattress. "Have you already made yourself so odious he can no longer stand the sight of you?"

Lelia flung a wad of toweling in Severina's direction, catching her by surprise. Her friend's gasp and uttered exclamation made Lelia giggle. But when her friend started around the corner of the bed toward her, Lelia squealed in alarm, half laughing. "No! No!" She held up her hand in protest as Severina attacked her with the fabric, drawing it around her neck as if she would choke her with it.

They were both collapsed in laughter when a deep voice startled them from the doorway.

"I hope our neighbors aren't trying to sleep."

Both women drew in startled breaths and turned toward the door, red-faced and guilty.

Donatus laughed. "It's all right. I'm only teasing. You haven't any neighbors yet. I checked."

"Oh, you!" Lelia turned away, almost embarrassed to be caught in an unguarded moment, and unwilling to admit that her heart had done a peculiar cartwheel at his appearance. His eyes had met hers too suddenly, filled with a mirth that immediately fled away, replaced by a hunger he did not try to hide.

Severina muttered some hasty excuse and moved to leave. Donatus caught her arm as she tried to sidle past him, and looked down into her face with a gentle expression. "No, don't leave. I won't be staying. I just came to check on the room, to make sure it would be secure." He lowered his voice. "We can't forget, Severina, that someone wants her dead."

Severina raised worried eyes to his.

"It gives me a bit more peace knowing that both of you are trained to fight," Donatus said. "But please keep weapons handy, just in case we've been followed or…" he looked hesitant for a moment "…in case one of our escorts might not prove beyond a bribe."

Severina raised an eyebrow. "You think one of the men who escorted us might try something?"

Donatus shrugged. "I hope not. I debated long about bringing them along, but the risk of being attacked by robbers on the road was even more worrisome. I chose the lesser risk. I hope I've not made a mistake."

Severina looked across toward Lelia, swallowing hard. "We'll prepare. Perhaps we worry for nothing."

Donatus smiled. "Even so, I'll sleep among the men tonight, in a room on the first floor. I'll be nearest the door, so that any who leaves will have to get past me first." His eyes met Lelia's again, burning hot at the contact. "It's the least I can do for my dear wife."

Lelia wanted to scoff at the words, but his tone hadn't been mocking or sarcastic. Was she, then, so dear to him? Why would she be? She'd done nothing but bring him shame. She'd cost him a small fortune. She'd denied him pleasure and the heir he wished for. And still he could call her *dear?* Lelia looked away, afraid of the emotion she might see if she looked at Donatus.

Thankfully, he didn't stay long. Instead, he made a quick circuit around the room, lingering a moment near the window. He talked in hushed tones to Severina and seemed almost to ignore his wife completely. Lelia knew the lack of interest was a ruse, however. Her every nerve strained at the tension that hummed between them.

When he'd gone, Severina turned to her with a deep, relieved breath. "I don't know how you stand it," she said quietly.

"Stand what?"

Severina's features twisted in acute disbelief. "Oh, play like you don't know."

Lelia sat down wearily on the bed, and then stretched out full length. "I'm not playing, Severina. I'm too tired to play."

Severina raised an amused eyebrow. "Is that so? Funny, but it looked for all the world like you and Donatus *were* playing. Something primitive. Something exciting. It doesn't take a soothsayer to read the future in the looks he was giving you."

Lelia rolled onto her side and propped her head up on her hand. "I don't know. Everything's happened so quickly that I haven't had time to figure it all out."

Severina walked to the door, making sure it was securely latched before returning to sit beside Lelia. "I think he loves you," she said quietly, sending her friend a peculiar, slanting glance. "Are you sure Donatus is quite the villain you've made him out to be? Are you sure you're doing the right thing?"

"The right thing about what?"

"Keeping him at arm's length. Maybe you should just forgive him and tell him the entire story. Maybe you two could start again and build a real marriage, one that's good for both of you."

Lelia frowned. "That's easy for you to say."

"I know. But Lelia, Donatus is your husband now. What choices have you? You can continue to hate him, and both of you will endure a life of sadness and bitter memories. Or you can begin anew and make the best of this situation."

Lelia bounced off the bed and busied herself with untying the bundle which held some of her clothing and personal items. She didn't speak. Severina watched her, frowning at the way Lelia snatched a hairbrush and yanked it with scarcely concealed irritation through her thick tresses.

"You're angry with me," Severina finally ventured.

"No, I'm not."

"You are. I know you are."

Lelia drew in an aggravated breath, tossed her brush back into the bundle, and faced Severina with her hands on her hips. "Maybe I am. Then again…" She paced for a moment, rubbing the tension from the back of her neck. "I'm not a fool, either. I know you're my true friend, and that you're concerned for me. It's just that this situation with Donatus is so strange. I haven't had time to adjust, to find my way through the maze of feelings."

Severina met her gaze. "It's hard, isn't it?"

The words were not meant to prick her. They were spoken gently, and the compassion in Severina's gray eyes was genuine. But the words brought stinging tears. One slid down Lelia's cheek before she could wipe it away.

"Yes, it's hard. Two days. I've been his wife two days. And in that time I've flown through so many emotions I don't know who I am anymore. It was easier when I could hate him. It was easier when I could call him a careless bastard without decency or honor. It was easier when he wasn't here. But now he's back and declares he cares for me. He looks at me, touches me, and I—" Lelia broke down, a sob catching on the words.

Severina moved to her, wrapping her arms tightly around her friend in a gesture of comfort and friendship. "I'm sorry I brought it up. I didn't mean to make you cry."

Lelia wiped at her nose. "No, it's not really your fault. It's this whole situation. I can't live with Donatus. He makes me crazy."

Severina nodded. "You still care for him, don't you?"

Lelia froze. "Does it show that much?"

"I'm afraid it does."

"It's not that I love him. Please understand that. Part of me still despises him. Part of me still wants to make him suffer."

Severina nodded, more serious. "And the other part?"

Lelia groaned and sank down again onto the mattress, resting her head in her hands. "The other part of me wants him, Severina. He... We..."

"You've never forgotten how it felt to love him."

Lelia looked up, wondering if her face was as stricken as her heart. She closed her eyes and swallowed hard. "I've never forgotten."

"I can't tell you what to do," Severina said. "But if I were you, I think I'd consider one important thing."

Lelia opened her eyes.

"He's the father of your child. Somewhere out there is that child you two made together in a moment of love. You want to find him, and I have faith that you will. But I think it would be better if you and Donatus searched for him together. I think it would be better if, when he's found, his parents were loving partners rather than subtle enemies. Give Donatus a chance to find his son. A chance to love his son's mother."

Lelia wiped at her nose with the back of her hand. "You're asking a lot of me."

Severina nodded. "I know. It shows how much faith I have in you, Flavia Lelia."

Lelia looked down at the rough wooden planks of the floor. She traced the head of an iron nail with the toe of her sandal, considering the words, wishing she could have as much faith in herself.

Severina's suggestion bothered her for the next three days—mostly because she knew it was sensible. She and Donatus were married. He'd done all he could to make amends; she knew that. The problem was, knowing something and *feeling* it were two different matters, and right now Lelia was too confused to risk anything. To let herself be vulnerable to Donatus, to his dark beauty and his seductive words, was a risk she wasn't quite prepared to take. Not yet, anyway.

She knew, logically, that she couldn't hold out forever. She wanted him as a man. When his eyes followed her, she felt breathless. When he touched her, fire burned in the pit of her stomach, setting flame to the dry tinder of her too-hungry desires.

And where her body went, her emotions wanted to follow. She feared her willingness to forgive him, to let herself care again. Donatus had surprised her by setting aside the promise she'd made him. She hadn't expected it. He had every right as her husband to demand it of her. There had to be a reason. But still, his sacrifice had warmed her heart.

And that, too, bothered her. It was difficult to stay angry with him when he kept doing things that were compassionate, like when he held her after one of her bad dreams and whispered kind words, with nothing of passion to mar the delicate intimacy of the moment.

Lelia groaned. Donatus didn't know the truth and yet he cared. He assumed she cried because she didn't want to make love with him. He assumed she hated him too much to bear his child. He knew so little.

She cried because she *did* want to make love with him. She cried because of the child she'd already borne him.

Her conscience hissed at her. She could tell him the truth, and then he'd understand. But the thought of it made her ache.

She'd made herself vulnerable to him once. He'd ripped her heart out of its place. To do it again seemed an idea so foreign as to be unimaginable.

Physical desire—she could do that without fear. She knew the moment would come. She was a woman of passion. Donatus had shown her that much about herself. At first he'd led her into that tentative joy. But soon, emboldened by love and the trust between them, she'd grown confident and voracious. It had caught Donatus by surprise that one as innocent as she could burn with so hot a flame.

It hadn't surprised her. She'd always known that when she gave her heart, all else would follow. Donatus had come, and inexplicably she'd chosen him for her lifelong mate. In her mind it was to be forever, and she'd held nothing of herself from him.

Well, some dreams died very hard, and they left the residue of memory to stain the soul. Memory reminded her of those exquisite moments of giving and taking, of murmured love-words and breathless sighing, of running and leaping and flying and falling into a lover's secure embrace, exhausted with joyful weariness when all was done. She'd never wanted another man, not before and not since. Donatus alone drew her like a beacon, made her heedless of the rocky shore. Inevitably she'd acquiesce to her own unfulfilled needs.

Surprisingly, the thought of joining her body with his did not frighten her.

It was the joining of their souls that made her blood run cold. It was knowing that their union would join them emotionally, bind them irrevocably into one being. It was the thought that even if she could lock her heart into a walled fortress, even if she could protect her vulnerable core from pain, there might be a child.

She could hold herself from Donatus, but she could not hold herself from his child. One look into cloudy baby eyes, one breath of softly scented baby curls, and her heart would lie like a naked sacrifice upon a stone table, awaiting the obsidian blade.

That was the reason she cried.

Chapter Ten

Lelia tried not to be nervous as they neared the village that was the centerpiece of Donatus's country estate. They stopped to eat lunch in a small copse of trees, the leaves providing a respite of shade after a morning of riding through gathering warmth and plentiful dust. As they ate, Donatus talked about the land through which they passed, and about his property that they would reach in the late afternoon.

He talked mostly to Severina, although Lelia knew by the familiar tension of her nerves that Donatus watched her surreptitiously. Had their eyes met just once… Lelia's gut tightened with the mere thought, a painfully acute reminder that her control was hard-won and completely superficial. If Donatus felt the same way, then she understood why he avoided her. Because if he didn't, it would be hard to speak coherently, hard to appear calm, when the most urgent wish of their young bodies was to find a refuge among the trees and consummate desire.

So Lelia ate quietly, listening to her new husband converse with her friend. Severina seemed to have easily put aside all her earlier doubts about Donatus, a fact which bothered Lelia surprisingly little. Donatus also seemed at ease with Severina. With her, he teased and smiled and offered amusing jests that, Lelia noticed, poked fun mostly at himself and never at others. Strange how she'd never noticed that about him before.

Watching them made her chest ache. She wasn't jealous in the traditional sense, because she trusted both of them. The pain she felt now wasn't the usual sort of jealousy. But it was jealousy just the same. Pure, unadulterated, green-eyed, monstrous jealousy. Jealousy for the laughter, for the simplicity and ease they felt in one another's presence. Jealousy for the way Severina made Donatus laugh until his eyes fired with joy and the sun-deepened bronze of his skin creased, until his white teeth flashed and the muscles of his chest rippled with mirth.

It was the way they made her remember the past, called back the days when she had laughed with him, when their eyes had met as something more than lovers. She and Donatus had once been friends.

The ache grew with that remembrance. Lelia moved in response to it, gathering the remnants of their meal, wrapping the bread in its leather pouch, brushing leafy debris from her *palla*—*anything* to deny the truth that twisted within her. She missed the companionship she'd shared with Donatus.

Thankfully, the mirth all around her soon quieted. Lelia felt Severina's gaze upon her and looked up, determined that her friend should not know her true thoughts or guess that she was disturbed.

It wasn't Severina who watched her. It was Donatus. His eyes caught hers, eloquent in their silence. His expression hid nothing—not his longing, not his lust, not the pain that told her he remembered it all, too. Lelia waited for those tender feelings to give way to mockery. She expected chastisement, some silent reminder that he'd already offered companionship and more. She waited, but no rebuke came. Instead his gaze gentled into a caress, a touch as delicate as dew, as beautiful as polished silver, as tender as love.

Lelia broke away, unable to comprehend that which passed between them. Or perhaps comprehending it too well.

Severina's low voice interrupted the moment. "Tell me, my lord Donatus, all about this villa to which we travel."

It was a moment before he answered, but Lelia didn't risk looking at him again. Her emotions were a whirlwind, her heartbeat rapid and unsure.

"It's not a grand villa," he answered quietly. "I hope you won't be disappointed. It's simple, but I love the place. For me it's a haven, a peaceful retreat. Some might decry it as hopelessly rustic, but that's what I like most about it. When I'm there, I work at honest labor. I toil with my slaves. But I return home each night content with myself and at peace within my soul." Donatus stopped and shrugged, looking almost uncomfortable with the confessions he'd made. "I've never thought to make the place more than what it's always been, since I need so little when I'm there. My house has only four small rooms, with furnishings simple and functional."

Severina laughed again, more softly. "Cozy."

Lelia looked up just in time to catch the look of understanding that passed between Donatus and her friend.

"I sent Micon on ahead," Donatus said, brushing an insect off his sandal with lean fingers. "The overseer and his wife will be prepared for us. They'll have prepared separate quarters for you, Severina. I trust you'll be content to have it so."

Severina smiled, her eyes narrowing slightly. Her expression reminded Lelia of a cat. "Of course," Severina assured him. "Unless you'd prefer that I sleep near Lelia for her protection."

Donatus crossed his arms over his broad chest. One dark eyebrow lifted at the mischief cavorting openly across

Severina's delicate features. He gave a snort that was nearly a laugh. "I thank you most heartily, Lady Severina. You're a true friend and quite the *thoughtful* gladiatrix. However, while this ex-soldier still has breath in his body and strength in his limbs, he will himself be rightly pleased to wield his blade on his lady's behalf."

"Oh, I'm sure of that, sir. Quite sure of that." Severina's chuckle made Lelia redden. Then, as the implication became understood, Donatus's face also darkened. He turned away quickly, excusing himself to see to watering the horses.

It was a long while before Lelia could look Severina in the face. A very long while indeed.

Now, as they passed through the most lovely valley Lelia had ever seen, she began to understand why Donatus's voice had held such a hush of reverence. For miles and miles the road wound through fields of growing things, all owned by the man who now sat beside her, his keen eyes surveying endless vineyards and pastures filled with sheep and cattle and horses.

For the first time in their journey, Donatus began to talk to her, telling her of this farm he so obviously cherished, and she was pleased that he'd asked her to sit next to him. She'd thought it only that he wished to keep up appearances when they arrived at the farm. Now she realized that Donatus loved the land and wanted to share it with her. It didn't matter that she understood little of the things he was explaining—how the vines were tended, how the livestock was rotated from pasture to pasture, how the shearing of the sheep was conducted. What mattered was that his eyes were lit with fire, that his voice was strong and deep and steady, and that he was sharing it all with her.

"You'll like my overseer and his wife," Donatus said,

glancing at her with a smile. "But pay little heed to Didia when you meet her. Age hasn't slowed her tongue. She's always truthful, whether I wish it or not. Her husband, Amandio, is the very opposite, a man of few words. He directs the labor of the men in the fields. Didia directs the female slaves and sees to the domestic hearth. And either of them can probably still work circles around me." Donatus laughed softly.

Lelia studied his face, deciding she liked what she saw there—the gentle touch of self-deprecating humor, the respect for a couple who were probably freedmen and of much lower status than he, the excitement that energized him when he talked about land and fields and sheep.

Her eyes lowered. She was afraid to trust herself to study him more. He seemed to grow more beautiful with each mile they traveled toward this place he cherished. But even looking down she could not escape. There were his lean fingers, so expert upon the reins, so expert upon her... Lelia closed her eyes.

Donatus didn't seem to notice her discomfort. He was talking, pleasure still flavoring the warm timbre of his voice. "Didia...she fancies herself almost my mother. In truth, she and Amandio were like parents to me in my youth." He smiled crookedly. "Didia will doubtless show no respectful fear of me, though I am the master. I've no idea what her forthright tongue will say to you. Prepare yourself, my sweet. Her fondest wish has been for my return and my marriage, and for all that should naturally follow."

Lelia glanced up sharply. "She wishes for you to produce an heir."

Donatus sighed. "Yes." He turned slightly, his eyes meeting hers only briefly before looking ahead to the horses again. "Lelia, I promise she'll love you. She'll be delighted that I've taken a wife."

Lelia nodded, thinking that Didia might be pleased. At least until she discovered that Lelia did not carry her master's seed. And likely, never would.

Donatus told her the history of the farm, that it had been for generations in his mother's family and had been part of her dowry gift to his father. Lelia wanted to ask him about his mother, but the stony expression he wore whenever he talked about the woman warned her away. She contented herself instead with listening to his memories about long vacations spent on the farm, fishing and swimming in the river which ran through the valley, learning to ride the magnificent horses that were bred and trained for war there, practicing javelin with the local boys until he could throw straight and true.

His happiest memories all seemed rooted in the dark soil of this land, and Lelia found herself hoping that being here would help her understand him. The key to the mystery of Donatus was in this place, and she looked around her with growing interest.

However, nothing he'd said could have prepared Lelia for the pristine beauty she viewed when they topped the last small knoll and found their destination stretched before them. A farm? It was more like a village, laid out neatly in a grid, crisscrossed by roads graveled with clean white pebbles.

There were buildings, a multitude of them, all sturdily constructed with thick stone walls. Donatus pointed out what they were as they passed.

There the tanners and fullers plying their trade, on the far outskirts so offensive odors wouldn't bother the townsfolk. There were the rows upon rows of small houses for the slaves and their families, most with fenced-in gardens in front. There was the bathhouse, where women bathed in the morning and men in the late afternoon. The large building far from the road housed the stables, and beside that were livestock sheds where the sheep were sheared. To their left was the shop of the man who repaired carts, and that of the woman who sewed garments, and of the potter who made jars and... The list went on and on. Lelia grew more amazed at the diverse people who made this "farm" operate efficiently. She sensed in Donatus a complex mixture of pride and deep responsibility.

"There," he said, pointing with a hand still wrapped in the reins. "Up there on that hill is your new home. I hope you'll find it comfortable, even if it is somewhat small."

Lelia lowered her lashes, surprised by the hesitation in his voice. Surely Donatus didn't think she was too fine a lady for his humble farmhouse? *She,* a woman who'd fought upon the bloody sand of the Amphitheater just days before, who'd lived in a tiny filth-infested *insulae* in a crowded, poverty-stricken part of the city?

Lelia shook her head. "Donatus, it will be fine. I've learned to be pleased with little. Your farmhouse will seem like a mansion to me after the existence I've lived these last two years."

He turned then, abruptly, his expression sharp enough to rake her face. She looked away, unsure what to make of the sudden, intense pain she saw in his eyes.

"The past is done," he said quietly. "You are now and forever the wife of a senator of Rome."

"Yes," she answered. "My fortunes have changed. But forgetting? That takes a while."

He looked away, his expression grim. "I would never have left you if I'd known what my choice would do to you."

She looked at him then, answering without hesitation and without malice. "I know, Donatus. But, like you said, the past is done."

He glanced at her, his expression guarded, wary. "So what does that mean, Lelia? Are we ready to begin anew? Do we wipe the slate clean and go from here?"

Lelia looked away, watching trees and buildings and shy townsfolk pass by. "I don't know, Donatus. How to go from here...how to begin again... I don't know."

Donatus's voice was warm and earnest, filled with the timbre of deepest need. "Let me teach you, Lelia. Let me guide you...*us*...into a new and stronger relationship. All I need is your trust."

Lelia looked down at the hands folded in her lap, very much aware of the man beside her, of his magnificent broad shoulders and the iron thigh pressed against her own, of his skillful hands on the reins and the pulse which throbbed at his throat. "I want to trust you, Donatus," she whispered. "But one cannot simply *decide* to give such a thing."

"You trusted me once."

She nodded, closing her eyes. "I did. I gave you my heart, my soul, all I had. And then..."

The unspoken hung between them. She saw Donatus's face harden and wondered what he felt. Regret? Anger?

He was slow to speak. When the words came, they were spoken calmly, too calmly, as if he controlled his emotions only by sheer dint of will. "The only way for us to begin again is for you to open the door and walk through it, Lelia. I've opened the door. I've given you my name, made you the mistress of my home, pledged my heart. If that's not enough to prove I'm worthy of your trust, then nothing else shall do it. I made a mistake, and freely have I admitted it. I wronged you, and freely have I repented it. But, Lelia, I damn well refuse to grovel for the remainder of our married life."

He drew in a deep breath. "The door is open. I stand before it with outstretched hand. Take your time if you wish. All the time you need. Study it, study me, study the situation from every conceivable angle. Then put your hand into mine and walk into the future with me, or…"

Lelia was stung by the bitter tone of his voice. "Or…?" she prodded, tilting her head with an arrogance that she only pretended. "Or what?"

"Or return to the arena and be damned."

Lelia gasped, caught completely off guard by this rapid change. There was a note of steel in his voice that frightened her, made her sense a core of almost brutal strength. "Donatus? What do you mean?"

"I mean that divorce is always an option, should you wish it. I love you, Lelia, and I'll never ask it of you. But neither will I allow my family's name to be tarnished. Not again. Not ever again. I'm not asking for your love. I'm only asking for your trust. If you can't give that, then you have only to speak the word. I'll set you free."

Lelia sat back, as stunned as if he'd dealt her a physical blow. What had just happened here? She couldn't understand—hadn't sensed it coming and knew not what to make of it. All she knew was that Donatus's eyes had narrowed and his nostrils had flared with an anger she'd never seen before.

She was still reeling from the revelation when the *raeda* pulled up in front of Donatus's farmhouse. She vaguely noted the serene beauty of it, its stone walls flooded with the reddish orange light of the late afternoon sun, a dramatic juxtaposition of shadow and texture that gave the place an almost hallowed beauty.

She vaguely noted that Micon rounded the corner at a fast trot, that Donatus climbed down and handed the slave the reins. She vaguely noted that Donatus came around and drew her down, firm hands around her waist.

Her senses came alive when he let her body slide down the

firm length of his until her feet made contact with solid ground. They stood, thighs touching, breath mingling. Lelia became aware of sensation, of her breasts firming and tingling against the warmth of his chest, of his hips pressing into hers with a blatant masculinity that made her pulse quicken.

Lelia looked up into his face and found it a chaotic mixture of harshness and longing. "Oh, Lelia," he whispered. "Sweet gods, I don't want us to hurt each other."

His lips descended just as the door to the house burst open and people rushed out, their excited tumble of words faltering and dying at the scene before them. Lelia barely noticed, her senses thoroughly consumed by Donatus—by his taste and his tongue and the hungry pressure of his lips, by his warmth around her, by the hands pressing her hips against his in a fitting that could hardly have been more intimate if they'd been alone and thoroughly naked.

A woman's shriek of joy broke into their awareness. "The gods be praised!"

Lelia felt Donatus pull back slightly, though his arms still supported her because she'd grown weak. Their bodies yet rested heavily against one another. She could scarcely breathe, or register the speed with which her emotions had run through the gamut of feelings.

Donatus. Only Donatus could make her come alive so quickly. Only he could make her forget herself with such frightening intensity. All propriety and all thought had fled away in the wake of desire. Lucidity returned slowly, burning her face with chagrin that she'd been caught by strangers in such a compromising position.

A woman appeared at her side, her elderly face alight with such happiness that it made Lelia want to cry.

"The gods be praised!" the woman repeated, hugging both Lelia and Donatus in a sturdy embrace. "Oh, Donatus, my lord! You've returned and brought this lovely creature to be our lady! Oh, the gods have been good this day, they have!"

Donatus released Lelia and stepped back, but only slightly. Lelia immediately understood. Donatus needed to shield himself with her skirt until the evidence of his passion lessened. The knowledge made her face flame. Donatus, noting it, met her gaze with amusement. After a moment he turned from her.

"Didia." He held out both arms and the woman flew into them. Lelia got her first full look at Didia, and liked what she saw. The woman was small, barely reaching Donatus's chest. Her hair was long, braided down her back, steel-gray with only a little of its original black remaining. Her embrace showed nothing of hesitation or subservience, only adoration.

She was talking breathlessly, patting Donatus's cheek even after their embrace ended. "Oh, that fellow Micon told us your big news—that you'd chosen a wife. But I could hardly believe it. I had to see such a thing for my own self. You've always been so loath to attach yourself to anyone—and my stars! I thought you'd *never* settle down!"

Didia turned to Lelia, capturing the younger woman's hands in her own. Sharp eyes of charcoal-gray traveled over Lelia quickly, softening with pleasure. "My goodness, child, just look at you! Worth all the wait, you are! What a beauty! What a lovely, lovely lady to be our master's cherished wife!" She looked back toward Donatus. "I'll say one thing for you, Flavius Donatus, you certainly know fine stock when you come across it. Oh, she's lovely, she is!"

Donatus laughed and pulled Lelia to his side with an arm entwined about her waist. "My fears are all at ease now, Didia, since you so heartily approve of my choice."

"Approve! Why, I couldn't be more pleased if I'd chosen her myself." Didia turned to the man who'd come up behind her and now stood smiling at the scene before him. "Amandio, come here and welcome our new mistress."

Amandio stepped forward. Lelia smiled and extended a hand, thinking as he took it that he was, indeed, the very opposite of his wife. Where Didia was petite, he was a hulking, big-boned mountain of a man, towering even over Donatus. For all his great size, though, his craggy face held kindness and his dark eyes were warm. "Mistress," he said, bending low in an awkward bow. "Welcome."

"Thank you," Lelia said, her gaze now flicking outward to the slaves who'd appeared behind the couple and stood watching. "It's a pleasure to be here among you. Donatus has spoken well of this place, and well of all of you who make it so special to him."

It was the right thing to say. Lelia could tell by the pleased expressions on their faces. Didia gave Lelia little time for pause, however. She caught her by the arm and pulled her toward the house, welcoming her with a pleasant stream of conversation that made Lelia smile. Donatus and Amandio watched them go, amused expressions on their faces as they shrugged and shook their heads.

"I know it's not the master's best mansion," Didia said as she led the way up the path. "It's not got all the finery you're probably used to. But it's got one thing those big fancy houses haven't got."

"Oh? What's that?" Lelia raised an eyebrow curiously.

"Why, mistress, it's *sheltering*. That's what it is. Such a wonderful place for two newlyweds to learn of one another. I could have slaves sent up from our home down the hill, but you'll probably want to be alone—in the beginning, at least. No wonder Donatus brought you here first thing. Where better to celebrate your love?"

She leaned closer and lowered her voice to a whisper. "It's

plain to see there's love between you, child, and oh, that does fill my old heart with joy. We feared Donatus would be a soldier forever. Mind, we understood all the whys of it, what with the way his mother did his father. Hard, *hard* for a son to get over that." Didia shook her head sadly.

Lelia frowned. "What? What did she do?"

Didia looked up, startled. "You don't know? Donatus hasn't told you?"

"No."

"Then I'm afraid I've spoken too freely." Didia sighed. "That's too often my way. Open my mouth in haste and repent it at leisure. But this thing, Donatus must be the one to explain. He'll do it when he feels ready. Give him a little more time, dear. Give him time. It's a very sore spot for him to this day. In the meantime, be tender with him. You have the power to bring him the healing he needs."

Lelia tilted her head. "I'm sorry, but I don't understand."

Didia patted her arm. "No, of course you don't. But in time you will. All will become plain. Just give Donatus time to trust you."

Lelia frowned. Donatus had asked her to trust *him*. It hadn't occurred to her that he might not yet trust *her*.

Didia made a soft sound and patted Lelia's cheek. "Give it no more thought, my lady. Come inside now, and let me show you your new home." She released Lelia and pulled at the sturdy plank door, gesturing for her to enter.

Lelia stepped in, blinking in the cool shadows. As her eyes adjusted she became aware of her surroundings, and found them just as Donatus and Didia had promised. Not grand. But, yes, the place was sheltering and cozy. The walls were thick stone, rough cut and providing a pleasing note of texture. There were only a few windows, with grilles made of baked clay. Wooden shutters stood open to admit the sun, but they'd be closed in the cool evenings to retain heat.

"This is the main room," Didia said, gesturing with her hand. "The one just beyond is the bedroom. Beyond that is a bath that was added by Donatus's father, and a small kitchen that's never been used much. I've always made a point to bring the master food from my kitchen and vegetables fresh from my garden." She straightened with pride. "I'm the best cook in the village, and I wouldn't be having the master served by any other. Unless you'd wish it otherwise, mistress?"

Lelia smiled. "Of course I wouldn't," she said. "I want everything to be done as before. Especially since I must confess to you—" she leaned near to Didia's wrinkled cheek "—I'm a *terrible* cook."

Didia raised a surprised eyebrow, then smiled in near-satisfaction. "Well, then. Of course I'll be pleased to continue to provide the meals. Donatus won't know of your lack of skill, not as long as you're here on the farm. Leave the cooking chores to me, and you… Well, you just do what a woman was made to do, my dear. Take care of your man in other ways." She chuckled. "That's probably what he's truly hungry for, anyway."

Heat flared in Lelia's cheeks. She turned away, feigning interest in the room. She walked slowly around it, patting a pillow into place, righting a candle in a candelabrum.

The room was solid and comfortable, with furnishings that were handmade and sturdy and cushioned with plump mattresses that invited relaxation. A hearth at one end of the room held a small bank of coals. Lelia stood before it, stretching out her hands.

"The days are warm, but the nights still hold a little chill," Didia explained, following the direction of Lelia's gaze.

"There's more wood for the fire stacked in the corner. Child? Let me be honest. I'm pleased my lord's found a wife. He's a fine man and will treat you well. I'm beside myself with the notion that he's finally married at last. He'll love you in this little home, and soon I'll be at your bedside, bringing his child into the world."

Lelia couldn't help the groan that escaped her lips, or the way her world shifted oddly sideways. When she steadied herself and opened her eyes again, Didia studied her with a worried expression.

"I'm sorry," Lelia whispered. "It's just that I'm not quite ready yet to envision such a scene."

The frown cleared from Didia's brow. "No, dear. I guess not. You've got a little more loving to do with your man before you'll be ready for his babe, but…" She gave a happy little laugh. "That day will come, mistress. It will surely come. And when it does, you'll think it the most precious moment of your life. To hold a sweet-smelling child to your breast and know it made of love, to see the pride in your husband's eyes as he holds his own little one, part of him and part of you… Ah, there's a joy too fine for words, let me tell you."

Lelia swallowed, fighting hard against the image the woman's words conjured. The pain brought tears to her eyes.

Thankfully, Didia didn't notice. Instead, she stepped further into the room and began to tell Lelia about the house—about the bedroom prepared for them and about the private bathing chamber, complete with its own hearth to heat the water.

Lelia followed behind her, barely able to hear the woman's excited chatter. All she could think about was her son, her own sweet-smelling son that she'd held to her breast, made of love, even though his father hadn't been there to taste the pride of one so made—part of Donatus and part of her.

Chapter Eleven

"Why in the world are we doing this?" Severina asked as she swung a wooden sword in a wide arc around her head, testing its weight.

Lelia tossed Severina a leather pad and watched as she began to strap it into place. "Because I'm bored out of my skull and because we're warriors, Severina. We're powerful. And there may still be someone trying to murder me."

Severina looked up with a wry expression. "And mostly because you're bored out of your skull."

"All right, I admit it. I try to work at chores like everybody else and no one will allow it." Lelia raised her voice in a high-pitched imitation. "'*Don't pick that up, my lady. Don't burden yourself, my lady. We're so proud to serve you, my lady.*'" She fell upon the grass of the clearing with an exasperated sound and looked up at her friend. "Severina, I've endured three full weeks of idleness. I want to do *something* to feel useful and needed, but aside from stitching clothing for my husband, there's no labor deemed suitable for the wife of Senator Flavius Donatus of Rome."

Severina smiled. "You have Donatus to blame for that. I heard him give Didia the command with my own ears."

Lelia's head jerked around. "Command? What command? When was this?"

"The morning following our arrival. He told Didia that you were his lady and a noblewoman, and that if she saw you doing anything strenuous she was to put an immediate stop to it."

Lelia groaned. "That explains it, then. And dear, sweet old Didia has not failed once in her performance of duty. I swear that woman is *everywhere*. No sooner do I lift a basket or an iron pot than she sends a slave to take it from me."

Severina laughed and drew on her leather helmet. "She thinks Donatus is solicitous of you because you carry his child."

Lelia's jaw dropped. She sat up abruptly, her hands clasping her knees until the knuckles turned white. "Good heavens! She told you this?"

Severina's eyes sparkled with amusement. "No, not to me. I overheard her say it to a slave girl."

Lelia groaned and flung herself back down onto the grass. "No! No! No! Now all of them probably think I'll soon be big-bellied with Donatus's seed."

Severina caught her friend's hand and drew her to her feet. "Well? Could you be? I mean…forgive me for suggesting this, Lelia…but if you could possibly be with child then I don't want to spar with you. It would be dangerous for the babe."

Lelia groaned again and grasped her head, feeling the cool smoothness of the leather helm beneath her fingertips. "No, Severina, I am *not* with child."

"Not even possibly?"

Lelia shook her head. "Not even possibly. Donatus and I have not…we're not lovers."

Disappointment flitted across Severina's face. "Poor man."

Lelia's eyebrows lifted. "Poor man? What about poor *me*? He watches me like a tiger awaiting the opportunity to feast on a weak gazelle."

Severina laughed, the sound ringing through the hidden clearing in which they stood, surrounded by mature, sweet-smelling pines. "No doubt. Like I said, *poor man.* Unless you also watch him with the same hunger?"

Lelia felt her face grow hot when she couldn't control the sudden image that catapulted through her mind—that of Donatus as he'd appeared that very morning, clad only in a piece of linen toweling after washing. His chest had been massive, his hips lean, his tanned skin still wet with moisture, the dark hair of his chest begging the caress of her fingertips. It had been all she could do to turn her gaze away to her sewing, and then only after she'd stabbed herself with her needle.

Severina laughed again, reading the horrified expression on her friend's face only too well. "Oh, Lelia," she said. "Poor Lelia. Why don't you get it over with and throw yourself at him? I daresay he'd not refuse."

Lelia's face grew warmer still.

Severina stopped and stared. "You tried it, didn't you?"

Lelia stammered. "No, I didn't… It's not what you think. Not…exactly. He… We…"

Severina shook her head. "Poor, poor Lelia. Married to a man too honorable to ease his pleasure for lust alone." She raised her wooden gladius and took her stance. "Come, Flavia Lelia. Come spar with me. Perhaps I can put you out of your misery."

Lelia lifted her own sword and took her position. Her words were partly serious, though heavily laced with sarcasm. "At the very least you must exhaust me. Maybe then I'll not be tempted to shame myself with lust for the man who is, after all, only my own husband."

Severina grinned, her muscles bunching as her feet shifted in preparation for her attack. "Will do, my friend. Will do. Though I do repent it already. *Poor, poor Donatus.*"

* * *

Several hours later Donatus was at work in the shearing barn, trying to hold a struggling ewe with one hand while shearing her with the shears in the other. He was also attempting to keep the wool in one tight piece, the mark of a skillful shearer. The other sheepshearers had teased him good-naturedly all morning about his ineptitude, and he wanted to show them all how wrong they were.

He glanced around, slightly irritated when he felt a tug on his tunic. Didia stood behind him, looking both worried and apologetic.

"Didia?"

"Forgive me for disturbing you at your work, my lord, but I'm concerned about your lady."

"Lelia? What's wrong with Lelia?" Donatus let go of the bleating ewe. He watched the animal bound away and turned hastily, wiping his hands on his tunic.

"I don't know. Something ails her, but she won't tell me the problem. I went to give her some of the fresh lamb stew I'd made, and found her upon your bed, groaning in pain. I couldn't get her to eat, and now I do fear something's terribly wrong."

Lelia was in bed and in pain? Could the murderer have struck again? Another dose of poison?

The thought galvanized him into action. He clasped Didia's hand. "Did Lelia eat anything other than what you put on our table?"

Didia shook her head. "I don't think so. Just some fruit for breakfast. She didn't touch the stew for lunch."

Donatus had already begun to pivot away. "I'll check on her."

He was running even before the last words were spoken, his insides writhing. The heavy door banged behind him as he entered their home, the dimness within like night after the brilliant sunlight outside. "Lelia!" he yelled. "Lelia!" He was at the doorway to their bedroom before she'd had time to answer.

She sat up in bed, startled by his unexpected presence in the middle of the afternoon. "Donatus?" Her eyes were wide.

He crossed the room in two strides and knelt beside her, his hand going to her forehead. Her skin was warm, but not feverish. "You're ill?"

"No, Donatus. Not really. Just—"

"Didia said you were ill—in bed groaning. You're not ill?"

Lelia looked uncomfortable and pulled the sheet higher about her shoulders. Donatus realized suddenly that she was naked beneath it. His chest tightened.

"I'm not ill, Donatus. At least not in any way that might be serious. I overexerted myself a bit today. I had too much sun. I'm blistered and all my muscles ache. I can scarcely move, but I'm not ill."

Donatus scowled. "How did you do this? I thought I gave orders that you were not to—"

"Oh, for heaven's sake, Donatus!" Lelia said in exasperation. "It's my fault. None other's but mine. Your servants have been following your orders well. They weren't around when I...when I did this to myself."

Donatus's lips tightened. "What did you do?"

Lelia did not answer.

"What did you do?"

Lelia raised her chin. "I'd rather not say."

Donatus straightened and turned, running his fingers through his hair. He looked back at her. "Sweet mercy, Lelia. I was so damned frightened. I thought you'd been poisoned. I ran all the way from the shearing sheds, sick with fear I'd find you already dead." He halted. He looked away.

Lelia looked down. "I'm sorry. I didn't know Didia would go to you. I told her it was nothing serious."

Donatus sat down on the edge of the bed and dropped his head into shaking hands, struggling to gain control of his still surging emotions. He looked down, silent for a long while. Then he stood, moving to Lelia's side. "Let me see your sunburn," he said gently.

"No, Donatus. It's nothing, really. I can—"

Donatus lifted the sheet.

Lelia shrieked and clutched at it. "No, Donatus! I can take care of myself!"

His strength won. Donatus snatched the sheet away, then immediately wished he hadn't. Her body was exposed to him, beautifully, splendidly, gloriously naked. He couldn't control the sharp intake of his breath, or the way his eyes raked her from head to toe, halting on the fullness of her breasts and the mound of dark curls where her legs joined. His manhood jumped in immediate response.

Lelia did not lie passive beneath his perusal. She immediately rolled to the far side of the bed and bounded up, snatching a garment from a stool and flinging it over her head, then groaning through lips that had gone surprisingly pale.

He was beside her in another moment. "Where? Where do you hurt, love?"

She shook her head. "Don't touch me, Donatus. Go. Go back to work. I promise you, it's nothing serious. I'll be fine in another day or two."

Donatus lifted the hem of her tunic. She tried to push it down, almost crying out at the effort of bending. He pushed her hands aside and raised it higher. She didn't resist.

Donatus whistled. "No wonder you hurt," he said quietly.

"I know," she moaned, easing herself down onto the bed. Donatus crossed the room and opened a chest, rummaging noisily within it until finding what he sought. He brought the small alabaster bottle back to the bed and pushed Lelia down against the sheets.

"What are you doing?" she demanded.

He pulled her tunic to her waist. She gasped and sat up, pushing it back down again.

Donatus gave an exasperated sigh. "No, don't fight me," he said impatiently. "Trust me. Right now I'm your coldly impassive physician, not your love-starved husband. Let me put this ointment on your skin. It will take the sting from the burn and relieve the soreness of your muscles."

Lelia's eyes met his, unsure, wary. Then as if she read the truth in his face, she visibly relaxed. She gestured toward the bottle. "What is it?"

"An unguent we cavalry officers carried to ease the day-to-day woes of military life." Donatus lifted the hem again and began to dribble a little of the oily mixture onto her calves, massaging it in with his fingers.

Lelia wrinkled her nose. "It smells terrible."

Donatus looked up with a smile. "Doesn't it. But it works wonders. We used it on both men and horses. No good decurion would be caught anywhere without it." He poured several drops into his palm. "This little bottle holds the elixir of war, my sweet."

Lelia closed her eyes briefly, relaxing beneath the firm ministration of his hands. "Then maybe I should steal it away from you. War is a very bad thing."

Donatus grunted. "War made Rome great, Lelia. A bad thing? Without a doubt. But a necessity. A damned inevitable necessity."

Lelia frowned. "You liked war, though, didn't you?" she asked. "I mean, you must have liked it. You left me to go back to it."

Donatus hesitated just a moment as the memories came.

He shook his head to clear them and resumed the gentle massaging, across her knees, up to the pinker flesh of her thighs. "I hated war. Every last moment of it."

"Then why did you leave me?"

Donatus looked up, his eyes finding hers. "Because I was more afraid of loving you than I was afraid of dying."

She drew in a sharp breath. "You were afraid of me?"

"I began to love you. I was afraid to love you."

"But why?"

Donatus looked away, feeling tension ratchet his jaw. He didn't know what to say. He couldn't explain; he'd never completely understood it himself. "I don't know," he said quietly.

Lelia didn't respond, and he was thankful. He finished pouring and spreading the oil upon her thighs. "Take the tunic off now," he said.

She looked up with a startled expression. "I don't think so," she said, raising her chin.

Donatus frowned. "It's for your muscles, Lelia, not to slake my lust. Your body aches everywhere, does it not? Your arms, your shoulders, your back?" He turned abruptly and snatched his cloak from a nail on the wall, spreading it upon the bed. "Here, lie face down on this so you don't get the bedclothes dirty, and I'll spread the ointment on your backside. You'll be better within an hour, not days."

Lelia met his gaze, assessing him. She sighed. "You win, Physician Donatus," she said, lifting the tunic over her head. Her breasts heaved upward and then bounced back down into place. Donatus stifled a groan and looked away, his male flesh throbbing. *Physician Donatus. Cool, impersonal, professional. Forget all else.*

She lay down on the cloak, the silken skin of her rounded buttocks gleaming pale in the dim light, her waist small above the flare of her hips. She waited. He sensed her confusion when he didn't move.

"Donatus?" she asked.

He drew in a ragged breath and shook the bottle in his hand. *Pour the liquid, you fool. Pour it on her body, massage it in. Don't think about it, just do it.*

He knelt beside the bed and began the work. But her skin, oh, it was warm. Her legs were long and graceful, her buttocks sensual perfection. He longed to press his lips against them. His hands began to shake.

He forced himself to concentrate on his own fingers, on their circular dance across her skin. But the image of her shape burned his mind, scorching him with lust.

"Donatus?" she asked, when he paused. She looked around at him with an odd expression, and Donatus realized he'd groaned. Aloud.

He leaned forward, unable to help himself, and touched the dimple in her lower back with his tongue. She jumped like a startled doe. He reined in hard and pulled away, biting back the need until it was a hard, painful lump in his chest. And other places.

She laughed, somewhat shakily. "That's not Physician Donatus."

"No," he said darkly. "It isn't."

"That's... What did you call him? Donatus the love-starved husband."

"Yes," he answered. "It is."

He sucked in a long, quavering breath and resumed. The ointment, he poured the ointment and massaged it in, trying to ignore the woman beneath his circling fingertips. Her buttocks, her back, her shoulders, her arms. Some cool, impersonal physician he, kneading the medicine into her flesh and trying to ignore his own, as hard as glass and hurting like hell.

He capped the bottle when he'd finished, and stood.

Lelia stretched out her muscles like a contented cat, making a low moan that ended in a sigh. The sound speared him, shattered him, burnt his restraint to cinders.

"That feels better already," she said, the words muffled by the mattress against her cheek.

"I know," Donatus said, reaching beneath his tunic. With hardly a whisper of sound, he eased his stiff member from the restriction of clothing. His lower garment slid to the floor.

"I can move now, and it doesn't pain me."

"That's good. That's very good," Donatus said, lowering himself onto the bed, almost touching her, poised to touch her, afraid to touch her.

"My muscles feel so much better now, so comfortable and warm."

"Warm, hmm." Donatus moved, stretched himself against her, his male flesh brushing her buttocks as his erection came to rest against the place where she was softest.

"No!" She started up in surprise and then fell back down again as she realized that her sudden motion had only brought her into closer contact with his body. "Donatus! We can't do this!"

He didn't move into her, only rested his weight against her, his breath stirring the hair that touched her ear. "Relax, Lelia," he said quietly. "I'll not force you. Only allow me this pleasure for a moment. Let me feel you against me, skin to skin."

"Donatus…"

"I'm not hurting you, Lelia, and I won't. You know I won't."

She made a small sound of protest even as she acquiesced. Donatus eased closer, pressing her hips back firmly against his aching loins, biting his tongue to keep from groaning at the pleasure that sheared through him. He buried his face into the smooth skin of her neck, breathing in her tangy citrus scent, wanting her so badly he could have screamed with it. He pulsed himself smoothly against the feminine folds, pleading silently for that which he needed. He would not beg with words.

Her body was slippery with oil, another sensual delight that pleased him. He moved against her harder, but friction brought too much need. It broke over him. He shook with it. His blade touched her warmth, so close. So damned close.

Lelia shifted slightly, a savage gesture to make him tremble. It would be so simple to push within her. He breathed deeply, racked with the primitive, urgent need to possess her.

She must have sensed the gathering tension of his body. "No, Donatus," she whispered. But the whisper was not as certain as it had been.

His hand moved up her arm and back down again, stroking her slick flesh. It slid to her waist and feathered up again, one careful inch at a time, drawing out the pleasure, making her breath quicken and her legs tighten against his.

His fingers found the bud of her nipple and gently squeezed. She gasped and moved, not aware that she ground sleek hips against his. More agony, that unexpected, delicious pressure.

"Have mercy, Donatus," she whispered. But she was shivering now, shivering with heat. It shimmered in waves around them.

He lowered his head. His tongue touched lightly to her sensitive ear. At the same time his palm cradled her female flesh, swollen with desire beneath his hand, feeling her curls wet and hot. She cried out at his touch, pushed up and arched, bucking slightly beneath him.

Donatus ground his teeth hard together, unable to hold back the sound that escaped him, part strangled curse, part groan. She jerked away with a startled exclamation, realizing the mistake had been her own. Donatus closed his eyes, waiting for sensation to subside, praying for torment to lessen, knowing it would not. He wanted more than that. He wanted all of her, the deepest depths of her.

"Oh, Lelia," he breathed against her neck. "I need you. Don't deny me."

"Donatus. I can't deny you. How could I deny you?"

But he could hear fear in her voice, mingled with disbelief, so he waited. No refusal came.

He moved against her, testing her, giving her another chance to hurt him. She didn't move away. She didn't utter a protest. He used his hips to plead for him, to whisper reminders of what they'd once known, promises of what they might yet know.

Her legs parted slightly, allowing him access. His heart clutched hard at the unspoken bidding.

He touched her, hard flesh to soft, probing the entrance to her secret places. She made a sound somewhere between pleasure and pain. Her body tightened, her thighs trembled. She did not call a halt.

His arms tightened around her. He held her steady in hands that now were sure. His breath sighed against her hair as his hips pulled back and then surged forward with no more thought of turning back. In the next moment Donatus slid himself into his woman with a deep, soul-shaking growl of pleasure.

It was a wild, feral sound, a calling to mate. He felt Lelia's breath catch on a sob, but he could not stop himself to comfort her. He saw her fingers curl against the mattress, but he couldn't think coherently enough to wonder at it.

Need drove him. Weeks of pent-up need drove him. He couldn't stop now—even if his fingers bit into her flesh, even if his hips ground hard against her. He needed her. He needed to own her, to brand her, to empty himself into her.

The thrusts of his body sang it. *Mine. Mine. Mine.*

The pounding of his blood sang it, sang possession, sang demand, sang triumph. She was his wife, his woman, his mate. *His.*

It was not a gentle possession. It was Donatus riding a cavalry charge down a steep hill. Reckless. Dangerous. Wind in his face, javelin roaring. It was Donatus fighting for a possession born of fiercest love.

He raced forward, tasting oil and sweat and battle-lust, desperate to pour his life into her. Desperate for the spasms when they came, and they came quickly, and they came with hard and overwhelming power. He raised his head and welcomed them, even though they made him grind his teeth and shake to the point of agony. He pulsed deep, finding her womb, seeding it. A cry came from deep within his throat, hardly recognizable, a keening cry of pleasure and pain and promise, all rolled into one sweet victory song.

Then it was over.

The pounding in his veins subsided. His mind cleared, his breathing eased. And Donatus realized what he'd just done.

He stumbled backwards, pulled away from her, felt the tug of her heated flesh against his own. He stood, looking down at Lelia's beautiful body upon the bed, and knew shame in ways he'd never known it before.

He heard her voice catch on a sob. He could only stand, helpless, while she began to weep.

"Lelia, I ..." He raked his hand through his hair. What could he say? That he was sorry for making love to his wife? For taking that which he had every right to take? And yet... And yet...

He moved forward, pierced to his soul by her tears. He knelt down beside her, soothing her, stroking her hair. He used one corner of his cloak to wipe his seed from her, as if he could just as easily wipe away the memory of what he'd done. But he knew how futile the action was, how late the gentleness and how empty the gesture.

"I love you, Lelia."

She looked up then, her violet eyes hot with tears and accusation. Her pain hit him forcefully, a blow directly to his beating heart. He stumbled backward, unable to speak beneath the guilt.

His hands clenched. He made a harsh sound. Unsure of words, and unaccustomed to feeling shame for being a man, Donatus pivoted on one heel. He bent and snatched his clothing from the floor and strode away from her, knowing there was little he could do. Knowing he'd already done too damn much.

Chapter Twelve

She had nearly told him. Lelia sat alone in the darkened bedroom for hours, staring at his cloak and at the evidence of what had passed between them, and wondered at herself. She'd let him love her and then she'd cried, so close to telling Donatus the truth. That she loved him, that she wanted him, that she'd borne him a son and then lost that child. And that she was a miserable failure as a woman, and as a mother, and as a wife. She'd hovered just on the brink of the truth, but he'd left her before the words had found a way out of the dark prison of her heart. He'd left her.

Always, always he left her when she needed him most.

He didn't come home when the work day was over. He didn't sup with her—though Didia brought plenty, setting it before her with an apologetic glance and hesitating, as if she wanted to ask why her young mistress had been weeping. Didia's eyes swept the room, but if her eyes had taken in the tangled bedsheet, the cloak with its dried stain, she didn't say anything. Lelia didn't care. All she wanted was Donatus and his arms around her. She wanted the dam to break, the flood to roar, the rains to cleanse her soul.

She wanted Donatus to know the truth, and if he couldn't love her afterwards she'd face it bravely. Of the tension between them, she could bear no more. She needed peace, one way or the other. Maybe the truth would work. Her way surely hadn't.

By midnight she was beginning to panic. She dressed herself and slipped out with a small lantern into the dark, intent on finding him, hoping he wouldn't have come to harm or—she trembled at the thought—found succor in another's arms.

She did find him in another's arms. Lucan's.

His best friend must have arrived in the afternoon from Rome. Donatus had mentioned that Lucan would come every few weeks to report on his progress in finding the murderer.

Right now, though, Lucan struggled to make progress of a whole different kind. Now he was bringing Donatus home, half-supporting, half-dragging her falling-down-drunk husband up the hill.

Lelia hurried to help, wrapping Donatus's free arm around her neck. Her husband roused when he heard her voice. "Lelia? You're here?" He leaned forward to kiss her, his breath reeking of wine.

"Good heavens," she said. "What in the world…?"

"He's drunk," Lucan said quietly.

"I *am* drunk," Donatus agreed in a too-loud, heavily slurred voice. "Damn stinking drunk. I haven't been this drunk in years."

"Hush, Donatus," Lucan said. "Don't let your bride see you like this."

"My bride," Donatus said. "She doesn't want me, Lucan. She cries when I make love to her."

The words pierced Lelia's heart. Was that what he thought? That she didn't want him? That was so far from the truth.

"Hush, Donatus," Lucan said again. "You talk too much when you're drunk."

Donatus nodded. "I do. I know I do." He said no more, and both Lucan and Lelia were thankful.

Donatus was a large man, and he was nearly a dead weight, so for the next few minutes, they had their hands full with the effort to get him up the hill and into the house. Holding the door open, Lelia directed Lucan toward the bedroom. She sat near the fire in the hearth room while Lucan undressed her husband and unlaced his sandals. Donatus snored soundly by the time Lucan pulled the covers over him.

A weary Lucan joined Lelia, sinking with a sigh into the chair beside her. He had an odd expression on his face, maybe one of embarrassment. "I'm sorry you had to see him like that," he said. "He's not usually one to drink much. I was surprised when I got here this afternoon and found him in the tavern, swilling wine like he'd never tasted the stuff before."

Lelia looked down. "It was my fault. We had a misunderstanding."

Lucan grimaced. He looked at her, his eyes gently apologetic. "I'm afraid I heard all about it. Donatus talks too much when he's drunk. Has for years. So I had two choices, leave or stay." He sighed. "Lelia, believe me. I didn't want to know all your secrets, but if I'd left, some other poor fool would have heard them. I didn't want your marriage to be fodder for gossip, so I stayed and let him empty his heart to me."

"Then you know everything?" Lelia didn't know whether to be relieved or embarrassed.

"Yeah, I guess so," he said quietly, looking away. "Your past with Donatus two years ago, the way he left you. And all that's happened since you wed. He feels guilty as hell, and fears you'll hate him for it."

Lelia shook her head. "I can't hate Donatus."

Lucan looked relieved. "I'm glad to hear that. He's a good

man. I know what he did to you two years ago. I know it was wrong, but he had his reasons."

"Reasons?" Lelia looked at him carefully. "I don't suppose you'd tell me what they were? It might help to know."

Lucan studied her for long moments, as if debating whether he should speak or not. "Donatus is afraid of love," he said finally. "He doesn't trust easily. He holds himself back from love. He left you two years ago because you got too close—because he'd fallen in love with you. It frightened him."

"But why?"

"An old wound. A deep scar. Donatus was seven when his mother abandoned him."

Lelia drew in her breath. "His mother abandoned him? Her own child?"

"Not exactly. Poor choice of words on my part." Lucan frowned, lips tight, as if searching for the explanation. "Donatus's mother was a beautiful woman, full of gaiety and life. I didn't know her, you understand, only learned of her later—and not from Donatus, because he never speaks of her. One of my aunts knew her and told me the tale."

Lucan leaned forward, his face dark. "Donatus's father was a good man, but one man wasn't enough for her. She took lovers. Many lovers. It brought shame upon Antonius and shame upon the Senate, for many senators were approached by her and more than a few acquiesced. So indecent was she that Antonius had little choice but the path of honor. He brought his case to the floor of the Senate, denounced her publicly and divorced her. The Senate voted as one man to banish her to some distant island."

"Donatus didn't know?"

"He was only seven. He wouldn't have understood things like adultery or the harsh laws against it. All he understood was that his mother had gone away."

"But later?"

Lucan nodded. "Later he did. It only reinforced what he'd already come to believe—that he might love a woman, but she could never be trusted completely. She might leave. She might hurt him. She might want someone else." Lucan sighed. "I don't think Donatus completely understands this truth about himself."

There was silence as Lelia considered the words. "So Donatus didn't trust me two years ago. And he still does not."

Lucan looked up. "No. But he loves you. His fear wars with his love. They go back and forth, each the victor by turns. Love won for a while. Donatus claimed you as his bride. But fear's been his companion far longer, and now it's making a bid for supremacy again."

Lucan stood and moved quietly to the hearth, stretching his hands out toward the warmth. "Even while he pushes you away, he aches to draw you closer. He cannot help himself because he doesn't understand himself. But you, Lelia, *you* have the power to heal him."

Lelia looked down. "And who will heal me, Lucan?"

He turned and looked at her, his gaze calmly assessing. "What healing do you need, Lelia?"

The day's strain had been too much. Now, beneath the compassion she felt in Lucan's gentle gaze, she let herself feel all the months and years of pain. Her eyes filled with tears. A sob broke though. She clasped her fist over her lips, struggling to hold it in. Her shoulders began to shake.

Lucan came to her. He lowered himself to one knee before her and took the fist clenched in the fold of her tunic.

Lelia began to weep in earnest then, great racking sobs that made her chest heave. Lucan held her, rocked her gently, whispered soft words of compassion until all her grief was spent, finally subsiding into heavy silence.

"Will you tell me what's wrong?" he asked quietly.

Lelia swallowed hard. Lucan let her pull away. She fished in her sewing basket for a piece of linen and used it to wipe her eyes and then her nose. She raised her chin and squared her shoulders. "When Donatus left I was carrying his child."

Lucan closed his eyes against the shock, making a sound of heartfelt pain.

"Donatus didn't know. I don't blame him."

Lucan's eyes opened. His gaze found hers. "Does he know now?"

Lelia looked down. "No, he doesn't. Not yet."

"I see." Lucan looked away, lost in thought for a moment. When he looked back at her his eyes held an understanding that seemed infinite. "Your secrets are safe with me."

Lelia flashed him a grateful look. "My father had betrothed me to another man. Needless to say, when I confessed that I carried Donatus's child, my father wasn't pleased. I had disgraced myself. I had disgraced my family. He sent me into the streets, called me a—" Lelia's voice cracked "—a *whore*. I was destitute. I had no money, and only the clothes I wore. I could find no work. For a few days I begged for food, but I didn't gain enough to feed myself, much less the babe within me, and the men…" She closed her eyes and swallowed hard.

Lucan's voice was gentle. "You don't have to tell me these things if they hurt you."

Lelia's eyes opened. "No," she said, almost frantic. "I need to tell you, Lucan. I need your understanding. I need your help."

"My help?"

"Yes. You see, I…I was taken in by a kind woman who found me scavenging for food behind a restaurant. She was good to me. She fed me, bought me clothes, took care of me.

She held my hand when I gave birth to my son. To Donatus's son. *Our* son."

"The babe…all was well?"

Lelia nodded. "Yes, he was fine. Healthy. Beautiful." Her voice softened and grew wistful. "He was so beautiful. He had Donatus's dark curls."

"What happened? You did not still have the child when you fought as a gladiatrix."

"The woman who befriended me stole him. One night I nursed my four-month-old babe into a contented sleep. The next morning I awoke to find them both gone. Gone without a trace."

Lucan frowned.

"I did everything I knew to do, but I could not find them. She'd used a false name, and the authorities were not able to do much—even after I sold myself to the *lanista* to earn better pay with which to further the search. I hired others, but they weren't successful either."

Lucan drew in a deep breath and scratched his chin. "Why do you think the woman took your child?"

"I don't know. I wanted to believe the best of her. She had been kind to me. I thought maybe she'd lost children of her own and needed another to cherish. But the authorities told me this sort of thing happens fairly often, that there are those who steal infants to sell them into slavery." Lelia's voice cracked again. "I can hardly bear the thought."

"It wasn't your fault."

Lelia looked up, her attention captured by the certainty in his voice. Lucan gave her an astute look and repeated the words, meeting her eyes with his mesmerizing gaze. "It was not your fault, Lelia. If you tell Donatus, he *will* understand."

Lucan leaned forward and clasped her cold hands into warm, strong ones. "Donatus loves you. You'll have to trust that. You didn't fail him. You're not a bad woman because you conceived a child and bore a bastard son. You weren't a bad mother because your child was taken from you. And you're not a bad wife because you've kept this pain from Donatus." Lucan's expression gentled. "Though I think it's time he knew."

Lelia's chest constricted. "No, I can't... I can't tell him yet. I'm not ready. I need more time. The feeling between us is still too fragile."

Lucan's brow furrowed. His eyes became the green of deep forests. He didn't seem angry at her answer, only concerned. "Don't wait too long," he said at last. "Donatus can help you. He'll want to find his son. That lost child is his *heir*. He could put his connections and fortune to immediate use—"

"I will tell him," Lelia said quietly. "When the time is right, I'll tell him. In the meantime, I thought you should know all this because it might be why someone's trying to kill me."

Lucan sat back. "You're right," he said. "I hadn't thought of that. There might be a connection. There might be." His face hardened. "But I'll go to hell and back before I let my best friend lose both his son *and* his wife."

Lelia smiled at him then, feeling lighter than she'd felt in a long time, certain that she'd entrusted her secret to one who understood.

Chapter Thirteen

$\sim\!\!\!\sim\!\!\!\sim\!\!\!\sim\!\!\!\sim$

Donatus woke early, wondering how a man could feel such relief and such wretchedness at the same time and within the same body.

The relief was simple—the permeating relaxation that eased a man who'd spilled his seed after long abstinence. How he'd needed it! No one but he could know what torment he'd endured, to have Lelia's softness always at hand but never able to touch.

He'd made a mistake in the garments he'd bought for her. They hadn't pleased him so much as tormented the life out of him, those sheer, diaphanous things that veiled without hiding. He'd had plenty of time to draw out the regret.

No one but he could understand why he rose before daylight and returned home long after dark, why he chose the most back-breaking of the labors, why he sweated to the point of exhaustion. Oh, he'd always worked the farm. His father had passed down that enduring legacy—the notion that a leader should be first and foremost the servant of all.

But he hadn't worked from any noble notion of leadership. worked, pure and simple, to keep himself from the strain of pure, unadulterated sexual need.

It hadn't worked.

Well, there'd be plenty of time for regret. At that bitter thought Donatus eased carefully from the bed, trying to ignore the pounding of his head and the stale taste of wine on his tongue. He moved gingerly through the room, finding his clothing in the pale shafts of sunrise that entered the window. He glanced back toward the bed where Lelia still slept, her breathing soft and even. The sight pierced him. She slept on the edge, her back to him. Even in sleep, being so careful not to touch him.

He drew in a deep breath, and then wished he hadn't when the pulsing of his head increased. He let his breath out again in a long, painful exhalation. He needed to get out of here, to breathe crisp air. He needed time to think before he faced Lelia again.

He'd find Lucan. He vaguely remembered that his friend had been with him during last night's drinking, though he knew Lucan had stayed for *him*, not the wine. Lucan didn't drink much anymore. His religion was a serious thing to him, and had changed Lucan's life in ways Donatus couldn't begin to understand, though he often envied his friend's peace and newfound decency.

Not that Lucan had ever been a bad person. He'd always possessed a kind heart, and had been a good friend from the first. But when they'd met, Lucan had been known to drink himself into a stupor. And the ladies... Lucan's fair good looks had won him the attention of scores of women, and he'd enjoyed it to the fullest. He'd once vowed to bed a thousand women before his thirtieth birthday. When Donatus met him, Lucan had been three months past his twenty-seventh birthday and had just enjoyed the company of female number seven hundred and ten.

Six months later, and shortly after female number seven

hundred and ninety-two, Lucan had been sent on assignment
to Antioch—mostly because two of Lucan's recent lovers had
been the wives of jealous officers with more authority than he.
It had taken Donatus several months of snarled paperwork to
get Lucan reassigned to his *ala* again, but when Lucan returned
he wasn't the same anymore. He told Donatus he'd found a
new faith, and talked a lot about being "saved from his sins"
through the blood of a Jewish teacher, Jesus of Nazareth.

Confusing stuff, that. Donatus had listened, but he hadn't
understood. The words made little sense, but the changes in
Lucan were substantial. He no longer kept rough company,
no longer drank, no longer kept count of the women he
bedded because he didn't bed any, married or otherwise.
When the weeks passed into months and the new faith didn't
wane as Donatus had expected it might, well…he'd begun to
admire Lucan's strength of character. Sometimes Donatus
even wished he, too, could have found something that gave
so much peace.

Instead, he'd found Lelia.

He sighed and shut the door behind him quietly, careful
not to wake her.

Lucan was an early riser. He usually rose at daybreak and
spent the first hour of his day in his room, praying aloud to
his strange god. Donatus hated to disturb something Lucan
thought so important, but he badly needed to hear what Lucan
had come to report. He hoped the murderer had been caught.
Lelia might be safe for the time being, but Donatus walked
through every day with a growing uneasiness, unable to shake
the feeling that someone, somewhere, plotted evil.

Maybe it was because his thoughts were already so
fastened upon Lelia that Donatus thought he heard her name
as he stood at the half-open door to Lucan's room, hesitant
to interrupt the low rumble of Lucan's prayers.

He heard Lucan say Lelia's name. Or did he? Donatus paused, his hand poised to knock, listening with deeper intent.

He heard it again. *Lelia...Lelia.* Lucan was praying—praying for her, or praying about her. Donatus held his breath, trying to make out the words.

A few moments later he backed away quietly, feeling sick. He eased toward the barns, or toward the fields—he didn't care anymore where he went. He just needed to get away from what he'd heard. It made him numb, it made him frightened, it filled him with grief and disbelief and rage.

It took a long while. An hour, maybe two. He wasn't sure because time had done strange things and halted, while his mind had done stranger things and raced. Finally, after whatever amount of time had passed, Donatus was calm. His head had cleared and the red haze of his anger had lessened. In its place had come a cool-headed determination, the product of long training at leadership and war. He could contain his emotions. He could contain his suspicions and his fury and do the job at hand with swift efficiency. Curse it all, he could do this.

He turned back again, knowing he must go back, knowing he must hear Lucan's report. It didn't matter what he'd over-heard. It didn't matter that Lucan had confessed to his Christian god that he lusted for his best friend's wife, that he felt uncommon desire and craved to touch her.

It didn't matter. It couldn't. Not right now. What mattered was that there was a murderer to be caught. If anything, Lucan's feelings for Lelia would only make him more determined to protect her. And for that Donatus supposed he should be grateful.

Lelia hated the taste of dirt, and she'd tasted it three times already this morning. She grunted as she heaved herself up, still breathing heavily and aching from the fall. Her sword lay nearby. She bent to retrieve it, pushing back the moistened tendrils of hair that had escaped the heavy braid she wore down her back.

Severina watched her from a few feet away, looking concerned but not nearly apologetic enough. "Have you had enough for one day?" she asked, wiping the sweat from her brow. She glanced up at the sun. "It's getting hot out here. Maybe that's why you're having trouble concentrating and—"

"No, that is not why!" Lelia snapped. "The heat has absolutely nothing to do with it. Besides, nobody ever asks a gladiator if the weather is pleasant enough for him to make his happy little foray into the arena."

One of Severina's eyebrows quirked upward. "My, my. Testy today, aren't we?"

Lelia frowned and leaned forward, assuming battle stance. "Testy as hell. Now, come on, woman. Fight me. I dare you to make me taste dirt again."

Severina surveyed her coolly, then positioned herself. Lelia watched her closely, waiting for her muscles to bunch. When Severina did not rush forward Lelia went after her. But her attack was too hasty, ill-timed, unbalanced. Severina easily defended her position. Lelia rushed her again, growing angry with herself. She growled as she swung the sword hard toward Severina's head. Severina ducked the blow and used the flat of her blade to whack Lelia across her ribs. Instinctively Lelia doubled over, forgetting her defense. Severina swept her off her weakened feet with one unexpected swipe. Lelia tasted dirt one more time.

She lay still in the grass for a minute, stunned by her defeat, trying to recapture the breath that had been knocked from her. Severina moved to stand over her. "Are you all right?" she asked.

Lelia nodded, still unable to talk. She felt her ribcage with her fingers. Nothing broken. Severina had showed the finesse of true skill, hitting her hard enough to bring her down but not hard enough to cause her serious injury. A more serious opponent would hardly have shown such restraint.

Lelia rolled over and forced herself to her feet, still gasping, bent over, hands to her knees. She looked up at Severina from beneath her leather helm. "All right, you win. Maybe I *have* had enough."

Severina nodded. "It will go better tomorrow," she said quietly. "Everybody has an off day now and then."

Lelia straightened the rest of the way with a groan. "An off day for a gladiator gets him killed."

Severina frowned. "Lelia, we're not *there* anymore. There is no more arena. There is no more fighting. I can't even understand why you want to spar like this."

"Because I do, that's why."

"It's Donatus, isn't it? You can't punish him, so you punish yourself. You can't control him, so you'll control whatever you can—your strength, your sword arm, *whatever.*"

Lelia hoped the scathing look she sent her friend was blistering enough. Severina deserved it.

Lelia had turned to walk away when Severina's head jerked upward and she grabbed Lelia's arm. "Wait! Stop! There's someone in the trees. Over there—behind you."

Lelia started to turn. Severina's hand tightened, making her halt.

"No, don't turn. Better to look like we're unaware of his presence."

"Can you tell who it is?"

Severina shook her head. "No, not from here. But let's ease away toward the other end of the clearing in case we—" Suddenly Severina burst out laughing.

"What is it?" Lelia asked, the unexpected sound catching her by surprise. She turned, seeing that Severina was looking back toward the stranger.

Donatus. It was Donatus. Damn him.

It wasn't just that he'd discovered their latest business—though that made her angry and defensive. It was that he'd surely be determined to put an end to it, and she'd be just as determined not to yield.

But more than that, she was disturbed by the sight of him across the field, striding toward them with a lithe, purposeful grace, his body tall and lean and sensual. It brought to mind all kinds of disturbing images from the day before.

She was suddenly angry, knowing she reacted to him like a…*woman.* A woman in love, at that. His body upon hers had changed everything between them. She could hardly think of anything else. She couldn't concentrate, couldn't focus. And she sure as Plutus couldn't *fight.*

She threw her sword down with a snort of disgust.

Severina grinned, nodding toward the one approaching. "Here he comes, a man on a mission."

Lelia spat on the ground, her hands on her hips. "More like a rutting bull sniffing out an unwilling heifer."

Severina laughed and put down her sword. "That may be. In which case you'll have to excuse me, *heifer,* if I beat a hasty retreat."

Lelia caught her arm. "Don't do it. Don't you dare leave me."

Severina raised a mischievous eyebrow. "What's this? Scared of your own husband?" She laughed and removed Lelia's hand from her arm. "Don't worry. He might be angry, but he'll never beat you—not with your training as a gladiatrix." She pulled a wry expression. "*Although*…with what I saw today…!"

Lelia jerked away. "Oh, for mercy's sake! Go, then! I'll face the raging bull alone—no thanks to you."

Severina laughed, waved to Donatus from behind Lelia's back, and trotted off through the grass.

Lelia stood in place, chewing the inside of her cheek as Donatus approached. He looked angry. But gracious, he looked good. She felt her stomach do a strange flip and knew that if he asked her to make love right here in this grassy clearing, she'd willingly taste dirt again. What was *wrong* with her?

Donatus finally reached her, green eyes glinting, raking over her, taking in every inch of the training apparel she wore.

"What are you doing?" he asked with a calm she was sure was deceptive.

She snorted and looked at him squarely. "What does it look like I'm doing?"

The corners of his lips twitched. "I thought so. I realized last night."

The words made her flush in unexpected response. He stopped, his attention suddenly riveted on her face. *Why, oh, why, did she have to act like a lovesick fool? Now he would know. He would know.*

He didn't know. He looked away, pushed slender fingers through the deep brown of his hair, and sighed. "Your sunburn was unusually distinctive. You were only pink where your armor did not protect you."

Lelia turned in surprise. She hadn't considered that. She had given herself away. In more ways than one. She flushed again, turning away quickly so he couldn't see.

"I guess you'll ask me to stop training?" she said, lifting her chin. "Well, I won't, Donatus. I *like* to train. I *like* the feel of my sword in the wind. I *like* knowing I can be strong and fierce and…"

His heat was suddenly too close behind her, warming her up and down her spine. She halted, the words all fled.

His hands found her hips, though he held his place, some small space between them. Not that it mattered, with lightning arcing between them. They might as well have been touching everywhere, her nerves hummed with such awareness.

"I like it, too," he whispered near her ear. "You don't have to stop."

She turned in surprise. "I *don't?*"

Donatus smiled. Lelia found her gaze drawn to his lips. She wanted suddenly to taste them.

"You don't," he said. "In fact, I've already talked to the metalsmith about making both you and Severina new helmets and greaves. Shields, too, if you'd like. I already have a *gladius* for you, of excellent quality and with superb balance. It saved my life in Dacia a time or two."

Lelia stared. "I don't understand."

He laughed and turned her body around to face him. Lelia couldn't ignore the warmth in his eyes. He raised a hand and wiped a smudge from her cheek in a tender gesture. "I don't want to limit you or kill your joys. You won't become less because you married me. I want to help you rise higher. I want to…" He trailed off, his eyes now fixed upon her lips. "I want to…"

Lelia felt her body leaning in toward his. His hands tightened on her shoulders as he realized it.

She finished the thought for him. "…Kiss me?"

He closed his eyes, fighting to steady himself. "Yes."

She laughed, surprising herself with the husky, seductive sound. "Fight me for it."

His eyes opened. "What?"

She pulled away, bent, straightened, then tossed him a wooden sword. "Here, Decurion. Show me you're man enough to take me on."

Donatus looked down at the sword, then back at her with a wicked grin. "I thought I showed you that yesterday."

She grunted and picked up the sword Severina had set aside. "That was not a fair fight and you know it. You caught me with my guard down."

He laughed. "And no clothes. That helped, it truly did."

Lelia's lips twisted. She pivoted and assumed fighting stance. "Come, warrior. Cease your prattle and raise your weapon."

Her throat tightened as Donatus moved into combat position. All the humor had fled his face. His eyes were determined. But it was his stance that gave her pause, for she suddenly saw the warrior, the feline grace and the deceptively light grip on the sword that warned her he was more than a match for her.

He came at her, but not in a rush. She met his first few forays easily, knowing he tested her. They circled; they pushed at each other with inquisitive strikes.

Donatus backed away. "Not bad, Lelia. But then, you always have made me work for it."

She gave him a haughty look. "Not nearly hard enough, Flavius Donatus."

He laughed and came at her again, meeting her with more force and speed this time. She defended well, but was still breathing hard when he pulled back, an intense expression on his face. "Well done, my sweet. Well done."

She nodded, and charged at him with a roar. He easily side-stepped the lunge and swatted her backside with the flat of his blade. She uttered a scream of frustration. He laughed.

She came at him again, her blade beating a furious rhythm against his. Now *he* was forced to defend, his face grim as he realized she used strategy against him.

Donatus had size and strength. In most situations they

probably served him well enough. But Lelia had speed and endurance. Donatus was not slow, but now appeared so when faced with such speed as she possessed.

She outmaneuvered him for a long while, circling him, attacking and retreating, circling again, forcing him to defend until rivulets of sweat trickled down his face, streaking the dust their struggle had washed over him. He wiped sweat from his eyes.

He seemed to be growing frustrated. Lelia hoped he was getting tired. Soon…soon… She wanted to smile, imagining how sweet would be the victory.

He surprised her. In her one unguarded moment of arrogance, Donatus made an opening. He leaped forward and delivered a blow that sent her sword sailing into the grass several yards away. At almost the same time he swept her feet from beneath her with a well-timed, well-aimed swipe of his powerful leg. Even before she could taste dirt he stood over her, the tip of his sword pressed lightly into her breast. She looked up into eyes that were alight with green fire, his chest heaving as he watched her.

"I let you win," she said.

He laughed. "You did not."

"Not this time. Yesterday."

The muscle in his jaw flexed. "I know. Next time we'll *both* win."

Lelia met his gaze. "I have no doubt."

He lowered the sword and turned away.

"Donatus?"

He didn't answer.

She sat up, hands grasping her knees. "Donatus?"

He turned, hand still gripping the hilt of the sword.

"You didn't kiss me."

Amusement flickered in his eyes. "I didn't, did I?"

"You won. You get a kiss."

His lips twitched. "No, Lelia," he said quietly. "I won. I get it *all*."

Their eyes met. Lelia's heart twisted. "No wonder you were such a good soldier for the glory of Rome."

Donatus grinned and raised a mocking eyebrow. "No wonder."

Chapter Fourteen

Donatus hadn't come for gladiatorial combat. He'd come to make amends, to restore the tenuous peace between them the only way he knew how. He'd come to say he was sorry.

But he wasn't sorry. He admitted that now as he walked away from Lelia. He was guilty, yes. He regretted having taken her selfishly. But he was not sorry he'd made love to his wife.

And now he was thoroughly confused. Last night she'd cried as if he'd broken her heart. Today she seemed *pleased*. Well, maybe not pleased. Maybe just resigned. But expectant, definitely. He knew he hadn't misread that.

He didn't know why he'd said what he had about "next time." For all he knew she'd leave him tomorrow and there wouldn't *be* any next time. But she'd met his gaze and agreed they'd share one.

He hadn't understood, so he'd walked away, believing she might have found a new, more ruthless way to punish him.

She caught up with him by the time he'd made it to his horse.

"Where are you going?" she asked, hands on her hips.

He turned. How was it he could be so attracted to her, even

when she wore that ugly leather padding and with her face and neck streaked orange with dust? He wanted to kiss her everywhere, lay her down on the grass…

"Have you eaten?" he asked. "I brought food if you're hungry."

"Will you stay?"

His gaze found hers and held. Her eyes were dark and full of some unfathomable emotion. He was afraid to breathe. "Do you want me to stay?"

She came closer until she stood next to him. "Donatus… about last night. I didn't cry because of anything you did. I wasn't angry with you."

"But you *were* angry."

"I was angry with myself." She bit her lip, then grimaced at the dirt she tasted on it. She turned away, hugging herself. "I'd just realized I still had feelings for you. I didn't want to acknowledge that. But this morning…I can't run from the truth any longer."

Donatus looked at her carefully, scarcely able to trust the words. "Feelings for me. What kind of feelings?"

She turned in exasperation. "The good kind, for Ceres's sake! You know what I mean."

Donatus hoped he knew what she meant. But he needed her to say it. "No, I don't," he said. "Tell me."

She glared at him. It almost made him laugh. She looked incapable of any "good kind" of feelings at that moment. She looked far more likely to take a swing at his head.

She looked away. "I hate you sometimes, Donatus, but I love you, too. I can't believe it. And I can't believe I'm admitting it to you."

He touched her, turned her chin and held it so he could look carefully into her face. "You love me, Lelia?"

She broke away from his touch and turned away again.

Donatus let her go. He'd seen the answer flash through the dark, confused violet of her eyes. It was enough. He wanted to cry, to dance, to whoop like a fool. More than anything he wanted to make love to her. Again. And better this time. With the love flowing like wine between them, over them, in them, through them. Making them both as drunk with joy as he felt right now.

But he knew Lelia well enough to know she needed time. She was like a fine-blooded filly. Beautiful, precious, and as skittish as could be.

He turned away from her and tapped a leather bundle tied to his saddle. When she looked at him with a question in her eyes, he smiled. "Food."

She shrugged. "I'm not hungry."

"I am."

"But you're as dirty as I am. Wouldn't it be better to go home and, uh, maybe wash off some of this filth?"

"I have a better idea. Come, ride with me." He vaulted with practiced ease into the saddle, then took her hand and pulled her up to sit in front of him. He lifted the reins, trying to ignore the soft buttocks pressed intimately against his loins.

A short while later he halted the horse, his eyes feasting on Lelia as she took in the beauty of water and sky, of lush greenery and the majesty of the tall trees that shaded the river. Lelia twisted around to face him. "It's wonderful, Donatus."

Her eyes had gone deepest violet, dark lashes sweeping down to hide her suspicions.

Slowly. Slowly. Let her learn to trust. Donatus groaned inwardly.

The saddle creaked when he swung his leg over and dismounted. His hands encircled Lelia's waist and he pulled her down, enjoying the feel of her curves as they slid against his. She drew in her breath. It made him smile. And hurt. He wondered if other men lusted for their wives like he did. Every day and all the time.

"Where are we going?" she asked when he took her hand.

"To get clean. In the river."

"But we'll get our clothes wet. We can't go back dripping wet! And if this leather gets soaked it'll be ruined."

He turned in mock surprise. "An excellent suggestion, my lady. So glad you've offered it."

She pulled away, looking worried. "What suggestion?"

"Why, that we remove our clothing, of course."

She shook her head. "Oh, no. I made no such suggestion."

Donatus smiled, taking her hand again and pulling her along, noting that her reluctance was surprisingly superficial. "Well, it was an excellent one, whoever made it."

"You're impossible," she growled behind him. "You don't truly mean to do this, do you? What if there are people about? What if someone sees us?"

"I have a solution for that."

And he did. He took her to his special place, a pool slightly upstream. Encircled by dense, overhanging trees and high banks of steep rock, it was as secluded a place as a man could wish for when he had every intention of seducing his lovely, half-reluctant wife.

Though maybe she wasn't so reluctant after all, because she let him untie her leather padding without a single protest. Her objection to his removal of her tunic and sandals was half-hearted at best. She gave him a hesitant sidelong glance and flushed prettily as she herself began to remove her undergarments. But she removed them, pretty flush and all.

When she stood naked before him, Donatus felt his jaw tighten and had to look away. She was Aphrodite in a woodland glade—too much of a goddess for him to carelessly touch. And he wanted to touch her everywhere, to ignite her with the fire that was burning him alive.

Slowly. Go slowly. Give her time.

He turned away to strip his clothing, not wanting to startle her with his arousal. He needed cold water and he needed it *now.*

The surprise was that the cold water didn't help—not when his wife swam beside him, their limbs touching with gentle, seemingly accidental bumps, legs gliding across legs. His hands brushed across her hips and her buttocks, and he could see the soft, pearly sheen of her breasts as water lapped around them.

Donatus didn't know how it happened—whether she came to him or he came to her—only that somehow his body embraced hers, warm skin to warm skin, fitting perfectly in all the right places.

Their faces were close, their lips almost touching.

"You're a patient man, Flavius Donatus," she whispered, arms arched elegantly to spear her fingers through his hair.

He lifted an eyebrow. "Patient? How would you ever imagine that?"

"You won, and yet you have not claimed your prize."

"Which prize is that, Lelia?"

Her lashes lowered. "Why, your kiss, of course."

"But I told you already. I won. I won it *all.*"

Her lashes fluttered back up, moisture clinging to them. The look within her eyes almost snatched his breath away. Desire. And *trust.*

She looked down again, her nervous tongue flicking out to moisten her lips. "Well, then. As victor, you must claim that, too."

A long while later they lay together on Donatus's riding cloak, stretched out on a mossy bank beneath tall trees, letting the wind dry their naked bodies. Lelia lay face down, pillowing her forehead against her folded arms, smelling the clean male scent of Donatus's garment beneath her, the smell of earth and sun, of growing things, of man. She inhaled and realized that the peace within her had little to do with the way he'd just held her and loved her and sated her desire—and not just once, but several times during the long afternoon.

Donatus had pleasured her to the point of weakness, and as she lay beside him, enjoying his stroking hand as it traced her spine, she grew languid and drowsy.

She hadn't slept well during the previous night. Her thoughts had been chaotic and disturbed as she'd peeled back layers and layers of feeling to come to the truth in the silent watches of darkness.

She loved him.

No matter what he'd done, no matter his reasons, she'd never been able to let go of the love she felt for him. Instead, she'd buried it beneath a mountain of bitterness. Even as she'd blamed him and hated him, she'd also ached with the loss of him.

Well, Donatus had returned. He said he loved her still, but her finely honed talent for self-preservation had made her hold her place, fighting him, denying the fact that if Donatus had wanted to hurt her again, he surely wouldn't have paid a fortune for her, or married her, or waited for weeks to claim his right to her body.

Lelia lay without sleep in the dark hours, slowly chiseling through rock to get to the truth—that Donatus acted like a man in love. His every deed was gentle and caring.

And that brought her, in the silence of the night, to a choice—the same one Severina had seen days before. Lelia could continue with the bitterness and make both their lives miserable. Or she could forgive and move on, making their marriage a beautiful thing.

And what of giving Donatus a child? Another child? She had to acknowledge her own mixed feelings about that, too. Especially since there was no turning back. Donatus had loved her. The seed could have already taken.

That hurdle was harder. It made her cry. But finally she understood that she could go on. She'd eventually have to tell Donatus about the child she'd lost, let go of the guilt, trust him to understand.

The moment of breaking had come when Lelia acknowledged that she might never see her firstborn son again. For the first time she forced herself to admit the possibility, even though the pain speared her so deeply she wanted to cry again.

And what then? Could she make herself vulnerable to that kind of hurt once more?

That night she had risen and stood over Donatus, listening to his breathing in the silvered blackness, watching the steady rise and fall of his chest. His face was softened in deep repose. His eyelashes lay like dark fringed shadows against the sharp angle of his cheekbones.

She wept quietly, moved by the severe beauty of his face, by this man with the powerful beauty of a fallen god.

Donatus wanted a child.

In an ideal world Donatus should have married someone whose family would provide him with status and wealth and political connections. In an ideal world the Flavian dynasty should continue on through his sons and daughters. That was the way of things.

But he'd married her, a woman of shame living a life of disgrace. Lelia bit her lip, thinking of the sacrifice he'd made...and *why?* Could his love be so strong?

She stared out of the window at the sleeping village below for what seemed like hours. She imagined the slaves in their houses, wives slumbering peacefully beside their husbands, their children nearby. It took so little to find happiness, so very little. Even a poor man could find love. Even a poor man could smile at his wife and know the pleasure of his children and grandchildren around him as he worked and toiled, grew old and died.

Donatus deserved at least as much as the poorest of his slaves.

Lelia drew in a deep breath and made her choice. She'd forget the past. She would place her hand into that of her husband and move forward into whatever future the Fates willed for them.

She didn't expect the transition to be easy. There would still be moments of regret, and moments of fear, and moments of pain. But Donatus had chosen *her*, for whatever reason. His actions proclaimed his love. She could do the same.

Lelia returned to stand beside the bed. Donatus lay carelessly upon it, his lean form almost too tall for comfort there. She wanted to touch him, but hesitated, not wishing to wake him. Instead she knelt, letting her fingertips barely touch his curls, a mere whisper of crisp softness beneath her hand.

The moment was a solemn one for her—even more solemn than the vows she'd spoken on their wedding day, when all she'd wanted was to get the ceremony past her. Now she studied him with tear-filled eyes, emotion expanding within her heart.

"You are my love, Donatus," she whispered. "I will be true to you."

Donatus did not awaken, but shifted in his sleep as if something of the moment penetrated his subconscious.

She swallowed hard, knowing the next words would be more difficult. "I'll not hold myself from you any longer. And if I should conceive your child, if your seed should bear fruit within my body, then…"

A tear trembled and dropped, falling onto Donatus's cheek, sliding down to leave a moonlit streak upon his skin.

"I promise to proudly bear your child and love the babe with all my heart."

The words were said, the vow surely made, and Lelia knew peace. After several minutes of silence she eased into place beside Donatus, cold from the chill of the stone floor, but warm within her soul.

Love could definitely change a man. Donatus marvelled at the difference the past few hours had made—in the way he felt inside, in the way he felt outside, in the way he felt toward the world, even toward Lucan.

A good thing, that. He had no desire to destroy his relationship with his best friend. They'd been through war together, had tasted sweat and blood and death together. They'd endured cold and heat and sat horses until their bodies ached. They'd done with scant food and threadbare blankets. They'd survived together. They'd survived because they *were* together.

Now Donatus had calmed enough to be rational. Lelia's love had helped, though the abrupt change had both startled and amazed him. He could find no reason for it—only knew that in some miraculous way his rough possession of her had broken through the wall.

He wasn't one to second-guess his good fortune, though he still felt the need to move about cautiously within the new relationship—at least until he found the boundaries, discovered the borderlines, tested the strength of the fortification.

But, damn, he felt good.

Donatus smiled now as he rode toward the village—grinned outright, from ear to ear—pleased with the world, feeling right within it for the first time in months. No, make that *years*.

He had loved his wife and he had loved her well. And she was the most passionate lover he'd ever known. So now he couldn't keep from smiling, even if somebody out there still planned evil, and even if his best friend lusted for his wife.

He found Lucan in the lambing shed. Alone, which was perfect for Donatus.

His friend looked up when his shadow fell across his feet. "Donatus. I've looked for you all afternoon. Where've you been?"

"My wife had plans for me."

Emotions flitted across Lucan's face in rapid succession. Pain, helpless frustration, embarrassment. He coughed lightly and shifted, looking away to hide his discomfort.

Donatus had never been one to shirk the necessary course, and he didn't now. He drew in a deep, steadying breath. "She's *my* wife," he said quietly. "I love her, Lucan."

Lucan looked at him then, a searching look. "I know." He sighed. "I know."

"I heard you this morning. I didn't mean to. I came to talk to you about the murder investigation, but I heard you at prayer. I heard you."

Lucan sucked in his breath, avoiding Donatus's gaze. "What can I say? Only that I'm sorry."

Donatus was silent, looking down the hill to where the shepherds were bringing to the gate more ewes heavy with lambs soon to be born. When he looked back Lucan was studying him. He didn't seem anxious, only subdued.

"You're my best friend in this world," Donatus said, meeting his friend's green-gold gaze. "I've trusted you, even with my life. But know this—Lelia is *mine.*"

Lucan surprised him. He actually smiled. "I'm glad to hear you say it, Donatus," he said.

Donatus lifted an eyebrow.

"You overheard my prayer to my God," Lucan said. "But did you hear it *all?*"

"I heard enough."

"We who serve Christ have to keep ourselves pure. And that means in mind as well as body. When I have impure thoughts I have to express them, ask for forgiveness, and receive from God the help I need to overcome them."

Lucan shrugged. "You know what I was before I received salvation, Donatus. You know how I was. What I did. I used women selfishly, for my pleasure. But, Donatus, I truly have forsaken that."

Donatus nodded tersely. "I'd like to believe so."

Lucan looked pained. "You've got to understand. There are sins of the flesh, and there are sins of the mind. I'm holding my flesh under my dominion, Donatus, though it's probably the hardest thing I've ever done. But my mind...what trouble I have with that."

Donatus would have smiled, had he not seen the genuine distress in his friend's eyes. "You're a man, Lucan. Men need women. It's just that simple. Does your god not understand this? Does he demand absolute chastity?"

Lucan swallowed hard and looked away. "Absolute chastity. Until marriage."

Donatus grunted. "Then you need to find a wife, Lucan, and find one quickly."

Lucan gave a short laugh, but the sound was filled with more pain than humor. "I can hardly choose a woman to share my life based merely on the needs of my flesh."

Donatus frowned. "So you'd rather lust after my wife instead?" He looked up at the rough-hewn rafters, choosing his words carefully. "I'm not usually one to bring up your past. You know that, Lucan. But married women were costly for you before, and I find I'm having trouble forgetting about that. I don't want to forsake our friendship because you find them intriguing."

Lucan frowned, looking down for one brief, uneasy second before his gaze met Donatus's squarely. It held honesty and regret. "Lelia's a lovely woman, Donatus, and I can hardly help being attracted to her. But I'll never touch her. I value our friendship. I'd never do that to you."

Donatus felt his chest burn. "You're right to fight what you feel for her, Livius Lucan. Lelia belongs to me. I will not share her."

Lucan nodded. Donatus looked into solemn eyes and found there what he wanted to see. There was no arrogance, no subtle challenge. A look of understanding passed between them.

Lucan cleared his throat. "I'm glad you do truly love her," he said. "She loves you, too, though she's suffered much because of it. Promise me you'll always deal kindly with her."

There seemed a strange significance in the words. Donatus turned, assessing his friend for a long minute. Then he relaxed. "Of course I'll treat her well."

Lucan nodded and absentmindedly wiped his hands down the front of his tunic. "We need to talk anyway—though my news may not please you." He met the question in Donatus's eyes. "I haven't uncovered the murderer. Not yet, anyway."

Donatus accepted the news with regret. "Well, come on. You can tell me over Didia's mutton stew. Sometimes a warm meal makes even the most dire situation seem more manageable."

But even as he said it Donatus knew that food alone didn't go far toward satisfying a man's deepest needs. That thought made him think of Lelia. And thinking of Lelia made him hungry for something far more delicious than mutton stew.

Chapter Fifteen

Didia was having a bad morning. She'd awakened with a headache, chills, and an awful ache in her bones, so Severina had offered to take Lelia's breakfast of bread, cheese, fruit and honey in a basket up to the master's house for her. But as Severina hurried down the dusty street, brushing back her long chestnut hair that seemed determined to fly in the morning breeze, she ran headlong into a stranger looking the wrong way as he swung out of the arched doorway of the granary. He grunted as she thumped hard into his side, dropping his bag of oats into the dirt.

Startled eyes of pale green met startled eyes of charcoal-gray as both began to apologize at once. They stopped in confusion, laughing at the sudden chaos of words. Then, at exactly the same moment, each bent to pick up the sack of spilled grain, colliding again as they did so.

Lucan straightened and stumbled backward, palm against his forehead. "Good Lord," he murmured. "I hope I didn't hurt you that time."

Severina snatched up the bag and jerked herself upright, already preparing to make some comical quip to cover the embarrassment of their mutual cracked heads. Instead she halted, and stared, all words fleeing in the face of the most handsome man she'd ever seen.

"No," she said quietly. "I think I'm too hard-headed for you to have damaged anything too badly."

She saw his eyes travel her form, saw them halt for a moment, but only for a moment, on her breasts. Then, in a slow sweep of honeyed lashes, they moved downward to her waist and hips and long legs. When his gaze found hers again, appreciation burned hot within them. He had feline eyes, she thought to herself. Tiger eyes, intense with the urge to prowl.

"I'm glad I didn't hurt you," he said. "Please forgive my clumsiness."

"It was an accident, and already forgiven," she answered with a nervous smile. She handed him the bag. He took it, his fingertips brushing lightly against hers. It didn't seem completely accidental. She was almost convinced of it when his eyes darkened at the surprised intake of her breath.

"Some accidents are rather fortunate," he murmured.

She glanced up, realizing for the first time that he was tall, much taller than she, though she was taller than most women. She forced her eyes to leave his face, such a beautiful face. But bless the stars above, he was beautiful everywhere, with a broad chest and trim waist and strong, straight legs.

He studied her as intently as she studied him, and seemed to be having just as much trouble concentrating on ordinary things. Like breathing.

"Who are you?" he asked. Severina decided she liked the warm, deep baritone of his voice.

"Severina."

"And I am Lucan. I've not met you before."

"No. I think I would remember."

He laughed then, a low-voiced husky sound that set her nerves tingling. "And I *know* I would."

She felt herself flush to the roots of her hair.

Lucan laughed again, then surprised her by reaching up to gently secure a wayward strand of flame-touched hair behind her ear. His hand seemed to linger a moment, then dropped to his side. Severina couldn't help the burn that ignited. Lucan was a new experience, as was this attraction—so immediate, so primitive, so *intriguing*.

He made a slight bow, his eyes never leaving her face. "Thank you for your kindness toward this clumsy oaf, Mistress Severina. I will mark it well."

She tried to smile politely, hardly hearing her expected response over the panicked plea of her heart. *No! Don't turn away! Don't leave me!*

But almost as soon as the golden-haired god named Lucan had entered her world, he left it, leaving her alone again in the narrow street, the basket of breakfast momentarily forgotten on her arm.

Donatus found Lucan in the stable, as they'd agreed the evening before. He walked through the wide doorway just in time to hear his friend soundly chastising the gelding he was attempting to saddle.

"What's got you in such a foul mood this fine morning?" Donatus asked.

"This horse!" Lucan said. "Blows his stomach up with air every time I saddle him so the girth won't be tight enough."

Donatus laughed. "That's a small thing to be so cross about."

Lucan came out of the stall, dusting his hands together. "I know. A small but immensely aggravating thing."

Donatus held out a piece of parchment. "Here's the information I promised last night. I don't know that it'll help, but we've got to try."

Lucan took the paper and scanned it briefly, before folding it again. He turned and tucked it into a leather saddlebag. "I'll do all I can. I know how frustrated you feel, because I feel the same. Nothing, *nothing* to go on. Lelia's generally well liked by everyone; nobody has motive to kill her. Not a soul saw anybody put anything into her food, and Livia was the only one who prepared it." Lucan's lips tightened. "How well do you trust that old woman, anyway?"

Donatus frowned. "Livia's served us since before I was born. Of all the slaves, she received the most from my father's generous hand, and she has the most interest in seeing my family prosper. She might be ill-tempered at times, but she'd never murder anybody—least of all the woman who might bear the next Flavian heir. Like you said, there's no motive." Donatus shook his head. "Somebody *must* have slipped in when Livia's back was turned."

"I'll keep at it. I'll exhaust these other avenues, ask more questions of more people. Maybe some random thing that is said will give us a trail."

"I'll see you back here in two weeks," Donatus said, rubbing the back of his neck with a firm hand. "And like before, travel alone, and don't let anyone know where you're headed."

Lucan smiled. "I'll try to keep the secret. But you know Druscilla. She's been after me like a dog baiting a bear, *insisting* that I bring her along. She begged with tears, saying how she loves Lelia like the sister she never had. That they share such a deep bond and—"

Donatus held up a hand, laughing at the scene he could imagine so clearly. "All right, all right. Enough already. Give my little sister a big kiss for me, will you? Right before you tell her she can't come along."

Lucan gave him a crooked grin, his eyes turning gold with amusement. "I had to wait until she was asleep to leave, you know. It was that bad."

"I wonder if she begged so fiercely because she loves Lelia or because she loves *you*. Her young female heart flutters every time you walk into the room. She fancies she might even be your wife someday."

Lucan smiled. "I know. She's a sweet little girl, a thoroughly charming little girl, but..." He paused, a strange, wistful look darkening his eyes to deepest green. "I already know the woman I want."

Donatus frowned, making no reply. For the first time in his life he found himself afraid to ask one simple question.

Several hours later, Donatus stood with Amandio, leaning against the stone wall that surrounded the barley fields. The smell of freshly turned earth, rich and heady, reminded Donatus of the deep connection he'd always felt to the land.

His father had shown more interest in architecture and engineering, but Donatus had always loved the outdoors. He'd learned to ride almost before he could walk. As a youth he'd felt most at home in the fields and in the woods, shooting his bow at wild boars or throwing his javelin at deer. Such pursuits had helped him forget his loneliness and grow into a strong, self-sufficient man. But it was the earth, this soil he saw before him now, that anchored his soul in bedrock.

"The plowing's going well," he said to Amandio.

Amandio nodded. "Yes, it is. Especially since I bought four more good oxen and you brought those six strong slaves when you came. They all know their business. The task has gone quickly." He turned to Donatus. "It'll slow down some, now that I've let Micon and Victorinus go. Not much, but a little."

Donatus twisted around. "You let them go? Go where? Please don't say back to Rome."

Distress captured Amandio's face. "I'm sorry, my lord, but I did let them return to Rome. I didn't know it was against your wishes. Micon was worried about his woman. She's about to give birth to their first child and he couldn't work for fretting. And I sent Victorinus to accompany him, so—"

Donatus drew in a deep breath. "Now our whereabouts will be known. Lelia's safety has been compromised."

Amandio's face changed, going white beneath his tan. "I'm sorry, my lord. I didn't consider!"

"The mistake was an innocent one. But tell me, when did they leave?"

"Yesterday, my lord. Around dawn."

"Then it's still possible to send a fast rider after them." Donatus sighed. "I won't ask Micon to come back, not when his wife needs him, but I can at least require their secrecy."

Amandio was already pivoting on one heel. "Consider it done, my lord. I'll see to it myself."

Donatus watched his overseer hurry away, thinking that twenty-four hours could give a man peace—and snatch it away again just as quickly.

Chapter Sixteen

Flavius Donatus and Flavia Lelia were in love, and it didn't take long for everyone living in the village to know it. It was evident in the way their eyes sought one another across busy stalls in the marketplace, or across the crowd at holiday games. They could hardly keep from staring, as if staring was just about as pleasant as touching.

Their eyes always spoke love, even when the lady sought out the lord among the workers to bring him lunch and a cool drink. It made the workers grin, but they did it behind the master's back, and quickly, so their expressions would all be normal by the time he looked around again. They had a lot of respect for this nobleman who'd work among them, and they didn't want him to think otherwise. But, ah, it was good to see two people so well-suited and content with one another.

Yet even the most diplomatic among them had to admit that the relationship was…well, it was *different*. They weren't quite sure what to think of a man who'd gift his wife with gladiatorial armor. Or a wife who'd be so thrilled with such a gift that she'd squeal and throw her arms around his neck and kiss him for it. And that in front of everyone.

Their master hadn't exactly encouraged his wife to content herself with a woman's usual pursuits, either. Instead, he let her help with the livestock, even the lambing. She'd aided several of the births, and rumor had it that now two orphaned lambs slept beside the master's bed, so she could feed them all day and night like babies. She'd tried her hand at other chores men usually did, and had learned, or so they'd heard, to do some of them fairly well.

She didn't cook. She sewed only passably. But everyone was pleased that she knew rather a lot about medicine—even how to pull a rotten tooth. She could stitch up wounds with sinew and mix a poultice of herbs to draw infection. She hadn't had cause to deliver a baby yet, or set a broken bone, but they were becoming convinced she could probably do it. Where or how she'd learned these things they didn't know, and even the bravest wouldn't dare ask. A strange, strange woman was Flavia Lelia.

But it was plain to see that she made their lord happy, and that made everyone else happy, too. Especially Didia. She'd already set the womenfolk to working secretly on tiny linen baby garments, she was *that* sure.

Perhaps Didia had something there, because the most superstitious among them had noticed how pleasant the springtime had been, how gently the rains had come and at just the right times. The sheep were bearing more lambs than usual, and healthier ones. The planted grain had sprouted well; the fruit trees had set what looked to be a better than usual yield. Even the bees prospered. The hives dripped with honey. The gods were favoring them all.

When they saw their master drop his task to stride eagerly toward the woman who'd ridden to the edge of the field, they winked at one another and grinned, certain that the look the couple passed between them was the reason for it all.

Donatus had heard the rumors. He smiled when Didia told him what his people said. He hoped the gods were indeed blessing his life, but he didn't trust any of it.

He trusted his instincts more, and his instincts told him Lelia was still in danger. And, worse, that the danger was increasing every day.

He didn't know how he knew this. Outwardly there was no cause to think it. Lucan had returned three times more, each time with little news to report. He'd followed up every lead he knew, talked to everyone who'd ever known Lelia, and turned up nothing.

Nothing. If not for the cold knot of certainty in his chest, Donatus might even have dismissed that first attempt as something aberrant and strange, a sheer accident. Except his gut told him otherwise.

And now he had more reason than ever to worry. Every day that passed he loved Lelia more. It was now late June, nearly three months since they'd become husband and wife in more than name alone. But in the last eight weeks of his intimacy with her Donatus realized that her monthly time had not come. He suspected Lelia already carried his child.

The knowledge burdened him. A murderer had tried to kill her once. Donatus sensed it would happen again. This time, if he failed to protect her, he'd lose two lives.

But it wasn't only the danger that burdened him. It was… How could he explain? How could he dare put it into words?

Donatus breathed in deeply and raked his fingers through his hair, wishing he could put his fear aside, wishing he could forget what he'd seen. He knew Lucan wanted his wife, and now he suspected that Lelia also had feelings for Lucan. Which might mean the child she carried…

He hadn't wanted to believe it of either of them. He'd tried to find explanations for the way they smiled at one another, for the way their eyes met often, and with shy understanding, for the secrets he sensed between them. But when he'd walked up unexpectedly and seen Lucan in a private moment with Lelia…

Oh, Lucan hadn't kissed her. He hadn't touched her. They'd been standing in a doorway facing the street, so they'd done nothing to make the gossips gawk. But they were discussing something important in low murmurs. Even from where he stood Donatus could make out Lucan's beseeching tone, and Donatus felt sick, imagining what the request might be.

Lelia's response had been slow to come, a long moment of hesitant consideration, and then a shake of her head. Her reply had seemed reluctant, though, and was accompanied by a deep sadness that etched her beautiful features.

Lucan reacted just as any lustful man might. He tried again, moving closer, so that he nearly touched her, his words a mere whisper in her ear. Lelia placed her hand on Lucan's chest as if to keep him from coming any nearer.

Donatus felt heat pulse between them. Lucan raised a hand to her shoulder, a caress. Lelia looked up at him, tears in her eyes. Donatus watched her lips tremble, watched them part. He knew what would happen next. He knew Lucan would lean forward. That their lips would meet.

Maybe he moaned aloud. Or maybe he moved forward involuntarily. Donatus didn't know. But something caused them both to turn abruptly toward him.

Guilt. It was all over their faces. Lucan blanched white beneath his golden skin. His lips tightened, his face went harsh with tight lines. He stepped backward, raising his hands as if to make it clear he hadn't touched her.

Donatus wanted to stalk forward and pull Lucan up into a tight-fisted grip. He wanted to throw him down the hill bodily.

He'd never wanted to thrash anybody as badly as he'd wanted to thrash Lucan in that moment.

And Lucan had known it. Their eyes had locked. Lucan couldn't have missed the rage. He'd pivoted and walked away without a word. Without a single word.

That was how it had remained for the last several weeks. They had not spoken of that moment again. They hadn't spoken of anything except finding Lelia's murderer. It was the only thing that mattered and the one thing they both wanted.

But Donatus had never known such crushing betrayal. It gnawed at him constantly now, poisoned every sweet moment. Even as he lay with Lelia, even as he loved her, he wondered if she'd already lain with Lucan, if she loved the other man more. And most of all, Donatus wondered what he'd do if he lost her.

Lelia trailed her finger down the center of Donatus's naked chest. "You're very quiet tonight," she murmured, pulling the sheet more tightly around them. "Is everything all right?"

Donatus made a soft sound of dismissal. He didn't answer, though she waited. The silence made her nervous.

She tried again, propping herself on one elbow to look into his eyes. They darkened to the deep green of a forest glade and shifted away, but not before Lelia saw anxiety flare within them.

"Donatus, what is it? Share your problem with me. Trust me."

His jaw clenched. He grasped her shoulders with two hands, almost roughly, and hauled her forward for a bruising kiss that made her wince with pain even as it sent a javelin thrust of need through her body.

The fierce passion startled her. Donatus was usually the

most gentle of lovers, always sensitive to her most subtle nuances. She didn't know what troubled him now, but she sensed he needed her in a different way tonight.

He released her from the kiss as abruptly as he'd begun it. "Oh, Lelia," he murmured. His features contorted with some inner anguish. He turned his face away.

She kissed the muscle pulsing in his jaw. "I don't know what's hurt you, my love," she whispered. "But use me. Use me to take the pain away."

He turned back, his face hard with tension. Lelia gasped when he jerked the blankets backwards, slid his hands around her waist and settled her with surprising swiftness upon his hot shaft.

"Help me, Lelia," he whispered. "Take the hurt away. Do it. Do it now."

The love she felt for him made her heart twist. Something was wrong. Something was very wrong. But she didn't know what it was or how to help. Only this—to restore him, to restore *them,* with her body and its power to heal.

She placed her hands firmly down upon the hard granite wall of his chest and began to move upon him, forcing him as deep within her as she could, grinding her hips against his in an effort to give him the utmost penetration. It was a gift to him that gifted her as well, for the feeling that speared her loins went white-hot in an instant.

Donatus groaned. His whole body convulsed in a shudder of desire. His eyes immediately turned cloudy and lost their focus. He pushed back into his pillow, twisting.

A feeling of triumph surged through Lelia, to know she could evoke such a reaction in him. Already he was forgetting whatever worried him. Already he was losing himself in her.

Her movements were instinctive, slow and sleek and

sensuous, sliding like hot silk over and around him. Pleasure twined around them, through them, drawing tighter, drawing them together. Their breathing grew harsher, ragged and intense. It was music, sweet music, the sounds of their love— their breathing a hoarse rhythm in the darkness, their skin wet and sucking, blood hammering dull percussion in their ears.

Donatus strained hard against her now, the cords of his neck growing taut as feeling tightened within him. Still Lelia drew out the pleasure, making him wait, keeping him from the moment of relief he craved.

He fought her decision. His hands moved from her breasts down to her hips, urging her on with gripping fingers, begging for more of what he needed.

No, not yet. Not yet, my love. Lelia held them both in a place of shimmering suspension, battling her own driving impulses as well as his, battling for more spirals in the pleasure, for more coiling of desire, battling to see him go insane with lust.

He was close, so close. He writhed beneath her now, his hips arching upward, his hands forcing her downward, word-lessly crying out for more speed and more pressure and more of her hot depths. His skin was slick with sweat. The hot, primitive smell of love thickened the air, a heady perfume that made desire rage.

He neared the edge, but still Lelia refused to let him plummet over it. She held them both in that place of exquisite torture, watching him, exulting in his agony, until the expression on his face became a beautiful, hideous thing, his eyes as dark as a serpent's, his cheekbones in the stark relief of near pain, his skin stretched with need. Soon, soon, her power would be shattered. Soon she'd not be able to control the shudders that racked him. Soon…

All at once Donatus jerked to one side, throwing her down

hard against the other side of the bed. Her skull cracked against the wooden frame. Lights exploded. Pain convulsed within her head.

She forgot to breathe. Donatus gave a cry that raised the hackles on her neck—the sound of a beast, part growl, part snarl, part scream of pain.

She struggled up, trying to get past her own hurt, aware that Donatus's body was no longer part of her. He'd turned upon their bed and wrestled with another man, his moonlit nudity a marble statue of straining muscle. He struggled with their attacker, locked in fierce combat to still the knife that quivered in mid-air.

That moment was a monstrous thing. At first Lelia could not move. Thrust so suddenly from pleasure into pain, paralyzed by the unexpected sight before her, she stood immobile within the grotesque dream, staring at the two men, seeing their forearms bulge with strain, seeing the blade that glinted with reflected moonlight.

The blood awakened her. Donatus's blood, spurting with frightening regularity from the wound that slashed across his shoulder. She moved forward, heedless of the danger, heedless of her nakedness and vulnerability, heedless of anything except that her mate fought and that he bled.

She launched herself upon their attacker from the side, nails and teeth bared, a cry of anger ripping through her throat. The attacker bore the brunt of her blow, and lost his grip on Donatus.

In another moment he lay dead at their feet. Donatus had captured the blade and slit his throat. Their assailant hadn't even had time to breathe.

They stood above the crumpled body, chests heaving, anger still a red haze around them. Donatus dropped the knife and reached for her, drawing her up into his embrace with a shudder. He buried his face into the warm pulse of her neck. "Lelia," he said.

Lelia couldn't answer. She'd begun to shake, the reaction involuntary and uncontrollable. Donatus held her, bracing her against the warm strength of his body. She tried to pull away when her fingertips touched the slick texture of his blood, but he whispered, *"No!"* and held her in place. They stood together for long, long moments, until their breathing eased and the tension lessened.

Then Donatus moved her away from the body beside them, moved her to the other side of the room. "We have to get dressed," he said. "We have to find out who *he* is." He glanced back toward the man on the floor.

Lelia looked back and drew in a deep breath, grateful for Donatus, for his strength and presence of mind, because she felt sick and trembling and frightened. And because at that moment she didn't know *where* Leda the Gladiatrix had gone.

About the time she was feeling most thankful, she heard a hard thump and looked around. Donatus had just hit the floor.

Some time later Didia placed a reassuring hand on Lelia's shoulder. Her voice was gentle. "Donatus will be fine now, my lady. He'll rest well with the sleeping draught."

Lelia didn't take her gaze from Donatus's pale face. She drew in a shuddering breath. "He lost so much blood."

"That's true. He'll need a while to rest, so his body can heal itself. But the wound was a clean one. Another few days and he'll be shoveling grain to the cattle like nothing happened."

Lelia nodded without answering. Didia withdrew her hand and gathered her supply of medicinal herbs and bandages into a basket. "Lucan will be back soon."

Lelia nodded again, still silent, remembering how Lucan and Amandio had carried the lifeless form of the attacker outside to a waiting cart.

The man would be buried in the morning. He'd been one of the villa's own slaves, one Avitus by name. He'd been a good worker, skilled with dressing the grapevines. He had a wife and three small children. He'd never given anyone any trouble. Amandio knew of no reason why he'd try to kill the master.

Lucan had caught Lelia's gaze and warned her into silence. Only they knew that Avitus hadn't intended to kill Donatus. Somehow, for reasons inexplicable, he'd intended to kill *her*. She'd been the one whose naked back had been the target. Even as she'd loved Donatus, even as she'd rejoiced in her husband's ragged breath and raging lust, a stranger had eased toward them with stealthy intent. Donatus had seen the glint of the moon-silvered blade with only just enough time to twist and protect her.

But not in time to protect himself. Lelia wanted to cry. She looked down at his pale face and wanted to cry.

"There's the cart rumbling out there now." Didia met Lelia's eyes with her worried, compassionate ones. "Lucan will stay. I doubt there's further danger, but we don't want you to be afraid."

Lelia nodded, turning back to Donatus. She hardly noticed when Didia slipped out.

Oh, Donatus, don't die. Don't leave me. I haven't even told you about your babe.

As if he understood the unspoken plea, Donatus shifted on the mattress and groaned. She reached down and smoothed his dark hair. His eyes fluttered and opened, confused and indistinct. He closed them again almost immediately, frowning as the ache in his shoulder penetrated the drug-induced haze.

Lelia sank wearily onto the floor beside him, pillowing her head against her husband's thigh.

It was all her fault. Death had been close. So close.

Almost she'd lost her love. An inch or two more of blade and the blood which seeped would have been the frothy pink of his lungs or the velvet red of his pulsing heart. Donatus might have died without ever knowing the secrets she held.

The knowledge was bitter.

She rested against the side of the bed, being careful to avoid the place where a stranger's blood stained the stone near her feet. *Oh, Donatus. How I've wronged you. How closely I came to losing you forever.*

She was tired. She needed to rest. But the thoughts churned. *Why? Why would someone want to kill her?* It made no sense.

The thoughts circled. Her hold on peace had been tenuous. Now it slipped, skewed. Life tilted toward fear again. Someone wanted her dead, and that someone knew where to find her now. Her life was no longer secure.

At last her mind quieted, more from exhaustion than from resolution. Her eyelids grew heavy, then closed. Her breathing deepened. And there, on her knees beside Donatus, she slept at last.

Some indefinite amount of time later, a hand gently shook her awake. She started up in fear, a gasp of horror dying on her lips as her muddled mind finally recognized Lucan's face.

"Easy, Lelia. Easy," he said gently, as if quieting a skittish mare. "I thought perhaps you'd be more comfortable in your bed."

Lelia pushed herself upright. He was right. The stone floor was cold and hard, and she was stiff from resting on it. She accepted his help as he pulled her to her feet, holding her in his arms until she'd steadied herself.

"What about you?" she asked, realizing for the first time that she hadn't been very considerate of his comfort. "Where will you sleep? Perhaps you could make a mattress of the cushions on the dining couches?"

Lucan shook his head. "I don't intend to sleep."

The words brought memory back. Lelia shivered with sudden chill. Lucan noticed it and drew her further into the warmth of his embrace, his hands chafing up and down her upper arms to bring warmth to her cold limbs. "Good Lord, but you're freezing," he said. He looked toward the bed. "We'd better get you tucked in."

Lelia glanced at her husband. "Will it disturb Donatus? I don't want to hinder his rest. He needs it badly."

Lucan shook his head. "No, I doubt it. Donatus will never know. Come, let me take you to bed."

She frowned and hesitated.

Lucan turned away, pulling her with him. "Come, Lelia. Come to bed."

Lelia was too weary to argue. She gave in to the delicious feeling of security as Lucan drew the blanket over her and dropped a brotherly kiss upon her brow. "Sleep now," he said. "I'm here. There's no danger. Sleep."

Lelia relaxed. Soon enough the danger would return. Tomorrow she'd have to deal with the fear. But for now Donatus breathed beside her and Lucan watched. She would sleep.

Two days had passed, and while Donatus felt somewhat stronger, he still winced as Lelia helped him pull a clean tunic over his wounded shoulder. He glanced at her, and her beauty nearly snatched his breath away. Her ebony hair was long and sleek, pulled back into an ornate silver clasp but otherwise hanging loose and luxurious. She'd chosen one of the prettiest of the tunics he'd bought her. It was simple, but accentuated her elegant beauty well. The white cloth shimmered. Donatus wanted to hold her, to somehow touch the life emanating from her, but held himself aloof. Hurt still knotted within him. He couldn't forget. He'd seen what he'd seen and he'd heard what he'd heard.

Lucan arrived just as Lelia had finished helping Donatus shave. He saw her eyes widen in surprise, and imagined he also saw pleasure within them, too. Pain wrenched his gut, and for just a moment he almost hated her. *How could you do this to me, Lelia, my love…?*

Outwardly, he remained calm. "Please leave us," he said to her. "Lucan and I have something to discuss."

She looked startled and disturbed. Her eyes flicked toward Lucan with barely concealed concern before she nodded silently and moved gracefully out the door.

"Sit down," Donatus said, gesturing toward a chair.

Lucan sat.

Donatus walked to the window and looked out at the early-morning haze over the fields. It was summer now. The workers were in the grain fields, harvesting the heavy heads of wheat that would see them all through the coming months. Ordinarily the sight would have made him proud. Now it just made him hurt.

He turned away to where Lucan waited, a slight frown on his otherwise perfect features. "I understand why you want Lelia," Donatus began, with what he hoped was a steady voice. "I understand the lure of the forbidden. I also understand the uncommon lust she can arouse in a man. But what I don't understand is how you could so easily forget your promise to me and make love to her. You said you would not."

Lucan's face went ashen. "No, Donatus!" he said. "Where did you get such an idea?"

Donatus frowned. "I've seen you together. I saw you in the doorway of the bath, talking low and intimately together. I didn't have to hear the words to know what you said." His eyes met Lucan's. "I'm a man, too. I know the language of the body, how a man hunts. I know what I saw between you."

Lucan shook his head. "No, Donatus."

Donatus held up a hand. "I also know you took my wife to bed on the night I was injured. I was drugged, but the belladonna didn't induce an easy rest. I heard you, Lucan. *'Donatus will never know. Come, let me take you to bed.'* I opened my eyes just long enough to see her put her hand into yours and you pull her away."

Lucan jumped up from the chair. "No," he said firmly, his hands clenching. "I did not make love to your wife. She was exhausted—had fallen asleep on the floor at your feet. I was only leading her to her rest. You can't think so little of me that you'd believe—!"

Donatus growled. "Tell the truth, damn you. I can bear it. I can forgive you. I can forgive her. I can take her away so temptation won't weaken you. Or I can let her go, even walk away myself… Whatever I have to do to resolve this situation for us all. But first I have to know the truth. I have to know how long you've been sleeping with Lelia. I need to know if…" Donatus swallowed hard, hearing his pain rush out with the words. "I need to know if the child she's carrying is my issue or yours."

Lucan paled. "No, oh no."

Donatus almost winced. Lucan hadn't known.

Lucan stared out of the window, hands clenching and unclenching, so agitated that he bounced hard on the balls of his feet. He turned back. "Lelia is with child? You're sure?"

Donatus shrugged. "She hasn't told me yet. But yes, I'm fairly sure." He met Lucan's gold-green gaze. "I need the truth. I owe my father an heir, Lucan. A *legitimate* heir."

Donatus saw a parade of emotions tramp across Lucan's face. Shock, dismay, fear…anger. It hardened on his friend's golden features and rasped in his voice. "Don't do this, Donatus. Think whatever you want of me. There's enough wickedness in my past that I can understand your doubts about me. But don't do this to Lelia."

Donatus made a sound of disgust. "I've done nothing to Lelia except love her. Trust her. But she—"

"Trust her?" Lucan growled. "You don't trust her. You love her so much that you've gone mad with it, but you don't trust her. You've *never* trusted her. And you don't even see it."

Donatus felt his eyes narrow, felt anger coil like a serpent within him.

Lucan wasn't finished. "Lelia's a fine, decent woman and she doesn't deserve what you're doing to her—what you've already done!"

"Lucan, I warn you—"

"You're so afraid of loving her that you're making a fool of yourself!" Lucan said. "You've always been afraid. That's why you left her before, pregnant and alone, and so hungry she had to beg for food. It's why you spent two lonely years trying to kill yourself in battle because you—!"

Donatus's head had jerked around. "*What* did you say?"

Lucan halted. He didn't answer.

Donatus stepped closer. His eyes locked upon Lucan's face. He read Lucan's mind, saw him backtracking through the words. He knew the moment his friend realized what he'd said, saw the horror overcome his face. "What did you say?" Donatus repeated.

"Nothing," Lucan said quietly. "Only that you do Lelia a disservice."

Donatus moved to him, taking the front of Lucan's tunic into a hard, unrelenting grip. "No. Not that. Tell me the truth, Lucan, and tell it to me now."

Lucan looked down at Donatus's fist, gripping his clothing. His eyes narrowed. "Take your hands off me, Donatus. I have not injured you. I have not made love to your wife. You wrong me."

Donatus's jaw hardened. "Lelia was *pregnant?* When I left her before, she was *pregnant?*"

Lucan didn't answer. He didn't have to. Donatus saw the answer flare in his eyes. It hit Donatus like a blow to his vitals.

He released Lucan's tunic and stepped backward, shaking his head to clear the sudden pain. Only the pain wasn't in his head. It was in his heart.

"She didn't tell me," Donatus whispered. "She never told me. I didn't know."

Lucan didn't answer.

"I didn't know, Lucan. I would have stayed. You know I would've stayed."

Lucan nodded.

Donatus looked up. "What happened to the child?"

It was bad. It had to be bad. Lucan would no longer meet his eyes.

"Lelia bore your son," Lucan said finally. "The child was healthy. When the babe was four months old, Lelia awoke to find he'd been stolen by the woman who'd taken her in and offered her kindness in her distress. For a long time now she's searched for them. There's been no success."

Lucan's gaze returned, heavy with sorrow and compassion. "I'm sorry I betrayed her secret. I tried to get her to tell you herself. Perhaps in time she would have. Unfortunately, you're not the only one who's afraid to trust."

He raised a hand to Donatus's shoulder. "I admire Lelia, but I swear I've never touched her. And, God help me, I never will. Believe me or don't. Whichever you will."

Donatus barely noticed when Lucan stepped around him to the door. He could only stand, numb with pain, thinking that Lelia hadn't told him. She hadn't said a word.

Chapter Seventeen

Lelia was on her way to help Didia with the spinning, though it was a task she usually despised. The morning was pleasantly warm, with dappled sunshine through leaves stirring in a slight breeze, fragranced by the scent of summer and newly mown hay. Lelia found her spirits revived. She refused to bow down to fear. She refused to live in shadow when she had so much for which to be thankful.

Donatus was alive and regaining his strength. And soon, perhaps tonight when they lay in bed whispering sweet love words, she'd tell him the truth. It was time. She realized how precious were the moments of mortal life. Nothing should be left unsaid, no opportunity to cherish left unfulfilled.

Surprisingly, her decision to tell Donatus the truth had lifted the burden of secrecy from her shoulders, and she almost anticipated the freedom that would come into the relationship once he knew all. From now on they'd work together to find their lost child, and to rear the one resting within her womb.

That thought brought a bubble of joy. She wanted to hug herself and twirl, thinking of Donatus and the family they'd have. He'd be a good father. She imagined him walking these fields with their strong sons, teaching their daughters to ride horses and swim in the river.

Lelia felt her heart warm at those beautiful images. She trusted Donatus so much now. He'd become lover and protector and friend. Their hands had touched, their eyes had touched, their bodies had touched. More important to Lelia, their souls had touched. Come what may, murder or the trials of an evil world, they'd face them together. Beginning tonight.

Didia opened the door, took one look at Lelia's happy expression and smiled, pulling her into the room with a pleased expression. "Ah, my lady," she said. "It's plain that having your man on his feet again has brought you joy."

Lelia nodded, smiling at the crinkling face of the older woman. "He's doing much better, Didia, thanks to you."

Didia beamed. "He's far too stubborn to be kept down long. He wants to be up and going, not flat on his back."

"I know." Lelia nodded. "But I'm glad for it. I was afraid I'd lose him, Didia."

"It was a frightfully close call, that, and we're all mighty pleased you'll not be a widow anytime soon. That would be too great a sadness to bear, what with the babe coming and all."

Lelia's head jerked up. Her face grew hot. "The babe? Oh, Didia. How did you know?"

Didia laughed and waved her hand in a gesture of dismissal. "I've raised a few little ones of my own, mistress. I can tell. There's a look that comes into a woman's eyes when she's with child, a softness that gentles her features." She sighed with happiness. "It's a beautiful thing to carry the seed of the man you love. To give life to a soul that will walk the earth for long years to come. A beautiful, precious thing." She squeezed Lelia's hand. "Does Donatus know yet?"

Lelia shook her head. "Not yet. Tonight, Didia. I plan to tell him tonight."

Didia raised one eyebrow. "Well, then. We have work to do."

"Work? Well, of course. I came to help with the spinning."

Didia laughed again, her gray eyes glinting mischievously. "No, not spinning. Not that. Not when such sweet news awaits. We'll prepare a meal—a special meal for a special evening. We'll gather flowers and hang the bedlinens in the sun to smell fresh. We'll choose your most beautiful tunic, soften your skin with fragrant oil and dress your hair." Didia's eyes gleamed. "Oh, mistress. We'll give Donatus a night to remember, because tonight will forever change his world. He's to be a father. The woman he loves carries his child. Ah, such a moment. I only wish I could see his face when he hears. He'll be so pleased."

Lelia felt her heart melt, imagining the tender scene. Tears misted her eyes. "Yes," she said, squeezing Didia's hand. "Donatus will be pleased."

Summer days were long. *Too* long when one was anxious to make a gift of a precious secret. Donatus was gone most of the afternoon. He'd ridden out with Amandio to check on the grain harvest. Lelia hoped he'd not wearied himself to exhaustion. It wouldn't do if, after all the effort she and Didia had made, he was too tired to enjoy the evening, or too distracted to hear her good news.

By the time she heard him enter the house she was almost beside herself with nerves. When he entered the candlelit bedroom and halted, looking around in confusion at the preparations they'd made, she waited with an unusual lack of poise, breath stilled in her chest until it hurt, waiting for his comment.

"What's all this?" Donatus asked, making a small gesture with his hand.

"A celebration," she answered, marveling at how low and sensual her voice sounded. He couldn't have missed the dark, vibrant texture of it, but he frowned.

"A celebration," he repeated. Lelia was discouraged to hear that he didn't sound pleased. He sounded tired.

Maybe food would help. She moved to the table and began to set out the dishes, telling him as she went what had been prepared. He lifted one eyebrow at the rare and unusual dishes—not common farm fare. Still he seemed to hesitate before he sat. She sat down, too, and tried to eat, telling herself the babe wanted nourishment even if she did not. But her nerves grew even more frazzled when she noticed that Donatus ate very little, and that her efforts at conversation were met with curt, taciturn responses.

So the food hadn't helped. Lelia tried another tactic. "You're tired, aren't you?" she asked, drawing near enough to stroke his chest with a gentle fingertip. "Come lie down, and I'll massage your back. I'll be careful with your shoulder, I promise."

Donatus's eyes narrowed. "What are you trying to do, Lelia?" he asked. "Just what are you trying to prove? Are you merely attempting to placate your guilty heart with this insincere show of love?"

The tone bit into her, even if the words took a minute to register. "What do you mean? I...I only want to love you, Donatus. You came so close to dying, and I—"

He cut off her words with a snort of disgust. "Such tender sentiment. Save it, Lelia. I'm not sure I believe it."

Lelia gasped. Her hand flew to her bosom as if she could hold her cracking heart together. "You don't believe me? What are you saying, Donatus? You know I love you. I haven't held anything from you. Not my heart, not my body, not my very soul. You have it all. I love you."

"You love me, Lelia?" Donatus stepped forward and grasped her chin in a grip so firm it almost bruised her. His eyes bored into hers. They were cold. "Then why did you share your secrets with Lucan and not with me?"

Lelia's heart clutched. *Secrets?* Her mind began to spiral. The only secret Lucan knew was... Suddenly she felt nauseous. She pushed at the arm which held her, needing to free herself from the harsh touch, from the eyes that burned, from the knowledge that Donatus somehow knew the truth, and that it hadn't come from her.

"Let me go," she said with a panicked voice. "I...I think I'm going to be sick."

He let her go at once, seeing her distress. He found a basin and brought it to her, standing quietly beside her as she lost her meal in it.

He moved away and back again, now wiping her face with a cool, wet towel. He drew her to the bed and pushed her gently down onto the sheets.

"I'm sorry," she whispered, still feeling weak. "I didn't expect that."

"You should have. It's not uncommon when one is carrying a child."

Lelia gulped, fighting the queasiness that was still with her. "You know?"

"Yes," Donatus said quietly. "I know."

Lelia glanced up and found his expression far too grim. "You are not pleased?"

Donatus didn't answer for a long moment. "I don't know yet."

Lelia breathed in deeply, deciding that it helped her feel better. "I want you to be pleased, Donatus. You *did* want an heir, and I may be carrying—"

"No, Lelia. This child is not my heir, is he?" The words

were harsh. Lelia turned to him. His face held deep anguish. *Donatus knew.*

"No," she whispered. She looked down, afraid to let him see the guilt in her eyes. "We have a son. But I guess you must know this already." She raised a hand in unspoken supplication. "Donatus, please understand. I wanted to tell you. I planned to tell you."

"*When,* Lelia? When the time was right? And when would that have been?"

"I don't know. Only that I didn't want your pity, or to think you stayed with me just because of—"

He made a growl of impatience. "I'm a man, Lelia, not a damned beast. Of *course* I would have stayed! What better reason could a man have for staying? But you never gave me that chance, did you?" He drew in a sharp, exasperated breath. "You toyed with my life. You took my son away from me."

"No!" she whispered. "You left *me,* Donatus."

He frowned. "I would have stayed. I didn't know."

Lelia fought tears. Long moments passed, the tension like taut cords between them. "I'm sorry," she finally said. "I should have told you, I know that now. Please forgive me. Forgive me."

"Forgive you?" He turned away, one hand raking through his hair. "And shall I also forgive you for the child you carry within your womb now, Lelia?"

She looked up, startled. "I don't understand."

He laughed, a bitter sound. "Oh, surely you do. Or will you pretend you haven't made love to Lucan? Will you pretend he didn't ask to bed you just two nights ago? I heard him, Lelia. 'Donatus will never know. Come, let me take you to bed.' Deny it. I dare you to."

Lelia gasped. This nightmare couldn't be happening. This evening she'd meant to be so beautiful just kept getting worse. And now he thought… He thought…

Donatus towered over her. "The child in your womb. Is it my babe or Lucan's?"

Fury hit Lelia like a gale, sudden and unabated. Without thinking, without reasoning the consequences, she pushed herself off the bed and toward him. The slap she gave him crackled like a drover's whip, and made her hand ache from the brutal force of it.

Donatus took the blow, his eyes narrowing. The look within them made Lelia instinctively crouch into battle position. Donatus's eyes raked her and he laughed, the sound bitter. "No, Lelia. I have enough respect for the child you carry not to lay a hand on you in anger, no matter who the babe's father might be."

Lelia launched herself at him. "You filthy bastard! How dare you accuse me of such?"

He caught her fists as they came up to pummel him. "Stop it," he said. "Stop this. For the sake of your child, show some good sense."

He pushed her back onto the bed and came to stand over her, arms crossed over his chest. He looked angry, imposing. As hard as granite and almost as cold.

"Tell me the truth," he demanded. "Do you love Lucan more than me? Do you carry his child, Lelia?"

Lelia wanted to rage at him. She wanted to rake her nails down his arrogant, angry face and hurt him as badly as he'd hurt her.

She bit out the words, watching them pelt him like stones. "And what would you do if I told you that, yes, I love Lucan? What if this child were his seed and not yours? What would you do, Donatus? Tell me—what would you do?"

He didn't answer her immediately. When he did, the words were so devoid of feeling that she grew frightened. "I would leave you, Lelia. Leave you to your lover, and damn your faithless heart."

Chapter Eighteen

The next afternoon, Lelia stared down at the folded piece of parchment in her hand—afraid to open it, afraid to break the seal, barely able to read the neat handwriting on the outside for the tears that misted in her eyes. She couldn't hold back the ragged sob, though she tried to contain it with the back of her hand against her lips.

Didia moved closer, touching her shoulder in a gentle gesture of reassurance. When the slight touch loosed more tears, she drew the younger woman into her embrace.

Thankfully, Didia didn't offer meaningless words of comfort. She didn't try to tell Lelia that all would be well. She knew the truth, too—that something terrible had happened, and that Donatus had gone. Ridden out without a goodbye, leaving Lelia pregnant and alone.

Again. It had happened again. Lelia could hardly believe it. She could hardly feel the hurt, it went so deep. She wanted to rage against Donatus, to curse his blindness and stupidity, to raise a fist toward heaven and call down wrath upon him. But most of all she wanted to run into his arms and kiss him senseless, to waken again that precious thing they'd begun. She wanted to understand. *Why?*

Lucan came to her in late afternoon, his face clouding with compassion when he saw her eyes swollen and red-rimmed. He'd received a letter from Donatus, too. His said virtually the same thing as hers—that Donatus cherished the love he bore each of them too much to stand in their way, and so was going back to Rome to find his missing son. Papers of divorce would follow within the month. He wished them well, charged Lucan with Lelia's protection, and promised to gift them with the villa when they wed.

Lucan couldn't take away Lelia's grief, but at least he could help her understand. He reminded her of all that had happened between Donatus's father and mother. Donatus had been only a child when his mother had betrayed both father and son, so he hadn't understood the blade that had sliced his heart, or the scar he bore still. His mistrust of women and his jealousy were the result of that deep wounding. The more Donatus loved, the more frightened he became. The more frightened he became, the more his imagination saw what had never been there to see.

"So what am I to do?" she asked.

Lucan looked at her with conviction. "Fight for him, Lelia. Don't let him do this to himself."

Fight for him. Fight for him. The words resounded like a drumbeat through her head over the next two days as she packed her things into the *raeda.* She left nothing behind. Not even so little a something as a hairpin. She'd give Donatus no reason to send her back. No reason at all.

Dead.

He was dead, he had to be. No other explanation existed for the way he felt. Donatus shuddered, thinking of how he'd gone through the last two days without feeling anything at all. He'd gone to the Senate and done his work there. He'd gone to the baths, strangely silent while the conversation of other men circled around him. He'd returned home to the company of Faustina and Druscilla, hating himself for the question in their eyes and the concern on their faces. Damn, he hated himself. What was *wrong* with him that he couldn't have made Lelia love him? What was wrong with him that he loved her still?

Twice he'd gone to submit the documents of divorce. Twice he'd walked away, fighting the hard knot in his chest, unable to do what was needed. *Give it time,* he thought. Another few days and maybe the pain would give way to anger, or hate. It would be easier then. Right now he loved her. Sweet mercy, how he loved her.

He'd told Lucan he'd never share her. But that had been before he knew Lelia's heart. Once he'd heard from her own lips that she preferred Lucan, the choice had been clear. He had to let her go. He loved her too much to keep her chained in a marriage she didn't want, had never wanted.

But how could he endure the loneliness? Everywhere he went he saw Lelia's face, the glistening fall and sway of her dark hair. At odd moments he smelled her fragrance, felt her presence. At night he dreamed of her. He'd awaken with his arms seeking her, his manhood throbbing, and she wasn't there. She'd never be there again.

He understood now what his father had once felt. Little comfort, but that thought led him to another, and Donatus realized where his focus must now lie. Not with Lelia. Not with her. Not ever again. But they'd made a child together, and he had to find that child.

He'd hired the best investigators in all of Rome and tried to ignore their frowns when he'd told them what little he knew. When they had suggested he ask Lelia for more information, he'd felt his lips compress, his face blanch. No, he wouldn't. What they had must be enough. He couldn't face

Lelia. Not yet. He'd want to touch her, to fall at her feet and beg her to love him again. He'd make an utter fool of himself.

So he'd endured the slight censure of the men whose skill he'd traded for gold. Maybe the gods would be kind, with or without Lelia's help. Donatus prayed it might be so. He needed his son. A son would keep him from being alone.

He arrived home, he ate, he walked to the terrace and stood in the red-gold glow of a splendid summer sunset. Still his mind did not quiet. Still he did not find peace. He'd been staring into the distance when he awoke to Faustina's voice behind him, and realized with a start that darkness had fallen and he still hadn't moved.

"Donatus, there are soldiers! Here, in our home! You must come!" Faustina came toward him quickly, with an urgency in her face that he couldn't ignore.

"Soldiers?"

"Yes, and not just any soldiers. Praetorian Guard. They have a warrant to search."

"Search here? Search for what?"

Faustina's face contorted with fear. "For Lucan. They're looking for Lucan. Somebody's told the Emperor about the Christian meetings and that Lucan leads them. They've come to arrest him, Donatus. It won't matter that he isn't here. Now that they know, they'll search until they find him. He's not safe at all. Not anywhere. And if they arrest him, Lucan won't lie. He'll never deny the truth, and they'll kill him! Oh, Donatus! What do we do?"

Donatus was already moving forward. "Calm yourself, Faustina. I'll go find out what's going on. Surely there's a way out of this mess."

Faustina followed him. "I trust you, Donatus. You're so much like your father. You always know the best thing to do."

* * *

"He did *what?*" Lucan paled, and stumbled backward into a chair. He slumped forward, holding his head in his hands. "Tell me he did *not.*"

Faustina wiped at the tear that slid down her cheek. "He did, Lucan. Donatus told the commander of the guard that he was *you.* They locked him in irons and took him away. I tried to protest, but he warned me away with a look so fierce I knew it was what he wanted. I don't understand, but it *must* have been what he wanted."

Lucan couldn't hold back the shudder. "It was." He drew in a deep breath. "I've got to somehow get him out of this, and when I do I swear I'm going to beat some sense into that dense skull."

"Whatever is he thinking?" Faustina asked. "Why would he do something so stupid?"

Lucan shook his head. "Why? Because Donatus is a man in love."

Faustina hardly noticed that Lucan stood and walked away with purpose in his step. He left her standing in deep confusion, frowning at the cryptic statement that, though it was supposed to explain everything, made absolutely no sense at all.

No time. There'd been no time to consider the situation, Donatus thought. Only time enough to make the decision that his heart demanded. Only time enough to realize that he loved Lelia and he loved Lucan, and that if they were ever to have their chance at happiness, then he, Donatus, would have to take drastic action, and quickly.

He looked down at the leg irons, at the red places they'd chafed around his ankles. The irony was that now there'd be plenty of time to consider what a fool he'd been.

Or at least there'd be plenty of time until the gladiatorial games began. He'd waived his—Lucan's—rights as a Roman citizen, waived the right to a hearing and a trial, so punishment would come quickly, with a minimum of publicity. To the world he was just another seditious criminal. They might crucify him, but more likely he'd die in the Amphitheater. He'd heard in the Senate that Trajan planned to celebrate victory over the Dacians with games for the people—lots and lots of games, and soon. The combatants would have to come from somewhere. The jails were full of them.

The irony of that struck him hard. He'd been part of that victory over the Dacians. His own *ala* had hunted Decebalus for weeks across the Carpathian wilderness. It was only because of his men's skill and perseverance that the renegade king had finally been cornered. Decebalus had managed to cheat the Romans of his death, committing suicide before they found him, but Donatus himself had been the one to sever the dead enemy's head for Emperor Trajan. He'd been rewarded—both he and his men.

Now he would die in the games that celebrated that victory. There wasn't a thing he could do about that. Unless he won, of course. Unless the gods granted him favor for this thing he did to protect Lucan and to give Lelia her chance at happiness. Maybe it would be his last gift to her.

Time would tell. Donatus looked at the walls around him, at the cold stone and the iron bars, and sighed out his despair, hoping that time was on his side.

Five days later, Lelia stood with Brocchus in the *lanista*'s private rooms. "I know it's an unusual request," she said quietly. "But it's the only choice I have."

Brocchus frowned, his eyes dark with concern beneath the

lowering of bushy eyebrows. "He means so much to you, then, this man who bought you?"

Lelia drew in a deep breath, thinking that one simple word couldn't *begin* to express what she felt. "Yes," she said. "I love him."

Brocchus turned away toward the window and the sight of his gladiators sweating in the sun. He stroked his chin with a callused hand, lost in thought. "All right," he said at last. "I don't know why I'm agreeing to this, Leda, and I swear by all the gods that if things don't go well—"

Leda the Gladiatrix rushed to embrace him. "Thank you. Thank you, Brocchus. I swear it *will* go well, and when it does—" she squeezed him again "—I'll give you all the gold this room can hold. Maybe more."

The big man flushed and reached up to caress her cheek. "I don't need gold, Leda. I just need for you to fight like I trained you. Fight well, and *live*."

"You know, when I told you to fight for Donatus, I didn't mean it quite so literally," Lucan said in a worried voice. "And I can't believe I'm letting you do this."

He shuddered as he looked around at their surroundings. They were underneath the Great Amphitheater in a narrow passageway—the one that led from the gladiator barracks to the huge gate where the fighting men entered amid pomp and ceremony.

Lelia could tell the close darkness made Lucan's skin crawl. He kept shuddering as they traveled through the shadowy labyrinth of underground chambers, animal cages, hydraulic lifts and winches, and water drainage tunnels. It was a dark world, a world lit by flickering oil. A world that reverberated with the roar of lions and the shouts of men. A world that smelled of dampness, musty earth, men's sweat and animal feces. A world that Lelia knew.

"We've been over this already," she whispered. "There's no other way. If you can't bear the thought, then go ahead and leave me now. I'll get somebody else to help me open the door."

"Donatus will never forgive me if something goes wrong. You know he won't."

Lelia stopped and waited for him to look at her. She bore into him with the most intense gaze she could muster in the semi-darkness. "Donatus knows me well enough to know I *chose* this. No one but I. He'll never blame you."

Lucan grunted—a sound of disagreement. Lelia ignored it, moving forward again until they were within sight of the great gate. "There it is," she whispered. "Brocchus should be here soon. If you're leaving, now's the time. Go back the way we came. And Lucan…" She waited for their eyes to meet. "Thank you for everything. I'll never forget it as long as I live."

"Just make sure you live a long, long time."

Lelia turned, her armor making a dull sound as it clanked against the sword at her side. "Where is Brocchus?" she demanded. "He said he'd be here."

At just that moment they heard the roar. To Lelia, the sound was familiar—only too familiar. She knew that roar, the roar of the excited crowd as two gladiators began their bloody business. "No!" she muttered with a frown. "We're too late, Lucan. Brocchus is not here because he's…" she made a sharp gesture with her hand "…out *there!*"

"But that means Donatus is, too."

"The game must've begun early. Donatus is already fighting." They heard the crowd roar again, and Lelia's heart clutched hard. She knew well that most gladiatorial bouts lasted only minutes. She had little time. She ran to the winch. "Help me, Lucan. Help me raise the gate."

Lucan was at her side in a moment, their hands sliding together against the wooden wheel that raised the chains. She heard the chains rattle as they tightened, then creak as the gate began to go up. They heard another roar from the crowd—a roar of disapproval. She looked backward toward the gate. "Hold it there, Lucan, just hold it. I can slide underneath it now."

She let go of the winch, seeing Lucan's muscles tighten as he struggled to hold the heavy door alone. She hesitated just a moment. "Lucan, before I go—if anything happens to me, take care of Severina."

Lucan nodded, unable to answer. Lelia pivoted sharply on one heel and flew to the gate, threw herself down onto the sand and pushed herself beneath it, vaulting to her feet on the other side. She looked back only when the gate fell into place behind her. Her heart hammered. There was no way out from here.

Brocchus startled her when he caught her arm. His voice was harsh and raspy. He looked nervous. "Get out there now, if you want to fight. And remember, I've got to make it look like I knew nothing about this."

"I know," she said, already trotting away. At least Brocchus gave her a decent head start before he came after her, waving his arms and looking for all the world as if he was angry she'd barged into this fight unexpectedly.

The crowd recognized her immediately. She'd worn the signature yellow plume in her helmet. As she trotted forward they responded. "Leda! Lee-dah! Lee-dah!" She should have been pleased, but at that moment all she could think about was Donatus.

She hurried toward the two men on the sand, assessing the situation through the eye-slits of her helmet, her breath ringing against the metal as she neared them. Thank the gods, Donatus was easily recognizable. He'd be the one beneath the armor. The *retiarius* he fought wore no helmet.

Lelia knew a brief moment of fear. Only twice before had she sparred with a *retiarius*. She had little experience against the trident and the net. But she knew Hermes well. They'd shared many a joke together over the food tables. She took off her helmet, letting her braid swing free so Hermes would know his opponent. Maybe if the fight didn't go well for her he'd be willing to grant her *missus* at the end.

She watched the men circle one another as she neared, her sharply trained eyes noting immediately that Hermes was without both his net and his trident. She felt a surge of pleasure at that. It meant Donatus had fought well, that so far he'd outwitted his opponent.

She reached his side. Brocchus came up behind them, red from pursuit and making a good show of his anger. He held up his arms as a sign for the fighters to pause. Donatus turned. She wished she could see his face and know what he was thinking, but the helmet hid him from her. Hermes stared— first at her, then at Donatus, then at them both. Confusion was all over his face.

"Why are you here?" Donatus asked. The question almost made her angry. She was here for *him*. Did he not know that? Did he not understand how much she loved him?

She put aside the momentary flash of anger. She had to do what she'd come to do. But she knew Donatus would never allow it if he knew. She breathed in deeply, steeling herself for the task. "Take off your helmet, Donatus," she said.

She waited, then saw his helmet turn toward Hermes, who cheated by sidling toward the net. Donatus took a step away, as if he wanted to resume combat. "Get out of here. Let me fight," he said. "I will kill him."

He pushed her aside in a protective gesture and raised his sword. But Lelia was determined. She wouldn't be put aside so easily—not when he needed her.

She stepped forward and put her hand over his on the hilt. She had to make him see. She had to make him understand, in case these were the last words she ever said to him. "Trust me, Donatus," she said, wishing she could say more, wishing she could condense all she felt into pure elixir and pour it into the three words. "Take off your helmet."

He shook his head roughly. She could sense his anger. He turned toward Hermes again and raised his sword, pointing it at the *retiarius*. Hermes stopped moving toward the net, watching Donatus warily.

Brocchus moved toward her now, as if he would lead her away. She'd run out of time. But, sweet mercy, how could she do what she had to do? *Donatus, forgive me, my love.*

"Please, Donatus. Just for a moment. Only for a moment. Take off your helmet."

Donatus didn't move. Brocchus was nearly upon her now. "The Emperor," she murmured. "The Emperor must see your face. Trust me." It was the only thing she could think of to say. Donatus had to remove his helmet and look away. She hoped she sounded authoritative enough, as if she had some plan in mind.

"Sweet mercy," Donatus groaned softly. "If I die, then I die for you."

"There's no need to die, Donatus. Remove your helmet and face the Emperor."

He hesitated only a moment, then lowered the shield and reached up with his left hand, unfastening the helmet's leather strap and drawing it off. He turned to face the Emperor.

Lelia drew in a deep breath, ignoring the pain that twisted her heart. She raised her sword, turning it, gripping the heavy weight of the hilt. She clenched her lip hard between her teeth, drew sharply back and then forward— and drove the blunt weight of the butt hard into the back of Donatus's skull.

She flinched at the crack, at his pained grunt, at the roar of the crowd as he crumpled. "Lee-dah! Lee-dah! Lee-dah!"

Brocchus looked relieved. He gestured Lelia and Hermes to the other side of the ring, then called for a slave to heave Donatus's prone body from the sand. The crowd rumbled in excitement, thinking the change of gladiators was a dramatic spectacle prepared for their entertainment.

Lelia allowed herself only one brief moment of satisfaction. Her plan had worked. She'd fight Hermes. Donatus would be taken to a physician. Brocchus's intervention would not be punished. It had worked.

Lelia allowed herself only the one moment.

Then Leda the Gladiatrix drew on her helmet, with its bright yellow plume, raised her sword, squared her shoulders and assumed combat position. It was time to fight.

Chapter Nineteen

Donatus awoke lying on a table in a small room, head pounding, blinking at the harsh sunlight which entered through a small window high in the stone wall. He tried to raise a hand to shield himself from the glare.

"Close the shutters, Tasius," he heard a male voice say. "He's coming around."

Donatus tried to sit up, but a stronger hand pushed him down again. He gave in, his head throbbing too violently to argue. *What had happened? Where was he?*

He closed his eyes and thought backward. The arena. Fighting a *retiarius*. Lelia… *Donatus, take off your helmet. Just for a moment. Trust me.*

He groaned with sick realization. It had been Lelia. It must have been her. But that would mean…! He struggled to sit up again.

"No," said the physician at his side. "You must rest."

Donatus shook his head, then wished he hadn't, it hurt so badly. "I've got to get out there. I've got to fight. You don't understand… Lelia…!" He knew he babbled, that he made little sense.

The physician smiled. "You're not going anywhere. You don't have to. Rest well. Your fight's over. The contest has been decided."

Donatus knew the most gut-wrenching fear of his life in that moment. He was afraid to ask, afraid the answer would end it all—his love, his life, his dreams. *Oh, Lelia! What did you do?*

"Who won?" he finally managed to choke out.

"I don't know," the man answered. "I'm sorry. I'll send Tasius to ask, if you wish."

Donatus drew in a deep breath. The ache in his head increased. "Send him," he said quietly. "I must know."

The crowd was in a flurry of confusion, the sound an indistinct rumble ending on a question. Lelia knew what they felt, because she felt it, too. The uneasy cartwheeling sensation of her stomach as she mounted the steps to the *pulvinar* made her frightened. She hoped she wouldn't vomit—not here, not now. She drew in some deep breaths and tried to ignore the queasiness.

The Emperor had called a halt to her combat. Even as she'd stood, muscles taut, poised upon the balls of her feet to launch herself in her first attack on Hermes, the trumpet had sounded. She'd looked up to see Emperor Trajan's gaze fixed upon her. And then he'd called for her to come.

When Lelia finally reached the top of the stairs, she heard the trumpet sound again. The big gate at the far end opened and a tiger was released onto the sand. The crowd gave a low rumble of pleasure. She heard another gate open, and the crowd cheered. Another combat had begun. So easily had she and Donatus been forgotten.

But not by Emperor Trajan. She moved forward to him, sweeping down before him, ignoring the sickness that the tilting motion made within her. She breathed in deeply. *Not here. Not now. Oh, please!*

Trajan's face reassured her. He seemed curious, not angry, and she hoped she was right. Trajan wasn't known for being harsh. Instead, this former military commander had a reputation for fairness and firmness. It was rumored that he knew his soldiers by name and took a personal interest in their lives.

He gestured for her to sit beside him. Lelia did so, grateful for the chance to steady her somersaulting stomach.

"I'm almost sorry to have halted your contest," Trajan began, leaning toward her. "I've little doubt it would've been the highlight of my afternoon."

Lelia glanced up into his face, surprised by the pleasant expression and slightly veiled amusement she saw there. "Thank you, my lord Emperor," she said, turning her eyes downward. "And yet I'm thankful for the reprieve."

"No doubt." He chuckled. "You are Leda the Gladiatrix. I've seen you fight before."

"Yes, my lord. You were generous with your gold."

"I remember. Then, as now, you displayed great courage. I admire courage. It's not as common these days as it used to be." He turned his attention briefly to the fight below, before turning back to her again. "Now, tell me how it happened that one of my best cavalry officers, now a senator of Rome, stood out there today to die a criminal's death? And why did you strike Flavius Donatus down and take his place?"

"It's a long story, my lord. I cannot explain in few words."

Trajan lifted an eyebrow. "I have time. All afternoon if need be. Start at the beginning. Tell the tale, and tell it all."

Lelia told him everything, beginning with the secret love affair she shouldn't have had, and all that had resulted from it. About her missing child, her marriage to Donatus, the attempts on her life, and finally, her decision to save her husband. She was careful, however, to protect Lucan, making it seem that Donatus's arrest as a Christian had been a mistake. It wouldn't do for Trajan's soldiers to come after Lucan—at least not before he'd left to go to Christian friends at Ephesus.

Trajan was mostly silent as she talked, asking only a few questions to clarify confusing points. When she'd finished, he sat back in his chair, stroking his chin.

"A startling tale," he murmured. "I wonder how Flavius Donatus found time in all his…uhm…*activities* to help me fight a war and pursue Decebalus." He turned an amused expression toward Lelia. "Though I understand why his attention was diverted. You're a lovely woman, and you possess the attributes of strength and courage which are bound to capture any Roman legionaire's heart."

Lelia flushed at the compliment.

"I'll help you," Trajan said. "I don't take it lightly that a senator's son and heir has been stolen from him, or that someone is trying to murder his wife. This grieves me. I'd like to see these matters set right."

Lelia bowed her head. "Your help would be appreciated, my lord. I'm honored by your offer."

"There might be more that I can do—"

Lelia interrupted, no longer able to ignore her rolling insides. She gulped air, her hand at her throat. "My lord, there is one thing. Could you call for a basin? I think I'm going to be sick."

Trajan wasted no time. Lelia met the slave halfway, turning her back away from the Emperor's entourage as she let her body have its way. She apologized as she handed back the bowl, wiping her mouth and face with a towel.

She went back to her chair, feeling better, but thoroughly embarrassed that the Emperor had witnessed her weakness.

He waved away her distress. "Nerves. Nerves will do that to a person—especially in a moment of great distress like you've had today—"

Trajan halted, one eyebrow lifting as he noted the changing expressions of her face. "But, ah…it isn't nerves, is it?" He laughed softly, looking at her in near disbelief. He shook his head. "Flavius Donatus, you're a lucky man," he said. "A wife who'll fight to the death for you even while she carries your child!"

He smiled at Lelia. "Such love should be rewarded. You and Donatus will be my guests tonight at the palace. I'll have servants take you there now, so you can bathe and be refreshed. Later we'll dine together and decide how a murderer can be caught and your child returned to you."

Lelia nodded, thankful that her hopeful words to Brocchus and Lucan had proved prophetic. This day had turned out well. Very well indeed.

Donatus was being escorted through the streets by soldiers of the Praetorian Guard. They hadn't put him into chains, but that was small relief. Their taciturn manner and tight expressions made him nervous. He didn't even know where they were taking him.

Neither had he been able to discover what had happened to Lelia. The slave sent out to discover the result of her battle hadn't returned before the soldiers arrived. *Ah, Lelia.* Regret tore at him.

The soldiers led him away, probably to his death. Even if Lelia lived, he'd never be able to tell her how sorry he was. That he loved her, would always love her, no matter that she'd chosen Lucan.

His thoughts were of her as he trudged silently along. He came out of them with surprise when they reached their destination. "Trajan's palace?" he said, turning to the guard nearest him. "What does the Emperor want with me?"

The guard glanced at him and then looked forward again. "We don't know—only that we were to bring you to the palace."

Donatus nodded, afraid to let hope supplant his fear. He was certain Trajan had recognized his face. And if he had…

The soldiers took him first to the bath, and instructed him to use it. For some time they waited outside with shifting stances while he steamed and washed and rinsed. Slaves oiled and scraped his skin, trimmed his hair, shaved the stubble from his chin. A new tunic was brought. To his surprise, it was ornamented with the crimson stripe of senatorial rank. Donatus's hopes rose higher. He was certain now that Trajan knew him. But if he did, then he'd want to know all. Donatus would appear before the Emperor and he'd better have answers. That thought made him wary, thinking of Lucan and of Lelia. How could he explain without endangering their happiness, even their very lives?

At least he was clean and decently dressed. That alone made him feel like a new man, and perhaps look like one as well. The soldiers' faces registered surprise when he came out, as if they could hardly believe the transformation.

They took him toward the guest quarters, passing through courtyards filled with lush plantings and flowers in bloom, decorated with marble columns and statuary and carved benches, with tall fountains pouring water into quiet pools. Serene—it all seemed so serene, contrasting sharply with the chaos circling through Donatus's brain. *Lelia…oh, Lelia.*

He had to pull himself together. He had to put thoughts of her aside and face the future—assuming he might yet have one. He was a senator. He was his father's son. He was father to a son. He had responsibilities to his family, to his clients, to his Emperor. He needed time to think. Maybe then the confusion would clear and he'd know what to do next.

The soldiers stopped in front of a door, heavily carved and ornate with gold. "Here you are," one of them said. "You're to rest until summoned to dine with the Emperor."

Donatus nodded and stepped forward as they opened the door. He sighed with relief when they pulled it closed behind him, leaving him alone.

He looked around, finding himself in luxurious accommodations, a suite of rooms, expensively decorated. Windows overlooked a walled courtyard, and a doorway led outside to it.

The furnishings were impressive. A huge bed dominated the room, constructed of ebony, carved and gilded with gold. It was cushioned with layers of mattresses and laid with embroidered silk sheets. Donatus moved toward it, realizing for the first time how exhausted he felt in the aftermath of nerves. Maybe he could rest for just a moment…

A movement startled him. He looked up and lost his breath. Surprise turned into shock, and shock into disbelief.

"Lelia?" he whispered.

She moved forward, a hesitant smile lifting the corners of her lips. "I'm here. And you…" Her eyes roamed over him. "You seem in fine health."

He touched a hand to the back of his head. "I'm alive, if that's what you mean. The physician gave me a draught for the ache. I have a tender lump the size of a hen's egg, but I'm alive. And you are here? I thought…" His throat closed up.

"The Emperor ended the contest, Donatus. He called for me and we talked. He knows all—except about Lucan. But about us, about our child, our marriage, the murderer…Trajan knows. He's offered to help."

Donatus could hardly bear to look at her. She was more

lovely than he remembered, clothed in a flowing tunic of cream embellished with tiny seed pearls across the neck and shoulders. Her glossy hair was swept up gently, soft and feminine, exposing the sleek ivory column of her neck. Donatus forced down the flare of lust.

"We dine with the Emperor this evening," she said. Then after a slight hesitation, "But first we need to talk."

Donatus looked away. To have her beside him made him think too much of the love they'd shared, of memories made, of whispered promises. He didn't want to talk. He wanted to love her again like before, to sweep her up and carry her to that bed there, to jerk the creamy skirt up to her waist and bury himself within her. To make her forget Lucan.

Instead, he waited, his jaw tightening beneath the hard rein of desire.

"We must talk," she repeated, her lashes sweeping up. Violet eyes fixed upon his. "I love you, Donatus. I've never loved Lucan—not in the way you thought. He listened to me when I needed him. He let me cry, allowed me to grieve. He's a cherished friend, but we were never lovers."

Donatus was silent, absorbing the words, walking around them slowly in his mind. "I saw you together. I sensed the desire between you. I heard him ask to bed you."

She shook her head. "No, Donatus. You imagined desire when there was nothing but concern. Lucan had been urging me for many weeks to tell you the truth about our son. The only desire you saw was his desire for truth. He is your true and faithful friend. He looked out for your interest, knowing well that you'd want to know about your son. I swear to you—"

"And what of the thing I heard? I heard him, Lelia. '*Come let me take you to bed. Donatus will never know.*'"

To his surprise, Lelia smiled. "Yes, Lucan said that. Just before he tucked me in, kissed my brow as a father would a child, and left me to slumber peacefully at your side. Your tortured mind made a thing of innocence into a thing of passion, but in truth there was no lust involved."

"But you told me you preferred Lucan. That the child you carried…"

Lelia bit her lip. Her eyes clouded with something that looked like pain. "I was angry. I was stung by your accusations. I let you believe what you wanted." Tears filled her eyes as she looked away. "I never expected you to leave me, Donatus." Her voice broke on a sob.

Donatus could not bear the sound. "Ah, Lelia," he groaned. He drew her into his arms, feeling her body shake against his chest. For a long while he held her, gently rocking, whispering soft words to calm her tears.

"The child is yours, Donatus," she said after she quieted. "I swear to you, I've been with no other."

Donatus drew in a deep breath, struggling with the desire to believe, wrestling with a fear he still did not understand.

When he didn't answer immediately, Lelia pulled back to look up into his face. "Let her go," she whispered. "Don't let her do this to us."

Donatus was startled. "Who?"

"Your mother," she said. "Lucan believes she's the reason you're afraid to trust, the reason that whenever you begin to love, you become afraid in some deep part of yourself that you'll lose it. And so you've imagined betrayal where none exists."

The words pierced Donatus. His chest began to burn.

Lelia watched him too closely. He turned away so she wouldn't see the pain. He turned away so she couldn't feel his hurt. He'd hidden it for too many years, that anxious knowledge, that burning question. *What is wrong with me that even a mother couldn't love me?*

It was too late. He couldn't hold it back this time. He tried to blink the tears away, ashamed of his weakness. They overflowed and slid down his cheeks. He blindly stumbled away, wanting, *needing* to escape. He heard himself make an awful sound, a hideous sound, a sound like the death cry of a beast. He stumbled again and fell hard to his knees, his face buried in his hands.

Lelia was beside him in an instant, her hand gentle upon his shoulder, smoothing his hair. "I'm here, Donatus," she said. He reached for her, wrapped his arms tightly around her thighs, buried his face into the soft folds of her tunic and cried out the hard grief of a child.

The hour was late, the night warm. Lelia couldn't sleep. She sighed and pushed herself out of the circle of Donatus's arms, easing off the bed to the window, seeking the fragrant air cooled by night shadows and garden fountains. Her movement woke Donatus. She heard him stir, his skin sliding in a whisper against silk.

"Lelia?" His voice was husky with sleep and darkness, a rich sound that immediately brought pleasant memories of their recent lovemaking. "What's wrong?"

Lelia sighed, wondering how she could explain. So much had happened within the last few hours, most of it too wonderful to comprehend. She should be elated, and yet disquiet gnawed at her.

"I don't know," she answered. "Maybe too many emotions in too short a time. Maybe thinking of our son again. I don't know."

Donatus rose and came to her. She went into his arms eagerly, needing comfort and the solid feel of his muscles against her cheek.

Donatus held her. No words passed between them. None

were needed. Maybe tears forged a bond. If so, they'd shed enough of them earlier to be united forever. Donatus had cried—a son grieving for a mother. Lelia had cried—a mother grieving for her son. Both had wrestled with shame. Both had ached with guilt.

In the end they'd sought out the only comfort to be found, their gazes locked in profound communication as Donatus lifted her and carried her to the bed. In the giving and in the taking, they'd found a rare peace. Love could never replace the losses, but love could heal the wounds.

That sweet connection sustained them through the rest of the evening, when they'd dined with the Emperor. Donatus held her hand under the table, reminding Lelia that she was not alone, that she'd never be alone again.

Lelia's heart warmed as she thought of the expression on Donatus's face when she'd answered the Emperor's many questions about their son. "Sweet mercy," Donatus had said, his eyes widening with amazement and pleasure. "You named the child after me? After all I'd done to you?"

"Yes," she said, finally able to admit that even then she'd believed Donatus would return. "His name is Valerius Donatus."

Donatus's expression softened, then hardened again with something like determination. "His name will be Flavius Donatus when he is found. I will hold up the child in front of the Emperor and all the Senate and proclaim him as my legitimate issue, my firstborn and my heir."

Trajan had smiled, but not as happily as Lelia. For a brief while she'd hoped for a happy ending. But now, in the darkness, she'd begun to doubt again.

"Talk to me, Lelia," Donatus whispered. "Don't hold yourself from me. Tell me what hurts."

"Oh, Donatus," she sighed. "It all hurts. I've spent months

trying not to feel. But tonight, telling Trajan everything, all the memories have come back. Of our son, of how it felt to be a mother, of that…that *woman*."

Donatus had no answer, only the gentle stroking of his fingertips in her hair. "At least you gave Trajan a description. His soldiers have something to go on. That's a start."

"So little, really. I wish I'd paid more attention. I wish I'd asked her more questions." Lelia made a sharp sound of frustration. "*Terentia*. She called herself Terentia. That's not even her real name. I should've been more careful."

Donatus groaned and covered her mouth with his own, silencing her with a deep kiss. "No," he said, when he finally pulled away. "Don't do it. Don't blame yourself. You were alone and frightened. You needed someone and she was there. You couldn't have known she'd prey on your vulnerability."

Donatus kissed her again. Lelia tried to hold back the sob, but it broke through anyway. Donatus pulled her closer, rocking her in his embrace. He used his voice to soothe her, weaving a warm cocoon of sound around her with a sweet, haunting melody.

Lelia wiped at her tears, letting the deep resonance of Donatus's voice wash calm over her. She relaxed within the sound, letting the melody carry her backward, then forward, like waves upon the ocean, the pull into the music almost irresistible. It was like something ancient, but also known and trusted and…*familiar?*

Immediately she stiffened. "What is that song?" she asked. "That song you're singing. What is it?"

Donatus stopped in confusion. "I don't know. Just something I know from somewhere, I guess. A lullaby, or—"

"Sing it again," Lelia demanded. "The words. Do you know the words?"

Donatus's brow furrowed. "Maybe." His lips tightened as

he searched his memory. "No," he said finally, shaking his head. "I remember there *were* some words. I just don't remember what they were."

Lelia frowned. "Terentia sang that song to the baby. I remember…" She thought backwards, living the memory again. Terentia with the baby in her arms, smiling down at him. Her voice had been sweet and sad. She'd sung, and the words…

The words came, and Lelia began to sing them. "*'An olive tree, a branch for me, a silver dagger sweet and true…'*" She paused, searching through memory for the next line.

Donatus drew in a sharp breath and finished it. "*'A child is born, a fresh new morn, a gift of diamond dew.'*"

Lelia grasped his tunic. "That's it, Donatus. That's the rest of the lullaby."

Donatus didn't answer immediately. He stood very still, lost in some deep reverie for long moments before he reached down and loosened Lelia's hand on his tunic, lifting it to his warm lips in a gesture of infinite tenderness. "I know. It all came back to me. And now I must leave you for a while, my love."

Lelia gasped. "You're leaving? But why? Where?"

He had already turned away. "I know who has our son. All I have to do now is find her."

Lelia gasped, the knowledge spearing through her with surprising certainty. But before she could recover and ask more, Donatus had left her, his dark shadow passing sound-lessly into the darker night.

Donatus had fought in war, and he'd known the rush of battle. He understood the lust for an enemy's blood. It was white heat, a pulsing in veins that burned, a song that rang through the soul with fierce ardor.

What he felt now was cold. There was no welcome exhilaration, no bloodlust surging through taut muscles. There was no quickening breath, no rush of heat.

Only rage. Cold, cold rage.

The cold was a deceptive thing, not at all like the fair contest of sword or javelin on a field of battle. Cold came upon the enemy with stealth, bringing death even before pain. Cold was subtle, an enemy of mist and shadow.

This cold made his mind keen and his movements careful. It didn't crave the taste of blood; that would have been too easy. It craved pain instead, feeding on it, growing stronger by it.

This cold was not a stranger to Donatus. That had surprised him, for he'd never acknowledged the feeling before, hadn't realized it must have dwelt within him for almost a whole lifetime—a serpent's egg within his heart, awaiting its time.

And now the serpent had been born, a cold, writhing, twisting thing with fangs of poison. Donatus felt it coil and prepared to strike.

Livia was asleep in her room in the slave quarters when he and Lucan found her. Donatus's eyes narrowed when the old woman began to berate him, irritable at being disturbed in the middle of the night. He almost enjoyed her gasp of surprise when he drew a dagger and pressed it into her neck. Her hot words died away beneath that kind of cold.

"Where is she?" Donatus asked.

"Who…? Who, my lord?" Livia's voice shook. Donatus was glad for it, glad for the cold she felt.

"You know who," he said. "And if you don't tell me where she is and what she's done with my son I'll kill you here and now, and with my own hand."

Livia hesitated too long. Donatus pressed the blade deeper into her neck until he knew she felt the prick. "Tell me, Livia," he said in a low voice.

Lucan's voice somehow penetrated the fog of ice.

"Donatus…Donatus, don't do this. Don't be like this. Let her go. She can't speak with that blade at her throat."

Donatus eased his hold, but only just a bit. "Tell me where she is," he repeated.

Livia gulped hard. He felt it against his dagger, heard a sound like a moan from the old woman's chest. "I'll tell you, my lord," she said with a whine of fear. "I'll tell you all. Just, please, take away the blade."

Donatus hesitated, his rage a tangible thing, while his hand still clutched the leather-wrapped handle. He lowered it only when Lucan seconded the slave's request.

Livia rubbed a hand against her throat. She looked pale and frightened. "She made me go along with her. Please don't be angry at me. She made me do it because of my sister."

Donatus frowned. "Your sister?"

Livia nodded, looking down at her hands against the pale sheets. "My sister's her slave, my lord, and she said she'd kill her if I didn't do all she asked." Livia's face contorted into a violence of fear. She threw herself down at Donatus's feet, her shoulders shaking. "I'm sorry. I never would have done what she asked if she hadn't threatened my sister, the only family I have left in this world."

Donatus was not moved. "You killed a slave. You tried to poison my wife."

Livia nodded, her breath coming in harsh, racking sobs. "Have mercy, my lord. Please have mercy."

Donatus felt the ache in his jaw, the struggle to contain the serpent. He closed his eyes. "Where is she, Livia? Tell me this, and you will live."

Livia answered without hesitation, though her red-rimmed eyes couldn't meet his. Donatus nodded and turned, hardly hearing Lucan's question as he moved into the corridor.

"Who?" Lucan asked again as he caught up with Donatus near the front door. "Who are we looking for?"

Donatus halted, his hand moving to the hilt of the sword he'd strapped around his waist. "My mother," he said in a low voice. "We're looking for my mother."

Chapter Twenty

$\infty\!\infty\!\infty$

Donatus and Lucan reached their destination just as dawn broke over the gently undulating hills of the city. The building at the address Livia had given him was not what Donatus had expected.

For one thing, it was in a clean, quiet part of the city. Tuscan Street, between the Forum and the Tiber. The shops were not yet open, but Donatus knew they catered to the wealthy with their expensive goods.

The building was sturdy and well-built, quite large in size. This surprised him. His mother had been banished by senatorial decree. She'd obviously escaped her punishment and lived outside the law under an assumed name or a series of them. When she'd left she'd been stripped of all her wealth and holdings. So the size of this building and its beauty, as well as the obvious prosperity of the surrounding neighborhood, made him uncomfortable and wary.

His knock was answered by a handsome male slave. The man was young and muscular and singularly attractive. His dark eyes raked over them quickly, with hardly any surprise. He didn't so much as raise an eyebrow when Donatus asked for the mistress of the home, and he led them in without hesitation or question. This also surprised Donatus at first—but he understood why almost as soon as he entered.

A painted fresco on the wall of the atrium through which they passed answered most of his questions. It was beautifully done, the detail breathtaking in its fineness, made to titillate the senses to the pinnacle of wanton desire as nearly life-sized men and women frolicked nude in a variety of lascivious poses. Nothing was veiled, nothing hidden, nothing denied.

A brothel. He'd entered a brothel. No wonder the slave at the door hadn't asked questions, probably supposing he and Lucan had come to partake of the pleasures offered within.

The male slave seated them on a bench and left. In a moment a lovely young woman came to them. She was tall, elegantly dressed, her dark hair braided in a complicated design of queenly form. Her facial features were aristocratic and classically beautiful. Gold bracelets tinkled against fine-boned wrists as she extended her hand in a genteel gesture.

"Senator," she said, her voice low and melodic, sensual in a practiced way. "So glad you and your friend have joined us this fine morn. May I help you?"

Donatus could have cursed that he hadn't asked Livia what name his mother used. But if his hunch was correct, she wouldn't be anything less than matron of this unworthy establishment. "We wish to speak with your mistress," he said.

The woman's smile never faltered, but her eyes flashed a brief moment of worry. "I'm sorry, sir. She's asleep in her private quarters and didn't give me leave to disturb her. If you've some business with her—"

Donatus's voice was low and as unyielding as granite. "We do," he said. "And I promise she'll see us if you'll escort us there."

Something flickered within the woman's gaze. She lowered her lashes, but not before she'd given them a quick, appraising glance.

Donatus knew what she thought and fought the anger. *It doesn't matter what she thinks. Let her think it.* It didn't matter that this stranger suddenly saw them as a woman's playthings, lovers to satisfy his mother's perverted desires. It didn't matter as long as it got them into that room.

Their hostess hesitated so long that Donatus had already begun to explore other options. He could leave quietly, return with a contingent of soldiers…

"All right," the woman said quietly, startling him from his thoughts. "Come with me."

She turned and led them through the atrium and the *tablinum,* past a colonnaded portico with a multitude of doors leading to private small rooms. Donatus tried not to imagine the activities behind those doors, but the female sounds they heard in passing—cries of pleasure? Of pain?—caused Lucan to glance his way. Donatus replied with a silent frown of warning.

The woman who led them seemed not to even notice. Donatus supposed she was accustomed to the daily milieu of her profession. She led them to stairs, upward to an apartment. Her knock was answered by a slave. A quiet murmuring between the two, a wave of her hand toward Donatus and Lucan, and the door widened. They were escorted inside. The lack of hesitancy made Donatus cringe. His mother's appetites were obviously well known. The slave seated them, and disappeared through a door on the right.

She was gone so long that Donatus had time to survey his surroundings, finding them surprisingly simple, refreshing after the more ornate and stifling sensuality of the rooms below. Tall arched windows let in air and light and overlooked a garden.

Donatus fought the urge to stand and pace, holding his place in the chair by sheer dint of will. Lucan glanced at him several times, his gold-green eyes conveying a depth of understanding that Donatus hadn't thought possible.

Donatus breathed in deeply, trying to keep his focus. In a moment he would face his mother. The enormity of the moment almost paralyzed him. He'd been seven years old when he'd seen her last, and all his memories of her were hazy and indistinct. He wondered if she still looked anything like the small portrait he had of her, the one his father had reluctantly given him so he could look into the faces of his offspring someday and see if they bore any resemblance to a grandmother they'd never know.

Why had she stolen her grandson? There were so many questions. How had his mother found out that Lelia had been his lover? That the child she carried was Donatus's son? Why had she befriended Lelia and taken the child? And why had she tried to kill his wife?

She'd answer those questions or he'd wring her wicked neck. Unable to help himself now, Donatus rose with a sharp, agitated movement and began to pace.

Thankfully, the slave returned, and led them down a dim corridor. A door opened, a hand waved them inside, and Donatus was suddenly face to face with the woman. His mother.

Strangely enough, her startled gasp comforted him, whet his anger and lust for battle. "Mother," he said, his lips twisting into a bitter smile. "I guess you weren't expecting me?"

She recovered with surprising speed, glancing toward the servants' startled faces and waving them away. Her gaze returned to Donatus when the door closed behind them.

"You look like your father," she said, her eyes narrowing in appraisal.

"Yes," he said. "I do. The gods favored me in that, I think."

She ignored the jab. "I, too, am pleased. Your father was a handsome man."

Donatus didn't reply. He waited, studying her. She was a lovely woman, though she didn't look exactly like her portrait anymore. Her hair was still dark and long, but subtly streaked with gray at the temples. Her body was attractively curvaceous, more rounded than the thin, svelte form he vaguely remembered. But the biggest difference was in her eyes. Their dark depths did not hold the warmth and life of the painting. They were cool, cynical, and wary.

She also studied him with unwavering regard, her eyebrow lifting at the swords he and Lucan both wore belted over their tunics. "Why have you come, Donatus?" she asked quietly.

"I want answers," he replied, just as quietly. "You have my son. You tried to murder my wife. I want to know why."

She raised her chin and looked away, smiling in an enigmatic way that frightened him. Donatus wanted to go to her then, grasp her shoulders, shake her until her teeth rattled.

Her eyes glittered with anger when she looked back at him again. "Ah, now I see. You truly are your father's son. Fiercely loyal to your little offspring, are you?" She made a small sound of disgust. "You hypocrite. Where were you when Lelia would've whelped your precious son in the street?"

Donatus ignored the stab of pain. "I didn't know."

Her lips twisted into a mocking smile. "No. Sweet little Lelia would never have tied you to her with those cords of paternal obligation, would she? But, oh, it made her such easy prey."

"Easy prey? Now there's an interesting choice of words."

She laughed, a bitter and unpleasant sound. "Yes. Isn't it? And yet a truthful one. That's the way of the world, Donatus.

The strong overcome the weak." Her eyes glittered with cold. "Lelia was weak. That weakness provided me with opportunity and I used it. I used her."

Donatus's eyes narrowed. He had to make a conscious effort to hold his place, to unclench his fists, to breathe. "Why?" he asked.

"Oh, come now." She raised her chin in a regal gesture. "Surely you aren't a stupid man. Why do you think?"

Donatus didn't answer for long moments. He studied her dark eyes, discovering the harsh truth. "I wanted to believe you took my son because you cared for him," he said finally. "That since you weren't a mother to me, you wanted to do better with your grandson. In that I was wrong."

She didn't answer, merely gave a short, mocking laugh. "How did you discover me? I was so very careful."

"I have few pleasant memories of you. But I do remember you'd sometimes make up little songs to entertain me. You sang one of those songs to my son. Lelia remembered it. It was the key I needed."

His mother shrugged. "That's unfortunate." She met Donatus's gaze squarely, without any hint of remorse in her beautiful, classical features. "I hadn't planned to make you part of my revenge. You were just a boy, and didn't understand how deeply your father wounded me, how cruelly he humiliated me. It was Antonius I wanted to punish, not you."

"By stealing my son?"

Her face grew vicious, her words inflected with venom. "Yes," she hissed. "Your son represents the one thing your father felt strongly about—that noble Flavian name, the continuance of the line. How fortunate I was to discover the Flavian heir, quite by accident. I found Lelia, destitute and desperate. Girls in such circumstances will do almost anything to survive, and I needed more beautiful women here to pleasure my clients. I began to win her trust, but was disappointed when she confessed she carried a child. Until she told me you were the babe's father. Oh, I danced with glee, then."

Donatus frowned, his eyes narrowing. "My father didn't know about my son. I don't understand how this plot of revenge could have hurt him."

His mother smiled. "It didn't matter whether he knew. *I* knew, and that was enough." She crossed her arms in an elegant gesture. "At first I was pleased enough that the lad would be my most menial slave. I even imagined how he would hurt, his keen intelligence desiring knowledge without ever receiving it, his noble soul somehow knowing itself destined for greater things, and all without hope of ever achieving them. It pleased me to know that Antonius's true heir would clean my latrines."

She flashed Donatus a look of triumph. "But he looks so much like you, Donatus. Like his grandsire, too. And, like I said, Antonius was always a handsome man. That's when I conceived the rest of the plan."

Donatus sensed it before she spoke it. He could only stare at her. So beautiful she was, and so hideous.

"He grows quickly, and he's quite a beautiful lad. Smooth skin, curly hair. Just the sort my clients crave for their pleasure. There are two in particular..." She laughed abruptly. "The sons of your father's senatorial colleagues, the sons of men who debased me, who called me *adulteress* and *whore*. And now their own sons lust for beautiful little boys. Ah, that pleases me. I will take the child to them. He'll be so trusting, so pure, clad in white linen. He will not understand. I will watch when they take him, Donatus. I will watch and I will enjoy watching."

Donatus heard Lucan make a harsh sound and turned

quickly to flash his friend a warning glance. Lucan pivoted hastily away, his eyes a flame of anger. Donatus understood. He felt the same, though his own anger burned far colder. Yet he knew this was a battle, like any other he and Lucan had fought. Emotion clouded the mind. It impeded strategy. Donatus was determined to win.

His mother gave a soft, cultured laugh. "Or perhaps I'll choose a different fate for the grandson of Flavius Antonius. Perhaps I'll sell him to a *lanista*. Maybe I'll be there watching on the day the noble Flavian heir dies, his throat slit to satisfy the bloodlust of proud Romans. I really haven't quite decided what to do with him, not yet—but you can be sure that whatever I choose will be carefully calculated to satisfy my need for revenge. Too bad you and Lelia won't be around to know his ultimate fate."

"So you will kill me and you will kill Lelia." Donatus was surprised that his voice sounded so calm. He nodded toward Lucan. "What about him? I suppose you'll kill him, too."

His mother turned, studying Lucan more carefully. "Certainly. But there might be other uses for him first." She stepped to the door, opened it in a swift movement and gave a sharp order. Men entered, a dozen men armed with drawn swords. Donatus and Lucan moved reflexively, their bodies tensing, their hands finding the hilt of their swords.

His mother laughed. "Don't do it, Donatus," she warned. "You'll not win—not against such numbers." She turned to a tall man near the door. "Tie them well, Gavros. Take this one—" she gestured toward Donatus "—take this one to the shed and lock him up until I decide what I want to do with him. Then take this one…" she smiled slyly in Lucan's direction "…to my bed."

Lucan made another harsh, strangled sound. She laughed. "What's the matter, golden boy? Does the thought of being forced to enjoy pleasure not arouse you? Or does it offend your *Christian* sensibilities?"

She smiled at Lucan's shocked expression. "Oh, yes, I know all about you, Titus Livius Lucan. Just who do you think alerted the authorities to your Christian meetings? But you were getting too close, asking too many questions."

She gestured again to the tall man. "Hurry, Gavros. Tie their hands behind their backs and be quick about it. I find I am eager to defile this Christian."

Donatus didn't resist as the man stepped forward and removed his and Lucan's weapons from their sheaths. He waited until Lucan's hands were jerked behind him, until the cords were nearly completely knotted.

He turned to his mother with a mocking smile. "If I were you, I wouldn't completely lose myself in the lovemaking," he said. "It might not do to be naked and flushed with passion when the Emperor's Praetorian Guard arrives."

Donatus enjoyed her reaction, the sudden upward jerk of her head, the sharp gasp for breath, the fear in her eyes when she pivoted to face him.

"You! What have you done?"

He laughed, taking his time with the answer, drawing out her pain and the pleasure he felt at it. "They'll be here soon," he said, tilting his head as if listening for the tramp of hobnailed boots. "I sent a request to the Emperor before I ever left home."

She froze, but only for one stunned moment before she became alive again, her body jerking with agitation while her voice rose in a mixture of fear and angry command to her men. "Forget everything I said. Our plans must change now. Hurry, Gavros. Tie them and have two of your men—only two, I'll need the rest to remain here—take them outside the city and kill them."

Donatus looked back only once as he was led away, just long enough to see his mother's even features contorted by a hatred he could hardly imagine on any woman's face—especially not that of the one who'd given him life.

Donatus had just been shoved into the oxcart when Lucan's green-gold eyes met his. "Remind me to thank you for that rescue."

Donatus grunted, not knowing what to say. He couldn't imagine why Trajan's soldiers hadn't arrived yet. He'd drawn out the interview with his mother as long as possible, but the timing was off—a mistake that might lead to his death, and Lucan's.

"I'm sorry," he managed to say, avoiding his friend's eyes. "I made a mistake. You might want to ask your god for some help about right now."

Lucan laughed, the sound strangely out of place given their dire circumstances. He lowered his voice. "The Lord's already provided. Listen—when the oxcart begins to move, fall down as if off-balance. Kneel near me as you arise and draw the dagger out of my left boot." He grinned at Donatus and nodded toward the men who'd just climbed into the wagon's seat. "Two of them. Two of us. And the element of surprise is on our side."

Donatus returned the grin. "Be sure to give your god my thanks. You know, your Christian faith is looking better all the time."

Chapter Twenty-One

Lelia had never been so relieved to see anyone as she was to see Lucan when he came for her some time later. As he hurried her through the streets to Donatus's home on the Palatine, he told her all that had transpired, how he and Donatus had managed to escape their captors, and how they'd encountered the Emperor's soldiers on their way back.

"And what about my son?" Lelia asked. "Did you find my son?"

Lucan's brows drew together. His lips tightened. "No," he said. "Not yet. When we arrived back there, Messalina—that's her true name—had fled. Her servants were questioned by the captain of the guard, threatened with scourging or worse. And though they told us where she'd gone, they didn't know about the child."

Tears stung Lelia's eyes. Lucan must have seen them, because he reached out to her with a reassuring gesture. "Don't despair, Lelia. Donatus has gone with the soldiers to find his mother. I'm sure your son will be in his arms when he returns to you."

Lelia nodded, unable to speak, holding fast to the image

in her mind, that of Donatus holding his wriggling son in strong arms, smiling with pride over the child he'd see for the first time. That image gave her hope. It helped quiet the confusion. Although she didn't know to what god she addressed her prayers, she prayed that somewhere in the great design of the universe some benevolent deity might hear and respond to the urgent cry of her heart.

Donatus had never been too fond of the Praetorian Guard. The regular legionnaires often despised them—a feeling that probably grew from outright envy. It seemed unfair to the average fighting man in the field, who daily faced hunger and deprivation and the fury of the Dacian hordes, that other fighting men stationed back home in Rome had a life of ease and relative comfort, wore the most handsomely decorated uniforms, served fewer years before retirement, and got paid a whole lot more. Donatus had unwittingly adopted the same attitude as his men.

Yet today Donatus had been glad to see the Praetorian Guard. They'd arrived just as he and Lucan had overpowered the drivers of their cart, slit their throats with the dagger, jumped from the wagon and raced the short distance back to Messalina's brothel on Tuscan Street.

As he'd watched the Praetorian Guardsmen go about their duties he'd even come to admire them, though it was a grudging admiration at first.

They were thorough. They were professional. The centurion who led them was younger than any centurion Donatus had ever seen, but he knew his business. He listened to their report without outward emotion, but Donatus sensed he was on their side and that he and his soldiers would do all they could to apprehend the woman who'd been so vile as to steal a senator's baby son.

Even the ostentatious decoration on the soldiers' uniforms, their ornate shields and their distinctly crested helmets with bold plumes made more sense to Donatus after he'd seen their effect on Messalina's slaves. The poor servants' faces had paled, their eyes had widened. They'd regarded the soldiers with such obvious fear that the speech the centurion had given them about the dangers of hindering the will of the mighty Emperor Trajan hadn't truly been necessary.

The slaves, from the highest to the lowest, were in serious awe—as indeed they should have been. The swords the soldiers carried may have been carried in lavishly beautiful sheaths, but their steel was sharp, polished, and ready for service. The soldiers may have moved among them with grim and sober restraint, but they also wielded the power to torture any or all of them, and to kill if the need arose.

The power of their intimidation was such that none of those tactics were necessary. It turned out that the slaves were more frightened of the soldiers and the Emperor than they were of the cruel mistress who owned them.

Donatus watched from a short distance away as the soldiers went about their work without delay. The centurion and three others questioned the slaves. One took notes on a parchment tablet.

Other small groups of soldiers painstakingly searched the house and adjoining shops, questioning each shop owner who rented the outer rooms about what he'd seen and the nature of his relationship with the brothel's owner. Each group returned grim-faced, corroborating what the slaves had told their interrogators.

Messalina and her two most trusted assistants had fled on horseback. The slaves had several possible suggestions for where she might be found, but none had overheard her give a certain destination. Everything was pure speculation, but at least it was something to go on.

The centurion had come to Donatus with a frown. "Don't be disturbed, Senator," he said. "My men are good and loyal soldiers of the Emperor, and they know how important it is that this woman Messalina be found. We've uncovered all we can here, and now we're going to follow up on these leads. You can go with us if you wish, or return home to your family to await notification after our work is done."

Donatus had looked across to Lucan, who nodded in response to his unspoken question. Donatus faced the centurion again. "My friend will return to my home and give my family the news of what's been discovered so far. I'll go with you. Messalina has my son. I won't rest until I see her come to justice."

The centurion nodded, pivoted, stalked away. Lucan clasped Donatus's hand. "All will be well," he said quietly.

"Maybe. But right now I need you to go to Lelia and tell her what's happened. Tell her I'll do all I can to find my mother and our son."

Lucan had nodded, clasped his friend's shoulders in a firm embrace, and turned away to the task.

Seven weary hours later, the soldiers found Donatus's mother hiding in the filth and stench of a chicken house on the outskirts of a small eight-hectare farm on the far side of the Tiber. It was the last place on their list of possibilities, and the soldiers were hot and tired and in no mood to be kind.

Her string of curses as they hauled her before their commander was met with glares of angry silence, until the centurion advanced and struck her firmly across the mouth. "Shut up your rough talk, woman," he said. "You dishonor your gender and shame yourself. We are soldiers of the Emperor and will not tolerate your abuse." He grasped her chin in a rough hold. "We've been charged with finding the son of Senator Marcus Flavius Donatus. Tell us where the child is."

Messalina's eyes narrowed. She looked over the company of the soldiers until she spotted Donatus. "You!" she growled. "You've done this to me."

"No, Mother," he said. "You've done this to yourself."

"I'll never tell you," she said. "I'll never tell you where to find him. And I hope you go to your grave mourning his loss, you—!"

The centurion slapped her across the mouth again. Her head lolled back beneath the force of the blow. She shook off the pain and spat blood upon his boots.

The centurion gave a low growl of anger and turned to Donatus. "This woman's your mother?"

"She is."

The centurion scowled fiercely. "Then I suggest you talk some sense into her. We're charged with finding the child. We'll follow those orders. They come from Emperor Trajan himself." He leaned forward, his expression intent. "We'll use torture if need be, but perhaps if you were to talk with her first and convince her to tell us, such tactics won't be necessary."

Donatus looked at his mother. She looked back at him, her dark eyes glittering with venom. For one long moment he didn't speak. For one long moment he tried to remember a happier past, anything loving or kind from his childhood. Yet all he could hear was her mocking laughter. Her words. *I will watch while they take him, Donatus. Or maybe I'll be watching the day the noble Flavian heir dies…*

"Do whatever you must," he said, turning away. "Just find my son."

Two hours. For two hours Donatus sat outside the stone building and waited for the soldiers to do their work. He felt sick and uncomfortable, unable to believe that it had come to this. That *he* had come to this. He leaned forward, cradling his head in his hands.

A shadow fell across the ground near his feet. The centurion stood before him, a look of compassion in his eyes, even if his face remained professionally impassive. "We have the information, Senator. I've sent my best soldiers to retrieve the child and bring him to you."

Donatus released his breath in a soft exhalation. "And my mother?"

The centurion nodded curtly. "She'll be fine in a few days. We didn't have to go far before she was willing to give us the information." His eyes met Donatus's squarely. "You do know there's a harsh penalty for what she's done? That death is a possible outcome? There will be more punishment, decided by Emperor Trajan himself. I doubt he'll be lenient, given her record of crime."

Donatus nodded, looking away. "The Emperor's a fair man. He'll decide what is best."

The centurion nodded, seeming satisfied. "At least the outcome for you will be a happier one. You'll soon take your son home to the loving arms of his own mother."

Donatus rubbed the tension from the back of his neck, trying to envision that pleasant scene. Lelia, holding her child again, tears of joy wetting the boy's dark curls. "Thank you," he said to the commander. "I owe you more than I can properly express."

The centurion smiled, the first smile Donatus had seen on the man's stern visage. "Save your thanks for the Emperor," he said. "He'll want to give your family a banquet of the finest order. He said I was to convey that news to you when I handed the child into your arms."

Donatus raised an amused eyebrow. "A little premature, aren't you?"

The centurion's smile widened into a grin. "I am. But I have a lot of faith in my men. They'll be here with your child shortly."

Donatus looked into the man's hazel eyes and couldn't help but believe. Soon he'd hold his son. Soon he'd give Lelia back one more of the things his wrong decision had cost her. That thought made him want to weep with joy.

The days were long and hot in Rome in the summer, but even so, the sun's rays had lengthened and the temperature had slowly given way to cooler evening air by the time the soldiers returned.

Donatus sat by himself on a bench in Messalina's garden, listening to the bubbling of the fountain and trying not to be impatient. He knew the news wasn't good when he saw the centurion approaching. The man's face was too grim, without even a flicker of joy. Donatus rose and adjusted the toga about his shoulders.

The centurion shook his head. "I'm sorry, Senator. I fear my faith in the success of my men *was* premature, though they're not to blame."

"What happened?"

"The child was gone. He and his nurse must have fled in great haste, for food was left half-cooked upon the stove and fruit being peeled was dropped half-finished into its parings. I'm sorry."

Donatus breathed in heavily. "What now?"

"I've posted soldiers to guard the house. It's possible someone will try to return for items left behind. And we still have Messalina. We'll question her again." He looked back toward the atrium where his soldiers were gathered in a subdued group. "But not tonight. My men need to return to their barracks. They need rest. It's been a long day for them."

Donatus nodded. "You've all done well. I thank you for

your service." He reached out a hand and the centurion clasped it.

As Donatus turned away he knew the bitter taste of defeat. Another dead end. Another failure.

How would he face Lelia's hopeful eyes with this news?

Donatus had never felt so helpless in his entire life.

Two hours later he entered the gate of his home, his curls wet with the damp of night. He'd delayed as long as possible, trying, over several goblets of wine in a noisy tavern, to find the words he'd need for Lelia. The wine took the edge off his pain, but it didn't give him comfort. There wasn't any. Not for Lelia and not for him.

At long last he'd decided that the only comfort they would find would be their mutual tears. She'd cry. He'd hold her. They'd cling to one another and the slim thread of hope that tomorrow would bring a better day.

He'd finally set the goblet on the table, left money beside it, and started the long walk home in the dark. It was probably the longest walk of his life.

The atrium was quiet when he entered, lit only by a single candle. He paused there, looking up at the wax masks of his ancestors in their wooden cupboards on the wall. His eyes moved to the most recent one, that of his own father. "I'm sorry," he whispered, fighting the tightness in his throat. "I failed you. I'm sorry."

A touch on his sleeve startled him and made him jerk around. Druscilla stood beside him, her eyes studying him intently. She raised on tiptoe and kissed him. "Donatus," she said quietly. Her presence, her voice, soothed him. He looked at her in surprise. When had she grown into such a woman? When?

She brushed a curl away from his eyes. "You've been drinking," she said, concern darkening her eyes.

"A little," he said.

She nodded. "Lelia's waiting in your room. She sent all the slaves to bed, but she's staying up for you."

Donatus closed his eyes. It couldn't be postponed any longer. He nodded and moved away, toward the private areas of the house.

He paused outside his bedroom door, praying that somehow he'd find the comfort Lelia needed. He lingered there, listening to the sound of his own harsh breathing, and heard Lelia's voice. She was singing. A soft melody, haunting and beautiful. *Singing?*

He opened the door, confused. Her head lifted and her eyes met his briefly, filled with happiness, before they lowered to the squirming child she held in her lap.

For a moment Donatus stood frozen, unable to comprehend. Lelia smiled, and shifted the baby around to face him. "You're home," she said softly. She stood and came to him. "I thought you'd never get here. I've been eager for you to meet somebody. Donatus, my husband, meet your son and heir…Donatus the Younger." She held the baby toward him.

Donatus shook his head. "How? I don't understand."

Lelia placed the child into his arms. Donatus looked down at his son and saw himself within the child. The same green eyes. The same nose. The same dark curls. His son. His firstborn son.

"It was Livia," she said. "Her sister had been entrusted with his care, and Livia knew that. She was so eager to make amends to us that she went and brought both her sister and the child here."

"She could've saved us a lot of trouble if she'd done that long ago."

Lelia nodded. "She was afraid for her sister's life. Only when she had cause to believe the soldiers had arrested your mother could she find the courage to do it. I hope you'll forgive her, Donatus. I've spoken with her and I think she's truly sorry."

Donatus couldn't think. He was under an enchantment, the strangest of his life. His son wriggled energetically in his arms and splayed sticky baby fingers across his lips. His wife looked upon them both with tenderness in her violet eyes. He couldn't think of Livia. He couldn't think of anything beyond this dream and the peace that filled his soul.

Chapter Twenty-Two

The Emperor's palace was a sight to behold at any time, to be sure, but as Valerius Leptis peeked out of the curtains of his litter he wondered if anything could be more lovely than the sight of so much marble lit by moonlight and the torches of hundreds of banqueters arriving for a grand evening. He turned to his wife. "We're almost there, Prisca," he said. "You should see."

Prisca smiled. "It's exciting, isn't it, Leptis? Imagine—the Emperor himself will be there. We've never been invited to anything so grand before."

Leptis couldn't halt the pride her words brought. His chest expanded with it, even though he knew every senator had been invited. All of them, even the younger ones who'd just recently been made magistrates and were just beginning to argue their first cases in the law courts. All of them. Even Flavius Donatus.

"Prisca," he said in a low voice. "I should prepare you in advance. I expect Lelia will be here tonight."

Prisca's eyes widened. "I hope so, Leptis."

Leptis turned away and lifted the curtain to peer out again.

They'd had this argument often enough. He knew how it would go. Truthfully, he was tiring of it. His entire family, even the slaves, had made their disapproval known. He'd had months to think about that, months for his anger to burn out.

He couldn't let any of them know that even *he* disapproved of the choice he'd made. It was true that Lelia had been a disobedient child. She should never have given herself secretly to Flavius Donatus. But even an old fool of a father like Leptis knew about the warm passions of youth.

Lelia had been his pet. He'd known her to be young and passionate, and should have guessed the man he'd chosen for her wouldn't have pleased her. Scipio Paullus had been too old and overbearing. Truth be known, Leptis hadn't liked him either, but he could hardly have refused the offer. It would have benefited his family and brought them incredible wealth.

Still, in retrospect he should have understood Lelia's behavior. He now regretted the fury he'd exhibited. Most of all he regretted tossing her like a chattel into the streets.

He couldn't, however, express those regrets aloud. He was a proud Roman, and he'd done what he'd done. Many of those most influential in the city knew the situation. Certainly his colleagues in the Senate knew. All agreed that he'd been within his rights to make such a stand. It wouldn't do to coddle the younger generation, to look passively upon their weaknesses. To do so would only encourage more of the same. No, parents had to draw the line somewhere, and he'd done that much at least.

The only problem was that now he couldn't rescind the harshness, no matter how he regretted the pain his family had endured, and endured still, every time they saw Lelia.

It would be difficult to see her tonight, a daughter of rare and exquisite beauty upon the arm of a man who was her match in every way. Oh, he pretended scorn toward Flavius Donatus, but the truth was that he'd always liked him, even as a youth. The younger man had distinguished himself well in war. He'd served well in the Senate; he seemed to possess the noble attributes of his father and grandfather, both men of esteem.

Leptis could see why Lelia had been drawn to Donatus. He was handsome, young and bold. They suited one another and would doubtless make offspring that were both beautiful and gifted.

That thought brought Leptis a shaft of pain. He'd never know those grandchildren. Such was the cost of his pride.

He shoved the morose thoughts aside as he and Prisca left the litter, made their way up the marble steps, and were escorted to their table by one of several stewards overseeing the banquet.

It was an enormous affair, the largest Leptis had ever seen, and the guests were still arriving. He was in awe as he surveyed the palatial décor, the jewels glittering in the hair of the women, the silver and gold platters heaped with delicacies far beyond the ordinary scope of everyday meals.

In one corner musicians entertained the arriving guests with flute and lyre, and a water organ even grander than the one in the Amphitheater.

They were led to a couch at the table in front of the Emperor's dais. From here they'd be able to see everything. They'd catch snatches of his conversation, see him pick at his food—everything.

Prisca's eyes grew large as the steward pulled out the chair for her and indicated that she be seated. "Here?" she asked in a startled whisper. "Are you sure? We're to be right in front of the Emperor?"

The steward smiled. "At his very feet, mistress, if you are indeed Valerius Leptis and wife Prisca?"

"We are," Leptis said. "But such fine seating? You are sure?"

The steward consulted his parchment list again, looked up and smiled. "Quite sure, Senator. Please enjoy your meal."

Leptis scratched his head in puzzlement and sat down slowly as the steward left to seat others. "That's odd," he said quietly. "I don't know why we've merited this much attention."

Prisca smiled and squeezed his arm. "Of course you do, Leptis. You've worked hard lately, and the legislation you've overseen has done well. Surely your efforts to make Rome a better place have not gone unnoticed."

Leptis smiled at her. She was a good wife, Prisca was. Discreet, chaste, loyal. Such a shame she'd borne him only daughters. At least she'd been fertile, and even daughters could be of use if they married well.

His thoughts came back to Lelia. He scanned the crowd, looking for her. The tables were rapidly filling up, and so far she was nowhere to be seen. He tried to relax. At least the wine would be excellent, Leptis thought as he reached for his goblet. The food would be plentiful and tasty. It wasn't every day that one was invited to the Emperor's banqueting table. He wouldn't let uneasy feelings ruin his evening.

It was sometime later that the doors at the far end opened and a blare of trumpets announced the Emperor. Everyone stood as he and his entourage made their way to the table on the dais.

It was then that Leptis saw her. Lelia was with the Emperor—right behind him, in fact. Her husband was behind her, his hand resting protectively against the small of her back.

Leptis felt his heart twist painfully, filled with sadness for the relationship he'd lost with his child. She was beautiful, more beautiful than he'd remembered. Her hair was arranged elegantly, and she wore a tiara of gold and diamonds, looking as regal as an empress.

Leptis was certain now that she was the reason he and Prisca had been seated in this place. Somehow, he didn't know how, she and Donatus had found their way into the Emperor's good graces. Maybe Lelia wanted to rub salt into his wounds. He probably deserved it. Leptis tried to look away from her, but he could not. He was looking right at her when Lelia turned in his direction and smiled at him.

That smile broke his heart. It wasn't the sarcastic, bitter smile he'd expected. It was tentative and hopeful, as if she were holding out an olive branch of peace with the gentle curve of her lips. He couldn't help himself. He smiled back, even as tears filled his eyes and made him angry at himself for such an unmanly display of paternal feeling.

The Emperor gestured for everyone to be seated, then waited, still standing, for the rustle of the crowd's movement to cease.

"My friends," he said at last in a clear voice. "Tonight you've all been summoned for a special event, one that celebrates the very foundation of the virtues that made our city Queen of the World. Now, lest you think that this ex-soldier-turned-Emperor speaks once more of the glories of *war*..." He paused to let the crowd's soft laughter subside. "Lest you think that once again I'll bore you with my exploits, let me be quick to put your fears to rest. No, my friends. The celebration tonight is to honor the best of Roman life. A man, his wife, the making of a home, and a child."

Trajan turned toward Donatus and gestured. "Marcus Flavius Donatus, stand forth." Donatus stepped forward and lowered his head in a respectful bow.

"This man epitomizes the best of Rome," Trajan said.

"His father and grandfather you all knew as esteemed men, your colleagues in the Senate. I knew them also, and daresay they'd be proud of young Flavius Donatus here, and of his service to me in the conquest of Dacia. Indeed, his sword was the very one which severed the head of that vile renegade chieftan Decebalus."

The crowd broke into applause at that. Donatus bowed again to acknowledge it. Leptis was pleased to see such humility in Donatus that he almost looked embarrassed at the praise.

After the crowd had grown quiet, Trajan spoke again. "Unfortunately, when a man is serving his Emperor in a foreign land, he's not able to attend to other important matters at home. Donatus, when he returned, met his infant son for the first time."

Trajan clapped his hands and a slave entered the room, walking briskly through the long line of tables with a squirming infant in her arms.

Prisca grasped Leptis's arm. "Leptis!" she breathed. "That's our grandson. Our grandson." Tears filled her eyes. "It's the first time I've ever seen him."

Leptis nodded. He couldn't speak for the knot in his throat. The child was lovely, what he could see of him. His skin was white and creamy, he was plump with health, and his head was covered with a thick mass of beautiful dark curls.

The slave girl handed the baby to Donatus. Trajan gave a short laugh when the child immediately reached up and squeezed his father's nose. The Emperor looked back to the crowd. "Tonight you are here as witnesses to a solemn moment. Ordinarily, a Roman father performs this ceremony shortly after the birth of his child, but as I told you, Flavius Donatus was rather busy at the time in Dacia." He turned to Donatus. "This moment is yours, Donatus."

Donatus nodded and walked forward, to the very edge of the dais. He looked unusually solemn as he addressed the crowd. "My friends and colleagues. Thank you for attending tonight. Your presence here means much to me." He looked directly at Leptis and Prisca. "And it means much to my wife, Lelia, as well."

He shifted the child in his arms so that the boy faced the crowd. Immediately those nearest the dais began to whisper. Prisca turned to Leptis. "He looks like Donatus," she said. "Exactly like him. Oh, what a handsome babe."

Donatus nodded. "You see that my son is indeed my own, but just so there will never be any doubt…" He held the child high above his head in a firm grasp. "I, Marcus Flavius Donatus, do hereby proclaim this child, also here named Marcus Flavius Donatus, to be my firstborn son, my own legitimate issue, and my future heir, in the sight of all of you as witnesses."

Applause broke out as he lowered the baby.

Donatus handed the child once again to the slave girl and she carried him out. Trajan stepped forward. "That, my friends, is the sight we Romans crave to see. A fine young family. *That* is the foundation of civilization—ours or any other." He turned and smiled at Lelia. "And soon we hope the favor of the gods will fall and there will be more healthy fruit upon your vine."

"Lelia's blushing," Prisca whispered. "You don't suppose…"

Leptis grunted. He should have figured it already. Donatus was as strong and healthy as a rutting stag, and Lelia was as beautiful a wife as any man could wish for. It looked to Leptis as if he'd have to repent the loss of not just one grandchild but two.

Leptis broke out of his reverie when he heard his name

called. Trajan gestured for him to come forward. He stood and made his way awkwardly to the front.

"Congratulations, Valerius Leptis, on the continuance of your family," he said when Leptis had reached him. "I have already rewarded your daughter and son-in-law with a small property, and Donatus with a post as Aedile, in gratitude for his service to his Emperor and to Rome. For you, sir, I have a gift of two golden statuettes. Your daughter tells me you have a lavish garden, and it would honor me if you were to place these lovely dolphin figures somewhere within it."

Leptis bowed before the Emperor. The crowd applauded.

Trajan then lowered his voice so that only Leptis could hear. "I know, Valerius Leptis, that your daughter and her husband are not currently in your good graces. I do beseech you to forgive the past and to restore the relationship as a wise father should do."

Leptis nodded and bowed again. "I shall do so, my lord Trajan."

Trajan smiled and stepped backward. He signaled for the banquet to continue. The musicians were already playing a lively tune as Leptis made his way back to his couch.

"What did he say?" Prisca asked.

Leptis smiled. "He gave me permission to be a grandfather," he said, patting her hand gently. "A grandfather, Prisca. Think of it."

Prisca sighed happily and looked toward the dais. She raised her glass to Donatus, who met her gaze across the short distance and smiled.

That night, as he held his wife within the circle of his arms, Donatus was a man at peace. Life could get no better than it was right now, and he wanted to capture this feeling, distill it into a sweet elixir and savor it for the rest of his days. The moonlight rested gently upon the bed, upon their bodies entwined within it, and upon the crib where their son dreamed nearby, making soft baby sounds in his sleep.

"Donatus?" Lelia asked quietly. "What are you thinking?"

He nibbled the nape of her neck. "About you."

She laughed softly. "You always say that."

"That's because you're all I think about."

She was silent for a moment. "Tonight went well, don't you think? I mean, nobody dared castigate the Emperor for his friendship with Leda the Gladiatrix."

"And they never will, Lelia. The Emperor has spoken."

"Even my father didn't look angry."

"He isn't."

She turned and scanned his face in the dim light. "How do you know?"

He chuckled. "I've got my ways. My information, however, is valuable to me. Costly for you."

She looked wary. "What cost?"

"Love me, Lelia. Let me savor your beauty."

She laughed. "Donatus, my love." She wrapped her slender arms around his neck. "You shouldn't ask me to make payment with that which you already own."

"Ah, you're too logical. Too, too, too logical," Donatus said. He gave a mock growl and kissed her with a vengeance.

She moaned when he finally pulled away. "Logical? Not when you kiss me like that. I'm lucky if I possess one rational thought."

Donatus chuckled and slipped a hand around the fullness of her breast. His thumb teased her nipple. "Then don't think. Just let me love you."

Lelia sighed and arched against him. So sweet. So willing. Her hand moved to him and encircled his warm shaft. Then it was he who lost all rational thought.

The moon had climbed much higher in the sky before they lay sated, relaxed, but still too pleased with the evening to sleep.

"I can't imagine why Trajan gave you Messalina's establishment," Lelia said thoughtfully.

"I can."

Lelia twisted to look into his face. "You can? Why?"

"Because I asked him for it. I wanted to buy it, of course, but he gave it to me instead. Recompense, he said, for the grief she'd brought us by stealing our son."

"You wanted to buy it? Whatever for?"

"For Severina. I overheard her tell Didia that she'd like to learn to cook better, that she'd always dreamed of owning an inn some day. As I considered Messalina's home for wayward ladies, I knew the building would be perfect. Provided I give that lewd entranceway a new paint job first."

"That's a wonderful idea, Donatus. But you know women aren't allowed to own property of their own."

"Oh, Severina won't *officially* own it. Lucan will."

"Lucan?"

Donatus grinned. "Yeah. Lucan will make a decent pretense of overseeing the business and will sign all the important legal documents for her. He might even have to live on the premises to look like the official owner. But for all practical purposes the new inn on Tuscan Street will belong to Severina. She'll not have to share her profits with him or anyone else. She'll be a wealthy lady before long."

Lelia tilted her head and laughed. "Severina and Lucan? This could get interesting. You're either a dolt or extremely clever."

"No dolt. Clever. Lucan needs a wife. Severina needs a husband. I'm just making it easier for that to happen. It might even change his plans about going to Ephesus."

"But if he's in danger here…"

"I don't think he is. Trajan's not against Christians, really—as long as they don't cause trouble. He doesn't order his soldiers to seek them out. As long as Lucan's discreet and doesn't cause a problem, he should be all right."

Lelia nodded. "Druscilla will be upset when Lucan finds another woman to wed. She's got her heart set on him."

Donatus gave a soft snort. "Druscilla's not ready to be any man's wife. I don't want to lose my baby sister just yet."

"Then prepare yourself to face her wrath."

Donatus laughed. "I think I'd rather face the Dacians."

Lelia traced the line of hair on his chest with a fingernail. "Speaking of wrath, Donatus… You never did tell me how you know my father's not angry."

"Because he sent me a message before the banquet was ended."

"A message?"

"Yes, Lelia. He invited you and me and little Donatus to come to *cena*, to dine at his home tomorrow evening. It looks like we're being reinstated into the family, after all."

Lelia drew in a deep, sighing breath. There was a long pause before she spoke. Donatus thought he saw the glistening of tears in the moonlight. "Then it's over," she said at last. "All the pain—it's over now. The nightmare's ended."

Donatus smiled into the darkness. "It does look that way, my sweet. I can't promise you there will be no more hardships, no more tragedies that come our way. But I can promise you that while I have breath in this body you'll never face them alone again."

"Oh, Donatus," Lelia said quietly. "Even in the darkest days I somehow knew you'd return to me. I wasn't wrong."

"No, you weren't. I just had to realize you meant more to me than anything. More than my life. More than my fears."

"More than anything, Donatus?"

He grew still, instantly made wary by the note of teasing in her voice. "What do you mean, Lelia?"

"More than anything, Donatus?"

"I suppose. What game do you play now, vixen?"

She laughed. "More than a night of rest? More than your sleep?"

He growled and rolled over to pin her down onto the bed. "I was a cavalry officer in the midst of war. I learned to do without sleep. You can't wear me out, woman, no matter how sweet the enticements."

Her laughter was husky and sensual, filled with rich undertones. "Prove it, Flavius Donatus. Love me again."

Donatus kissed her then, thinking that he was more than ready with all the proof she'd ever need. A whole *lifetime* of proof. Beginning tonight, in these crisp sheets dappled with moonlight, with one child sleeping beside them and another on the way.

As he slid his body deep into his wife, he heard a snatch of song in his mind. This time it reminded him of Lelia. Only of Lelia, and the love they shared and the children they'd made.

An olive tree, a branch for me, a silver dagger sweet and true.

A child is born, a fresh new morn, a gift of diamond dew.

He smiled and moved with slow, precise rhythm, the same rhythm as the lullaby, loving his wife, letting her know he would always be thankful for his beautiful life and for all the sweet, sweet diamond dew she'd brought to him.

* * * * *

0807/04a

MILLS & BOON

Historical

On sale 7th September 2007

Regency
A DESIRABLE HUSBAND
by Mary Nichols

Lady Esme Vernley's unconventional first meeting with
a handsome gentleman has damned him in the eyes of
her family. His departure from protocol fires Esme's curiosity
and Lord Pendlebury is taken with her mischievous smile. But
his secret mission could jeopardise any relationship between
them — especially when his past amour arrives in town.

Regency
HIS CINDERELLA BRIDE
by Annie Burrows

The Marquis of Lensborough was appalled! Who was
this badly dressed waif in his aristocratic host's home? And
why was the proud Marquis so drawn to her? Convinced
that she was a poor relation, the noble lord was about to
receive the shock of his life…from a lady who would break
all his very proper rules!

Available at WHSmith, Tesco, ASDA, and all good bookshops
www.millsandboon.co.uk

0807/04b

MILLS & BOON

Historical

On sale 7th September 2007

Regency

THE LADY'S HAZARD
by Miranda Jarrett

Major Callaway returned from war a damaged but determined
man. Thrown together with copper-haired beauty Bethany,
he must uncover a mystery that involves them both. They are in
grave danger…and the truth could tear them apart.

TAMED BY THE BARBARIAN
by June Francis

Cicely Milburn has no intention of marrying a Scottish
barbarian! But when Lord Rory Mackillin rescues her from a
treacherous attack she reluctantly accepts his help – even
though his kisses trouble her dreams.

THE TRAPPER
by Jenna Kernan

Wealthy socialite Eleanor Hart finds forbidden pleasure
in the arms of the rugged, passionate Troy Price.
How can Eleanor return to the privileged prison of a
world she's left behind?

Available at WHSmith, Tesco, ASDA, and all good bookshops
www.millsandboon.co.uk

On sale 7th September 2007

THE MASQUERADE
by Brenda Joyce

Shy innocent or experienced woman?

At her very first masquerade, shy Elizabeth Fitzgerald is thrilled
by Tyrell de Warenne's whispered suggestion of a midnight
rendezvous. But that one night is only the beginning…

Two years later, she arrives on Tyrell's doorstep with a
child she claims is his. He could not be the father. Is
Elizabeth Fitzgerald a woman of experience or the gentle
innocent she seems? But neither scandal, deception nor
pride can thwart the desire that draws them together.

'A powerhouse of emotion and sensuality…'
—*Romantic Times BOOKreviews*

Available at WHSmith, Tesco, ASDA, and all good bookshops
www.millsandboon.co.uk

Medieval
LORDS & LADIES
COLLECTION

When courageous knights risked all to win the hand of their lady!

Volume 1: Conquest Brides – July 2007
Gentle Conqueror by Julia Byrne
Madselin's Choice by Elizabeth Henshall

Volume 2: Blackmail & Betrayal – August 2007
A Knight in Waiting by Juliet Landon
Betrayed Hearts by Elizabeth Henshall

Volume 3: The War of the Roses – September 2007
Loyal Hearts by Sarah Westleigh
The Traitor's Daughter by Joanna Makepeace

6 volumes in all to collect!

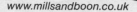

www.millsandboon.co.uk

M&B

*Victorian London is brought to life in
the stunning sequel to Mesmerised*

London, 1876

Though Kyria Moreland is beautiful and rich enough to
attract London's most sought-after gentlemen, she has yet to
find love and refuses to marry without it. When she receives a
mysterious package, she is confronted with danger, murder and
a handsome American whose destiny is entwined with hers...

Rafe McIntyre has enough charm to seduce any woman, but
his smooth façade hides a bitter past. Still, he realises Kyria is in
danger, and he refuses to let her solve the riddle of this package
alone. Who sent her this treasure steeped in legend? And who
is willing to murder to claim its secrets for themselves?

Available 17th August 2007

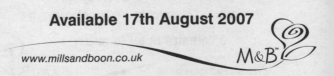

www.millsandboon.co.uk

FREE

2 BOOKS AND A SURPRISE GIFT!

We would like to take this opportunity to thank you for reading this Mills & Boon® book by offering you the chance to take TWO more specially selected titles from the Historical series absolutely FREE! We're also making this offer to introduce you to the benefits of the Mills & Boon® Reader Service™—

> ★ FREE home delivery
> ★ FREE gifts and competitions
> ★ FREE monthly Newsletter
> ★ Books available before they're in the shops
> ★ Exclusive Reader Service offers

Accepting these FREE books and gift places you under no obligation to buy; you may cancel at any time, even after receiving your free shipment. Simply complete your details below and return the entire page to the address below. You don't even need a stamp!

YES! Please send me 2 free Historical books and a surprise gift. I understand that unless you hear from me, I will receive 4 superb new titles every month for just £3.69 each, postage and packing free. I am under no obligation to purchase any books and may cancel my subscription at any time. The free books and gift will be mine to keep in any case.

H7ZEE

Ms/Mrs/Miss/Mr...Initials ....

BLOCK CAPITALS PLEASE

Surname ....

Address ....

....

....Postcode ....

Send this whole page to:
The Reader Service, FREEPOST CN81, Croydon, CR9 3WZ

Offer valid in UK only and is not available to current Mills & Boon® Reader Service™ subscribers to this series. Overseas and Eire please write for details. We reserve the right to refuse an application and applicants must be aged 18 years or over. Only one application per household. Terms and prices subject to change without notice. Offer expires 31st October 2007. As a result of this application, you may receive offers from Harlequin Mills & Boon and other carefully selected companies. If you would prefer not to share in this opportunity please write to The Data Manager at PO Box 676, Richmond, TW9 1WU.

Mills & Boon® is a registered trademark owned by Harlequin Mills & Boon Limited.
The Mills & Boon® Reader Service™ is being used as a trademark.